the captain and the coach

ASHLYNNE KRISTINE

To younger me—you did it.

basil

I didn't know what was worse, accidentally buying decaf coffee or the unexpected snowstorm.

I juggled my coffee, keys, and a snack in one hand while I wiped away the snow covering the door handle with the other. The tiny snowflakes clung onto the close-knit material of my sweater, and I attempted to shake them off, only for them to sneak down my sleeve. With my arm cold and wet, I put my things down and shifted through the center console. I grabbed an old gift card and turned on the car. Then, I worked on scraping away the ice.

I knew an ice scraper would make this easier. However, mine was an unfortunate victim of a heat wave that passed through Denver this past summer. The plastic had warped beyond use, and I threw it out. I should have bought one at the grocery store the other day while they were on sale. But I didn't because I thought I had another month before I had to even start worrying about snow. So, I left the store with my decaf coffee purchase, a new pack of red pens, and a great attitude that was meant to carry into the week.

That attitude hung by a thread, and it was only Wednesday.

I waited until the car was warm enough to melt the remaining ice before I drove to work. The roads, while clear of snow, were covered in thick patches of ice. Resulting in my usual fifteen-minute drive, being closer to thirty.

I finished my snack as I pulled into the parking lot of The Rockies Performance Training Center. The building used to only be accessible to professional athletes, but after a multi-million dollar renovation a couple of years ago, they opened some parts of it to the public. During the renovation, they added another ice rink, a basketball court, and a separate gym for the community. The athlete's wing was separate and could only be accessed by a badge.

I gathered my things, braced myself for the awaiting cold, and got out. My legs carried me fast to the building doors, and I avoided the patches of salted ice on the ground. As soon as I stepped inside, I relaxed into the heat that wrapped around me. I stomped my feet on the mat, then continued forward. My gaze met the familiar blue eyes of the front desk worker.

"Hi Daniel," I said as I leaned over the wood counter.

The college student smiled, and his eyes seemed to brighten. "Hey, Basil. How's your day going?" Daniel asked as he stretched. He crossed his arms on the desk and tilted his head as he waited for my answer.

I glanced out the glass doors and sighed as I rubbed my chilled hands together. "It was fine until I looked out the window and saw snow."

"Did you ever replace your ice scraper?"

"No," I mumbled to myself. Daniel chuckled, and I smiled before I started tapping a finger on the counter. "Enough about my day. How has yours been?" I asked.

"Caught someone trying to steal some towels. Other than that, it's been good. Oh," Daniel sat up and reached for a plastic container behind his computer, "want a cookie?" The contents made my stomach grumble as he held up the plastic container and wiggled his dark brows.

I searched through the options and picked one with pink frosting. "Who keeps bringing you guys this stuff?"

Daniel shrugged and placed the container back behind the computer. He grabbed a napkin from a neat pile and handed it to me. "Someone who works the morning shift. I don't know their name, but they always leave a note," he said as he held up a yellow sticky note.

"Well, that's nice of them. And surprising considering everyone here is such a health nut," I said before I bit into the cookie. I wiped away some stray frosting on my lip. "Well, I gotta get to practice. I'll see you later."

I gave Daniel a kind smile and continued toward the employee locker rooms. Once I made it to my locker, I wrapped the rest of the uneaten cookie in the napkin and shoved it into my purse. Then I hung it in the locker and grabbed my skates. As I made my way to the ice rink, I admired the fall decorations lining the walls. Colorful ceramic pumpkins sat outside office doors while leaf garlands hung from the high ceilings.

The decorations even bled into the arena. The garlands hung from the sideboards, and the arena smelled of spiced cinnamon.

The Rockets—the youth hockey team I had coached the past two seasons—met three times a week. When I was hired, I accepted this as a temporary placement until a coaching position opened up for soccer or volleyball. I played both those sports in high school and I wanted to coach them now. I knew nothing about hockey coming into the job. However, by the end of the first season, I had fallen in love and requested a permanent coaching position. Now, I couldn't imagine coaching anything else.

I finished setting the cones up for some passing drills when the doors opened and laughter filled the arena. "Hi

Coach Andrews!" the kids yelled in unison. I skated over to the sideboard and greeted everyone with a warm smile.

"Hey guys! Are you ready for practice?" They all nodded their heads with enthusiasm and rushed to get their skates on while I talked with their parents. When the last child skated past me, I finished up my conversation before I turned to follow them.

A deep voice stopped me before my skate hit the ice. "Ms. Andrews, could I have a word, please?"

I glanced behind me and met Mr. Clein's hard gaze—which was emphasized by his thick-framed glasses. I gave him a curt nod. "Of course." I turned to the kids and saw they were waiting for instruction. "Start stretching! I'll be there in a minute!"

Mr. Clein's disapproving scowl only deepened the closer he prowled to where I stood. Of all the parents I had interacted with, Mr. Clein was the most unpleasant. I kept my expression neutral as I regarded him. "How can I help Mr. Clein?"

The movement of him adjusting his silver cuff links drew my attention to his tailored suit. It was blue today, with a gray button shirt and a patterned tie. My eyes skated over his hard features before they settled back on his dark, irritated stare. His words were tight when he answered.

"It's come to my understanding that Aiden is unable to participate in this week's game."

"That's correct. He has two warnings, Mr. Clein. Aiden has been using unsportsmanlike conduct. Being aggressive to his teammates during drills and it—"

Mr. Clein held up a hand to stop me, and my cheeks burned with frustration. "It's hockey. Force is part of the sport, Ms. Andrews."

I hated the way he undermined me, as if I still didn't understand the sport. I could admit that, when I first started, I made some wrong calls. But I learned from my mistakes, and it wasn't an excuse for him to speak to me like that.

I took a slow, steady breath to collect myself before I continued. "Sir. Our policy states that this kind of behavior is not tolerated. Physical force may be expected at the professional level, but not here."

He scoffed. "Ms. Andrews—"

"While practice is in session, you may call me Coach Andrews. If you have any other grievances, Mr. Clein, you can contact Mrs. Johnson and she'll be more than happy to help."

I didn't give him a chance to say anything else before I skated toward the kids. They had all finished stretching and were talking amongst themselves when I found myself in the middle of the semi-circle they formed. I clapped, earning their attention.

"Okay! We're focusing on passing today. I've got some cones set up. Split into groups of four and find a station." The kids scattered, and I skated to the side. I waited until everyone was ready to go, and then I blew my favorite whistle I found on Etsy.

———

It took ten minutes to pick everything up once the kids left. Then, I traded my skates for my well-worn sneakers and put the equipment back.

As I walked by the front desk, Daniel waved me over. I set my purse on the desk and leaned across it. The setting sun cast a soft, pink light through the windows and coated everything in a dusky hue. My eyes grew heavy, and I laid my head in my hands.

"Why do parents think they know everything?" I asked Daniel as I rubbed my hands over my face.

He shook his head as he continued gathering his things.

"I wish I could tell you, Baze." He jingled his keys. "Ready to go?"

I nodded and took the space beside him before we walked to the doors, where he opened them and let me go first. We got halfway to our cars when my foot caught a patch of ice. I fell backward and a heavy hand landed on my back. Daniel helped steady me before he offered a smile.

"Thanks," I said before we started walking again. This time, I was extra careful about where I stepped.

Daniel smiled from beside me. "No problem. So, do you have any plans tonight?"

I sighed and watched as my breath fogged in front of me. It was colder than when I left my house, but at least it had stopped snowing. "Help Hollis, eat ice cream, the usual. How about you? Hanging out with Sheila?" I asked as I wiggled my brows.

Daniel started dating Sheila five months ago, after weeks of admiring her from a distance. She coached the youth girls' basketball team and always spent time with Daniel before and after practice. It took him three months to muster up the courage to ask her out. Since then, though, they've been happier than ever.

Daniel shrugged. "Not tonight. She's doing something with her sister. I'm probably gonna hang out with Douglas."

"I still can't believe you named a lizard Douglas."

"Hey, it's a very refined name, okay? Don't make fun of him," he teased. We reached my car and Daniel cleared his throat. "Well, get home safe, okay?"

I smiled as I opened the car door. "Yeah, will do. See you tomorrow."

As he walked away, I started the car and rubbed my hands together. When I was sure my fingers wouldn't succumb to frostbite, my phone rang.

"Hey lady, you heading home?" Hollis asked in her cheerful tone.

"Once I get feeling back in my hands, yeah. Why did you want me to stop somewhere?"

I heard a rustling sound in the background before Hollis answered. "No, I was just curious. I picked up some Chinese and wanted to tell you the roads suck. Like, even more than they did earlier, so be careful and go slow."

I started driving out of the parking lot, and my stomach growled at the mention of food. I dug the half-eaten cookie out of my purse. "Really? Well, thanks for telling me, and please make sure you're careful too, okay?"

"Of course, B. I'm always—" Her voice was cut off by a muffled thud that made my heart drop. Silence stretched between us, and I stopped breathing.

"Hollis?" My voice was small as panic rose in my chest. My heart started beating faster, while I sat there frozen, waiting for her to say something.

After a soft thud, her adrenaline-filled voice came back on the line. "Hey, I'm here, I'm okay."

I let out a heavy breath and eased my grip on the steering wheel. "What happened?" I asked.

A door shut before she answered. "Someone skid and hit my car. The damage isn't too bad," Hollis said, and a deep, muffled voice sounded in the background.

Now, I should have taken those words and trusted Hollis to handle the situation herself. We were adults and could do things on our own. But knowing my best friend got into an accident made my blood boil. People needed to be more careful. Heat crawled up my back before it settled somewhere between my shoulder blades. "Where are you?" I asked, my voice tight.

Hollis sighed heavily before saying something to that mysterious voice. There was another thud, and when she came back, I could hear her hesitation. "I can handle this B."

"You don't sound very confident. You sure?"

"Well I was, but," Hollis sighed, "remember how I gave you the spare key to my car? Like, for emergencies?"

I held in a chuckle. Hollis's car had an auto-lock feature and would do it even if her keys were inside. So, she gave me a spare if she ever forgot them. I asked her for the street names and turned on my blinker. "I'll be there soon."

CHAPTER 2

case

Being a professional athlete had a lot of perks—but I couldn't think of any because I was about to die.

The small brunette with flushed cheeks pulled her finger back, then poked me square in the chest.

Jab. "How reckless of you."

Jab. "Do you have any idea how bad this could have been?"

Another jab. "You're lucky she wasn't hurt."

I held her gaze and took in the rich browns of her eyes before I reminded myself now wasn't the best time to think about how beautiful this woman was. She craned her neck and her mouth tightened with frustration as her breathing came in quick, short spurts. The street lamps cast a yellow hue over her face as she stared at me, and I searched for any indication she knew who I was. Her eyes glanced down at my Denver Peaks hoodie, and the flush on her cheeks deepened. From the cold or our current predicament, I wasn't sure.

A chuckle escaped me. I tried to hide it behind a cough, but it didn't work. Her brows furrowed as she pulled back. "You're laughing? Do you not realize how serious this is? You hit her! What were you looking at your phone? Or do you just not know how to drive on icy roads? Newsflash, you have to go slow!"

I let her throw her words at me while I fought a smirk. She had it all wrong, but I needed an opening to tell her that. The blonde woman, whose car now had a small dent in its green paint, tugged on her friend's sleeve and threw me an apologetic smile.

"Hey—"

"Do you have anything to say for yourself?" The brunette asked as she drove her finger into my chest again. My hand itched to reach out and grab it, to pull her close and tell her just how wrong her assumptions were when her attention shifted.

Scottie came running out of the store. His red curls bounced as he made his way to the car for his phone. Then he walked up to the blonde and ran his hand through his hair. "Again, I'm really sorry. What's your number? So, I can get you my insurance information for, well, insurance. And then if you need anything else, you can just text me."

I watched the flush deepen on the woman's face as her brown eyes narrowed on me. Her breathing changed from fast and shallow to slow and deep. Something hit me in my gut at her reaction, and I knew I needed to fix this misunderstanding. I held out my hand and smiled as she took a step back.

"Hi, I'm Case. And that," I tilted my head toward the rookie, who was in deep conversation with the blonde, "is Scottie. He's the one who was driving."

The Miami native, while extra cautious on the roads, was following too close to the sedan when he hit a patch of ice. Lucky for all of us, no one was going fast enough for any casualties. Well, except her car. Scottie was beside himself and thought he caused major damage. He and the blonde talked, but when he grabbed his phone to get his insurance information, it wouldn't turn on.

At some between getting food and getting into the fender bender, it died. So, he plugged it in and excused himself so he could use the restroom inside the small convenience. The blonde had locked herself out of her car, so she and I were having a nice, casual conversation while we waited for her friend to show up.

After the brunette handed over the key, she stormed up to me. Panic and rage consumed her soft features. Have you ever been yelled at by a woman who was almost a foot shorter than you? And it wasn't your mother? Let me tell you…it's terrifying.

The woman's head dropped, causing her deep brown hair to cover the entirety of her pretty face. I put my hands in my pockets and looked at her as I waited for her to say something. Scottie stepped toward us. "Everything okay?"

People walked by us, bundled in their winter coats and hats. Some stopped for a moment to catch a glimpse of Scottie and me, but continued when they saw what was going on.

When the brunette didn't answer right away, her friend stepped up and placed a gentle hand on her arm. "Hey, B. You okay?"

Hmm, what's B short for?

"Yup." She lifted her head and turned to her friend. "Totally fine. You go finish up so we can get home. I'm starting to freeze." Her attention turned to me, and I took her in. The way she bit the inside of her cheek, her brown eyes, which I was sure turned warm and caramel in the sun, and her body. She was bundled, but my imagination tugged in my mind, begging to be let loose and run wild. I cleared my throat, and she stood straighter.

With a steadying breath, she opened her mouth, and concern crashed into me. Was she going to apologize?

Why? I was the one who should have stopped her instead of letting her ramble and poke me.

"I'm sorr—"

"Look, I—"

We let the words fall into the cold space between us, but she never looked away. Her brows creased together and formed two lines I wanted to erase. I smiled and hoped my nervousness didn't show. This wasn't like me. Why was I feeling like this?

"I'm sorry."

Her tongue dragged over her bottom lip before she let out a huff. The air fogged in front of her face. "Why are you apologizing? I don't know if you remember, but I'm the one who laid into you. Not the other way around." Her tone tilted up in hesitation. But despite how long she kept her eyes on mine, they never gave away how she was feeling.

"It's my fault. I should have stopped you after that first jab. You have a strong finger, by the way." I rubbed the spot on my chest, feigning pain to lighten the mood.

As we stood there; with the sun dropping in the sky and snow falling above us, I noticed the shadows on her face darken. I dropped the smile and filled the words I was about to speak with something genuine. "So, I'm sorry. I was at fault, you don't need to say anything. I understand why you did it."

There was a tense moment of silence between us as she looked me over, and I couldn't help but watch her. I wanted to see if I could catch onto whatever she was thinking. But it seemed like she had some kind of shield up. I couldn't read her at all. Eventually, the tension between her brows disappeared, and the tightness in my chest lightened a fraction.

Her dark eyes, framed by snow-coated lashes, met

mine, and she straightened. "I'm going to say sorry, anyway. I may have overreacted."

I smiled and shifted on my feet. The snow beneath my feet crunched with the movement. "No, you didn't. You were sticking up for your friend, it was a perfectly reasonable reaction."

I didn't want her to overthink anything, and needed to let her know I wasn't upset. Something in her gaze softened, and the tension in her body seemed to melt away. She didn't smile, but she didn't have to for me to understand that my words had their intended impact. Without thinking, I leaned in. I caught a whiff of strawberry mixed with something else, and she froze when I was close enough that my breath caressed the hair covering her ear.

"And just between us, it's probably best you yelled at me. I don't think Scottie would have survived." When I pulled back, I found this woman with her mouth open in shock.

"Are—are you flirting with me right now?"

"Depends on your definition of flirting," I said with a teasing smirk.

She rolled her eyes and turned on her heels to face her friend. "You ready?"

The blonde nodded her head and said one last thing to Scottie, then she walked past the brunette to her car. The brunette turned back to me and licked her bottom lip again. I assumed to keep them from getting chapped from the cold. It took some effort to keep my eyes on hers when she did that. A question itched as we looked at each other, and I took what might be my only chance to ask it before she left. But she cut me off as soon as my mouth opened.

"Well, bye."

With that, she turned and started for her car, leaving me with my mouth open and my question forgotten. I watched as she sidestepped the ice on the sidewalk to reach her car, wanting to make sure she made it there safely. It had nothing to do with how good her ass looked in her jeans. That was just an unexpected bonus of me looking out for her safety.

Scottie came and stood at my side as the two cars drove off. He let out a heavy sigh. "I can't believe that happened."

I gave him a few solid pats on his back. "It all worked out in the end, no harm, no foul. Now, let's get going."

When we got to the car, though, Scottie stood at the driver's side door of his luxury sedan. I watched as the snow stuck to his jacket as he stared at the handle.

"You okay?"

He shook his head, and I walked around to meet him before I took the keys. "Come on, my balls are starting to freeze."

I didn't blame Scottie for not wanting to drive, especially after what had just happened. The main roads were better than the side streets, but the clouds had cast everything in a dusty blue and the lines were hard to see as we drove back to my house. When we pulled into the driveway, I was busy with my seatbelt when Scottie finally spoke. "Your girlfriend texted you."

"Hm?" I asked, seeing the notification on the screen disappear. I grabbed my phone to see what she needed but felt a tug in my chest at the news article she sent me.

AUBREY

We have an image to uphold.

Case Whitlock Seen with Mystery Woman Walking into Hugh's Friday Night with Model Girlfriend Nowhere to be Seen.

I sighed and typed out a response.

I sent a thumbs up and shoved my phone into my pocket before I grabbed the Thai food we picked up earlier. Scottie gave me a questioning look as he came to walk by my side. "Trouble in pretend paradise?"

I grumbled in response.

basil

"I can't believe you work with him!" Hollis said over the phone, as she tried to contain an excited squeal.

I hauled my duffel bag over my shoulder and made my way to the parking lot. When we got home the other night, I secluded myself in my room. I spent all night hoping the whole thing was a dream, and that I didn't, in fact, yell at Case Whitlock. Of all the people in this city, why him? I was super familiar with the side of his face. As well as the rest of his teams from seeing them around the training center. But the day Case turned around, and I saw him fully—I got distracted.

I almost ran into a trash can.

It almost hurt to yell at him the other night, but I couldn't give him a pass for putting my friend in danger just because he was brutally handsome. And when I realized it was a mistake, it hurt even more,

Running into my room though meant Hollis couldn't ask any of her burning questions, and my phone had been blowing up all morning with them.

Have you seen him practice? How are
his abs?

Do you think we can get invited to one of
those after parties athletes always have?
They sound fun.

Get toilet paper on your way home.

Were you ever going to tell me you worked
with him?

That was the last text I got before she called me—
almost immediately after—because she had my meet
schedule memorized. Teacher's brains were crazy. I let my
head settle on my left shoulder as I tried to stretch the tight
muscles in my neck. "Hol, I told you, I don't work with
him. I just happen to work at the training facility his team
uses."

"Same difference."

"Not the—" I was cut off when I noticed the
approaching program director's attention was on me.
"Hey, I'll see you at home, okay? Something came up." I
hung up right as Mrs. Johnson reached me. She clasped
her manicured hands in front of her deep green pantsuit
and smiled.

"Sorry to catch you on your way out, Basil. But do you
mind coming to my office for a chat?"

My grip on my duffel tightened, but I forced a calm
smile. "Of course." I followed behind her and focused on
the clicks of her heels against the floor to keep my mind
from wandering.

I hadn't done anything wrong, at least to my knowl-
edge. Unless—was it related to the conversation I had with
Mr. Clein at practice earlier this week? Mrs. Johnson was a
fair woman, and most times had my back regarding over-
bearing parents, but it was possible I overstepped.

She gestured to her office, and I took my place in one of the oversized brown leather seats. I glanced around her office as I sank down and let the inviting atmosphere pull me in, easing my anxiety. Her two bookshelves were filled to the brim with file boxes, and her personal knick-knacks lined the top. But everything was neat and organized, especially her desk. The only thing that littered the space were pictures of her family.

Mrs. Johnson settled in across from me and grabbed a manila folder from the neat stack already on her desk. "How was your game today?" she asked. Her smile was genuine as she held my stare.

"Great, the kids won today."

"I'm not surprised. They have an amazing coach."

The way her voice broke at the end had the hairs on my neck standing and I shifted in my seat. I stared at Mrs. Johnson. She was usually so confident and well put together, except for now. Her brows furrowed together, just enough for me to notice. I cleared my throat. "What did you want to talk to me about, Mrs. J?"

She sat straighter; her graying hair falling over her shoulder with the movement, and opened the folder. What she pulled out had me leaning closer as I tried to get a better look at it.

"Basil, are you aware of the opportunities that are available to the members here?" she asked, and I nodded in response. Since the training facilities renovation, there had been a constant flow of donations from the sports teams and the community. They were dedicated to the building's upkeep and provided the proper finances that made the youth programs possible. Mrs. Johnson smiled, and her crow's feet framed her brown eyes. "Are you also aware of the opportunities we offer the athletes here?"

I tilted my head and shook it. "No, I'm not."

She cleared her throat and opened the folder. There

was a lone piece of paper inside, and she took it out, only to hold it in her hands. Her fingers worried the top corner, but she kept her voice professional. "Well, there are numerous ways we allow the athletes to participate in our programs. However, they usually just show up for fundraisers." She waved a hand as if shooing away the excess thoughts that kept her from getting to her point. Her eyes met mine, and she took a steadying breath.

"They can also be requested to participate in various activities by name. The request goes directly to the team's coach, who approves or denies it, then it comes to me." She placed the paper in front of me and my eyes found a familiar signature at the bottom of the paper.

Next to another signature that sat above the Denver Peaks logo.

Tension found space behind my eyes and I asked, "What's this?"

Mrs. Johnson kept her voice even as she explained, "Mr. Clein submitted a formal request last time he and I talked. As of next week, you'll have an assistant coach."

A ragged laugh escaped me before I had the chance to suppress it. My hand flew to my mouth and my eyes widened. Mrs. Johnson looked at me, bewilderment filled her expression. "I'm sorry." I tried to contain my nerves as I talked. "But I must have heard you wrong. Who's getting an assistant coach?"

It couldn't be me. Not when my team was on a winning streak this season. When it was my team who could do the fundamentals of skating in their sleep. I worked too hard for anyone to think I was incapable.

The lines of her mouth tensed. "You, Basil. It's not ideal, I know that. But this isn't a decision I made, nor can I change it."

Her words hit my chest with a force that made me grateful I was sitting down. I could understand Mr. Clein, or anyone else, being upset about decisions made based on their children's actions. But to think I was incapable because they didn't agree with rules I had no control over? It was ridiculous.

When Mrs. Johnson spoke, I saw the concern in her soft eyes. "Basil, you and I both know how capable you are, and I'm sorry I can't do anything to help."

"It's fine. You said next week?" I asked. I started thinking of how I could get with their coach to convince him to change his mind.

She nodded and looked at me one more time. "You okay?"

"Yeah, I'll be fine. Is it okay if I go? Or was there something else?"

Her head tilted, and her words came out gentle. "No, that was all for today."

We said our goodbyes and during the entire drive home; I thought of how I was going to do this. I knew what hours the team's coach was at the facility, but how could I approach him without running into a certain hockey captain?

I had given a lot of thought as to what I'd say to him, but couldn't seem to come up with anything. Apologies were exchanged, and that was good enough for me. I had Hollis and a job I loved. A tall, handsome man—who I was sure gave hugs good enough to wipe away people's problems—was not what I needed.

My thoughts continued to work themselves out in my mind when I entered the apartment. They stopped as soon as I was through the door. There was a loud bang, and then confetti fell to the floor. I stared at Hollis in shock and took note of the gigantic smile she wore. "Guess who's a homeowner!" She yelled before she tossed the confetti launcher to the counter before she ran toward me.

My duffel bag dropped, and I held out my arms. "Are

you serious!" I asked as she plowed into me, her body vibrating with excitement.

She pulled back and skipped to the counter to grab her phone. "Come on, we're going out to celebrate." When I hesitated, still in the small entryway, her brows creased together. She pushed a curly blonde strand behind her ear before asking. "What's wrong?"

I tried to shrug off my bad mood. I shouldn't be acting like this. I was happy for Hollis and needed to act like it instead of wallowing in self pity. "I got some news after the game today that's put me in a funk, is all. Sorry Hol, tonight should be about you. Where do you wanna go?"

"What happened?" She asked, as she sat on the brown microfiber couch and patted the spot next to her.

"Do we have to talk about it?"

"If you don't want to ruin my night, then yes. Come on B, talk to me."

This was why I loved Hollis. Her unlimited capacity for understanding, love, and concern she held for the people in her life. She was such a mom. I plopped into the spot and pulled a flower-embroidered throw pillow into my lap. "I'm getting an assistant coach."

She pulled back. "That's a bad thing?"

In any other situation, I wouldn't have an issue with it. If they hired another coach who was learning, or if I asked for help, it would have been fine. But the fact this was done behind my back without talking to me first hurt. I wasn't going to dump all of this on her, though. This was her night and going out sounded great. A perfect chance to forget about today and all the twisted thoughts in my head. I smiled at her. "It's going to take some getting used to it all. Now, where do you want to go?"

She pursed her lips and regarded me before letting out a huff. Hollis knew better than to push, because I'd push back and our conversation wouldn't go anywhere. She checked her phone. "I'm waiting for Ryan to text me back before I decide."

I held in my groan at the mention of the egotistical asshat that was her boyfriend. Ryan had a habit of putting his needs and wants above Hollis, and I didn't understand why she put up with it. I picked at the dry skin on my thumb as I acted fine with the company.

"Who's it going to be? The coach, I mean?" Hollis asked as she typed away on her phone. I shrugged and set my head back against the couch.

"No clue, all I know is it's one of the players on the Peaks. Guess a special request was put in for it." I tried to visualize the team's roster in my mind so I could file through all the possibilities.

"What are the chances it'll be that guy you yelled at?"

I could hear her teasing smile grow bigger and bigger with each word. I snapped my head up and my jaw dropped in horror. "Don't you dare put that on me, Hollis Shay."

She laughed and put her hands up. "All I'm saying is it's possible. And why would it be so bad? He's cute."

"Did you not see me yell at him?" I asked.

"So? You both apologized to each other. That makes it okay, right?"

I scrubbed my hands over my face and sighed. "Oh!" I glanced at Hollis, who was grinning at her phone. "Ryan texted back! He said he's coming. Now, you go get ready," she commanded before sauntering off to her room. When her door clicked shut, I got off the couch and headed to my room. I opened the door and was overwhelmed with the new plug-in air freshener I bought. It smelled too artificial, so I quickly unplugged it and tossed it in the trash. Then, I started looking for clothes. A load of clean clothes sat on the computer chair in the corner, and I hoped I threw the dress I bought last week onto the pile.

It was right on top. I grabbed a pair of shoes from the closet, and my phone rang from where I tossed it on the bed. I considered not answering it when the familiar name popped up on the caller ID. A heavy weight pooled low in my stomach and goosebumps peppered my skin as I stared at the screen. I could just let it go to voicemail, and deal with the consequences later. Or I could call her back and pretend I wasn't staring at my phone.

I answered on the second to last ring.

"Hey, mom." I saw Hollis's shadow stop right outside my door.

"Hi sweetie, I was calling to see if you were still coming over for dinner?" she asked.

Of all the things I didn't want to do in my spare time, dinner with my mother was at the top of the list. So why I agreed to do it once a month was beyond me. That feeling in my stomach worsened, and I tossed the shoes from where I grabbed them. I found a pair of sweatpants and a t-shirt to change into as I tried to come up with what to tell Mom. This day had sucked, and the promise of a good time had been ruined. Not because she called, but because I forgot the one thing I was supposed to remember.

Mom didn't like it when I forgot our scheduled dinners. "Sorry Mom, tonight isn't a good night."

The thing about people who liked to mess with your emotions was they used words to hide their true intentions. Because, even though her next words were gentle, and were words that an understanding mother would say to her daughter. I could hear the disappointment. My chest welcomed the familiar heaviness of guilt as I tried to keep my breathing even.

Because in her mind, the things she wanted were above everything else.

"Okay sweetie, want to rain check? How does next weekend sound?"

I pulled up my pants and opened the door. Hollis jumped back but didn't hide the fact I caught her eavesdropping. I sighed and forced a smile as I told my mom. "Sounds good."

I hung up the phone and glanced at Hollis. I could see the question on her face before she even opened her mouth. "Go, have fun."

Her blonde brows creased, and I could see she was thinking of an excuse to stay. But she knew better than anyone when I liked to be alone. If I was going to dwell on a bad day or be miserable because I was sick, I'd rather not do it around anyone. Besides, Ryan said he was going, and he was an asshole when anyone but him canceled at the last minute.

The crease between her brows softened, and she tilted her head. "You and I are going to celebrate later, okay?" she stated before she left to grab her things. Then she poked her head through my door as I sat on the plush bed.

It wasn't until I gave her a solid nod and a weak smile that she left.

CHAPTER 4

case

I swiped my badge against the scanner and waited for the lights to blink green before I hauled the door open.

"Hold the door!"

My hand slid back onto the wooden door and kept it open until Townes passed me. The goalie ran a tattooed hand through his brown hair, and something shiny caught the light. A tired sigh escaped him. "Thanks."

"Rough morning?" I asked as I readjusted my duffel. We walked down the carpeted hallway toward the athletic lockers and when I glanced at him, awaiting his answer, I noticed that shiny stuff again, but this time, on his hoodie. *Oh, man.* "Is that…glitter?"

Townes's scowl deepened when his eyes darted down. "I had to help Hayley with a last-minute project last night. I overslept." He flicked a few pieces of glitter off the dark blue fabric. "How does this stuff get everywhere? This wasn't even in the same *room*."

Townes was preoccupied with the invasive material, and I did nothing to keep my amused smile to myself. In the three years since I met Townes, he had never touched glitter—until yesterday. It was entertaining, to say the least.

We entered the crowded locker room. Guys on the team chatted on the bench as we walked by, and Connor saw the glitter. The defenseman sympathized with Townes. "Hey man, I've got one word for you, lint roller."

"Con, that's two words." Townes said as he shook his head.

Connor shrugged. "It could be three words, but it doesn't matter. What does matter, though, is that's how you're going to rid your house of that shit."

I grabbed my skates from the locker, and Townes sat next to me with his. I kept my focus on my laces and asked, "Did the project at least turn out alright?" When Townes didn't answer right away, I looked up. He looked at me with a blank stare before blinking twice, like he was shocked I'd accuse him of doing anything less than perfect.

"Of course it did. I'll show you a picture after practice." Townes said with fondness and pride in his voice.

My phone vibrated in my pocket as I smiled at Townes. I removed it and scanned the text I had been anticipating all week.

AUBREY

Reservation's been made, you'll pick me up at 6?

Sure will. See you then.

Once my phone was put away, Townes raised a brow. "You still dating Aubrey?"

"We're fake dating. And yes, at least for now," I said, inclining my head toward the door. "Come on, it's not a good look if the captain's late."

As we walked, footsteps sounded from somewhere behind us. I glanced behind me and caught a glimpse of the familiar redhead. He grinned. "There you guys are!"

"Walk and talk, Scottie," I commanded as I trailed my

way out of the crowded locker room. He nodded and hurried to take the spot to my left. He opened his mouth, but then he caught a glimpse of Townes.

"Dude, why is there glitter in your hair?"

Townes' scowl reappeared, and he mussed his hair again. This time with more intent on getting the glitter out. "Damn art project," he mumbled.

Scottie shrugged and turned his attention back toward me. "Don't make plans for the twentieth. We're all busy."

I raised a brow and waited for him to continue, but he never did. Once we entered the arena, I sighed. "Care to explain?"

"Yeah, I need to know if Hayley's gotta go to her grandparents that day or not," Townes stated as he set his gear down.

Scottie sucked in the side of his cheek and glanced away. He was nervous, but why? "I may have told a friend we'd help her move that day."

The news had Townes and me regarding each other before looking back at Scottie. We both made fast friends with the rookie and knew it wasn't like him to be so hesitant. My smile pulled at the side of my mouth, and I finished removing my blade protectors. We all stepped onto the ice, and I bumped Scottie's shoulder.

"A lady friend, huh? Have we met her?" I asked. Between parties, press conferences, and team dinners, there was a very good chance we knew who Scottie was talking about. But we wouldn't know for certain who it was until he gave us a name.

Scottie took in a deep breath before locking his eyes with mine. "Remember that girl we got into that fender bender with?"

I remembered one of them *very* well, but I also knew he was talking about the blonde. I smirked. "No way."

"Wait. You got into an accident?" Townes inquired from beside us.

We both ignored his question.

"She reached out because her insurance needed something, and we got to talking. She just went into escrow and asked if I'd help her move, so I volunteered all three of us. At least one of us needs to help her move out of her apartment since her roommate has something going on that whole day." Scottie waved his hand. "So yeah. I'll let you know more details when I get them."

"I'm sorry. I'm still caught up on the fact that you guys got into an accident and didn't tell me." Townes skated around and stopped in front of us.

Scottie raised his hands in defense. "It was a small fender bender. And I didn't say anything because I didn't want to embarrass Case." A coy smile formed on his face as Townes nearly snapped his neck to face me. As he opened his mouth to press for answers, a whistle blew from outside the rink.

"Less talking, more stretching!" Coach Warner yelled from his position on the bench.

I glanced at Townes. "I'll tell you all about it after practice."

Before he could argue, I skated off and took a small corner of the rink to start stretching. I let my mind wander as my body went through its motions, reveling in the warmth that flowed to my muscles while I stretched and skated. During practice, my mind kept wandering; a new recipe for blueberry muffins, our game schedule, and the woman Scottie promised to help. But the blonde only passed through my mind as I wondered about the roommate. Was it the woman who yelled at me?

I couldn't remember her name, or if it was ever mentioned. Everything around me seemed to blur when she walked up to me. I was frozen, completely awestruck by beauty even the fading light couldn't cast shadows on.

I felt like an ass for not correcting her about who caused the accident, and also for knowing I contributed to her embarrassment. My parents raised me better than that.

After drills, we spent some time going over plays. Once everyone was given specific things to work on, we were free to go. I took a quick shower, and Townes found me while I was putting on a shirt.

"A car accident?" he asked with his arms crossed.

I raised a brow. "You're really worked up over this, huh?" I teased, not paying attention to what he was saying. My mind was torn between the fake date I had got tonight and that pretty brunette.

"—Cats have spiky penises."

I whirled around to Townes. "How did we get on this topic?"

"You weren't paying attention," he said with a scowl.

I cleared my throat. "Oh yeah. Uh—Scottie hit a patch of ice and hit a car. Everyone was fine, but the girl's friend showed up and thought I caused it."

Townes cocked his head at the same time his brows pulled together. "And?"

I shrugged. "And she ripped me a new asshole," I pointed at Townes' deepening scowl, "do *not* look at me like that. Seriously, everything ended up okay. I walked away unscathed." I wasn't sure when we started walking, but before I knew it, we were out of the athletic wing. We rounded the corner that led to the front of the building, and I could see the snow covering the ground through the large windows. I braced myself for the cold.

"New asshole and unscathed don't belong in the same sentence," Townes grumbled from my side.

As the front desk came into view and the hallway widened, something caught in my peripheral that made me stop walking. I turned to face the head of braided chocolate brown hair.

"Um—are you coming?" Townes asked, oblivious to why I stopped.

I waved toward the door, but kept my eyes on the woman as I tried to contain my surprise. "I'll catch up."

That was all I said before I sidestepped and placed myself behind a large snake plant that sat at the corner. Not my finest moment—I could admit that. But I needed to see if this woman and the one occupying my mind were the same.

I didn't catch whatever Townes mumbled before he sauntered off, and I didn't care. I just—I needed to know.

My eyes dragged over her side profile, the tilt of her nose and tanned complexion—it was her. I noticed the hoodie she wore had the facility logo on the back. Did she work here, or was she a gym member? I was positive I would have seen her around, regardless. She was too beautiful to miss. I glanced back up, eager to catch a glimpse of her again. But she looked away and shifted her attention to the man standing in front of her.

I couldn't see his face, but his hard, anger-filled voice drifted my way. The older woman I recognized as the program director nodded her head to whatever the man next to her was saying. I wasn't usually one to eavesdrop, but I didn't need to hear his exact words. The drop in the brunette's shoulders told me he was speaking to her in a way no man should ever talk to a woman. Upset or not.

Now, I planned on walking up and interrupting their conversation. But I knocked into the plant, and the ceramic pot made a loud sound as it circled its base. I reached out to steady it, and when I looked up, I had their attention. I glanced between the three of them, and slowly set the plant back where it was supposed to be. The sound echoed in the empty space, but I focused on the task as I tried to control my nerves. Goosebumps peppered my clammy skin, and the collar of my shirt became unbearably tight.

Case Whitlock; hockey captain, baker extraordinaire, and almost plant murder.

As I glanced at the group, I saw the man's eyes widen as a coy smile crossed his face. When he opened his mouth to speak, though, a booming voice sounded from behind me.

"Whitlock? What are you doing behind a plant?" I turned to face Coach Warner.

"Just—making sure it didn't need to be watered," I explained, sticking my finger into the pot to test the soil. I tsked when I held up my hand. "It's a little dry."

Coach stared blankly, and I cleared my throat before I dropped my hands to my side. "What did you need, coach?"

He scratched his bearded chin and nodded toward the hallway that contained all the offices. "Follow me, we need to talk."

We walked toward the long hallway on the opposite side of the room. As we passed by the group I was *not* eavesdropping on because, well—plant—I smiled.

"Katrina, nice to see you," Warner directed toward the older woman. She smiled, and the lines around her eyes deepened with the movement.

"Thomas, lovely as always," she said before she directed her attention to me. The way she tensed didn't go unnoticed, and her smile tightened as she nodded to us both. "Well, I see you're both busy, so I won't keep you. We'll talk soon."

With that, she turned her attention toward the brunette whose cheeks were painted with the lightest shade of pink. "Basil, let's discuss this another time."

Basil.

I rolled the word around in my mind, dissected every vowel, and practiced each syllable. Her name was perfect.

The program director walked past Basil to the older gentleman, who had been eyeing the interaction with a smile. She and I locked eyes a second before I walked off to catch up with Warner. I didn't look back until just before I turned the corner. And when I caught her staring, I flashed her a smile before I lost sight of her.

———

"Isn't that beneath you?" Aubrey asked as she sipped on her wine. Her blonde hair was pulled back into a low ponytail, and her dress was incredibly tight. She looked amazing but was overdressed for the casual restaurant we were at. The well lit dining room was full of younger couples and a few families, so Aubrey requested a small table in the back where we could have some privacy. And while we would get looks from the people around us, no one came up to ask for pictures or autographs.

Aubrey leaned back into the black booth.

"I don't think so. It'll be fun," I said with a shrug. I told her about the coaching position I had been volunteered for. According to Warner, the youth hockey team was struggling, and their coach needed a helping hand. I was more than happy to accept.

Aubrey sighed as she moved her finger along the rim of the wineglass. "So long as it doesn't take away from our dates, I guess it's okay."

I kept my mouth shut and sipped my water. Aubrey and I had been at this fake dating thing she suggested since she moved to the city. At the time, she had been trying to get into the modeling business and insisted our public image together would boost both our careers. I didn't care about my 'image' but took the chance to help an old friend. Her career skyrocketed due to being my *girlfriend*.

She didn't need me, though. Aubrey was already very talented and deserving of her success. If only she believed in herself as much as everyone else seemed too.

The first 6 months were fine, but lately, Aubrey had become more–difficult. More demanding of my time and energy, and had started pushing the boundaries we established so we could keep our feelings out of this arrangement. I wasn't sure how much longer I was willing to brush it off.

"It'll be fine, Aubrey," I said, as I placed my hand on top of hers. She smiled, and I realized how much of her old self showed in that expression. Before she turned into the picture-perfect sports model, she was now. She moved her hand and finished off her pasta.

"Do you know the coach you'll be working with?" she asked.

"No. I'm meeting him next week." I gestured to the waiter for our check when he walked by. "So, anything new going on with you? We've talked an awful lot about me tonight."

Aubrey raised a brow and smirked. "That's because your life is more interesting lately. I'm getting more bookings so that's nice. I'll be flying out to California and New York quite a bit in the next few months."

"That's great. I'm happy for you," I said. When the waiter brought the check, I briefly glanced at Aubrey and caught her checking him out. Which, again, we weren't actually dating, so my feelings weren't hurt. But for how often she got onto me for looking at women and being seen with them, you'd think she'd be more careful as well.

I cleared my throat and gained her attention. "You've been doing really well for yourself, Aubs. Uh—do you think this needs to continue?"

She tilted her head and creased her brows. "What do you mean?"

The waiter dropped off the check, and I handed him my card. I watched him walk away before I gestured between us. "This. I mean, it's been a year, right? Wasn't that what we agreed on?"

Aubrey froze. Her arms were already in the sleeves of the jacket I gave her when I picked her up. She kept her head down and didn't look at me until after we left the restaurant. Once in my car, she pinned me with a soft stare and I saw the redness in her eyes.

"A little longer, please? Then we'll call it off. Okay?" she pleaded.

I clenched my jaw, but nodded as I kept my eyes forward.

basil

There were quite a few things I was grateful for in life. Like, the friendly maintenance man at my apartment complex, for example. He never objectified the female tenants and would always give you light bulbs when you needed them. Iced coffee, of course. Rhonda's brownies, a car that hadn't given up on me—yet—and oddly enough, Case.

I still wasn't sure why he had been hiding behind that spider plant, but I appreciated how his presence distracted Mr. Clein from his tangent. I was talking with Mrs. Johnson about some equipment that needed to be replaced when Mr. Clein interrupted us. He was upset that he hadn't heard when the new assistant coach would start and demanded it be our next practice. I was only there that day to fill in for another coach and wasn't ready to have that conversation. In the middle of being berated for my poor performance, Mr. Clein's attention shifted to somewhere beside us.

I turned around and watched Case wrestle a plant back from where he knocked it over. His gaze glanced over the three of us before his coach called for him. When they walked past our small group toward the office-lined hall-way, I did my best to ignore him. I was hopeful that he didn't recognize me, but he proved me wrong with a wink before he disappeared. Mrs. Johnson then took Mr. Clein to her office to finish their conversation, and I headed home to enjoy the rest of my evening.

That smile plagued me all weekend, despite my attempts to think of anything else.

So I was extra cautious as I entered the facility for today's practice. The chances of me running into him on my normal day were slim, but I couldn't be too careful. Daniel and I exchanged our usual greetings, and I continued to the locker rooms. I grabbed my skates, then headed to the equipment locker, only to find my favorite cones were gone. They were new and shiny, and I had hidden away under the volleyball net someone threw in here at the end of last season.

I cursed whoever took my cones while I plucked the older, dirtier ones from the shelf. Once I made it to the rink and the door clicked shut behind me, I paused. The missing cones were set out on the ice and irritation warmed my cheeks as I scanned the ice. As I put my skates on, I noticed a blue duffel bag shoved under one of the benches, and it only added to my sour mood. I intended to find whoever was here so I could tell them to leave. I made it halfway onto the ice when I heard the door open, and I spun around, ready to face whoever it was.

Now, I should have stopped or looked where I was going before doing that. Because as soon as my eyes landed on the six-foot-something man walking into the arena, I tripped. My skate clipped the edge of a cone, and my ankles intertwined as I tried to avoid the fall.

It didn't work.

I laid on the ice with my eyes closed and kept my breathing steady as an ache in my hip made itself known.

The pain radiated up and curled around my spine before it settled somewhere in my mid-back. As I tried to remember if I hit my head when I fell, the lights overhead grew darker, and an imposing sensation washed over me.

Was this a sign of brain damage?

I opened my eyes, and my heart leaped into a steady gallop.

Case hovered over me, and he tilted his head as he stared. I didn't realize how close he was until something spiced and woodsy overwhelmed me. "Are you okay?"

I stared at him and willed my heart to slow before I spoke. "Did you see me hit my head?"

"I didn't. Do you think you need to see a doctor? Here," he held up a finger, "follow this. I've had enough concussions to know how to check for one."

I didn't follow his finger.

"Come on, Basil, follow it once and I'll clear you fit for work. Or skating, whatever you're here for, really."

"You're not a doctor, you can't clear me for anything," I said plainly. There was a beat of silence between us before Case raised a brow. With a huff, I gave in and followed his movements. He grinned and my gaze involuntarily darted to his cheek, where I knew a dimple hid. I cleared my throat and looked back at him to find him staring intently. The crease between his brows deepened as he leaned closer.

"What?" I asked, my words sounding softer than I intended. They were supposed to have some bite to them, something to give off the sense I didn't want him so close —I would overthink how that wasn't true later.

"Your eyes." Case's voice contained a rasp as it lowered, and I *tried* to ignore it. "They're not brown."

I didn't know why he was so intrigued by my eye color, but I let the comment slip. "Are you going to stare at me all day or are you gonna help me up?"

"I can't do both?" Case teased.

We looked at each other, neither of us blinking, until I sighed and held out my hand. Case—still smiling—reached out and gently took it while his other settled on my elbow for extra support. I was too aware of the warmth that crawled through my body from the places he touched me as he helped me to my feet. Pain shot up my back when I was fully upright, and I must have made a face. But I reassured Case before he could mention it.

"I'm okay," I stated as I removed myself from his touch. Another snap of pain radiated from my hip, but I kept my face neutral as my eyes dragged over him. He wore a pair of black joggers and a hoodie to match. His hair was disheveled, strands curled around the tips of his ears, and I hated how handsome he looked. It was odd—that he was here. As he picked up the cone that I tripped over, a question settled on my tongue.

"Was there something wrong with your rink?"

"What?"

I held his curious stare. That would be the only reasonable explanation why he was here, that the rink the Peaks used for practice was being worked on. I didn't understand why I never got a notice though, Mrs. Johnson was usually on top of things like this. I pointed to the cones. "You set those out, right?"

"Yeah, why?" he asked as he put his hands in the pocket of his hoodie.

I let out a heavy sigh and shook my head. "Look, I'm not sure who said you can practice here, but you can't. Come back this evening after six and the place is yours." I skated past him and toward the cones so I could rearrange them.

He followed after me and tugged on my sleeve. I whirled around to face him and was confused by his genuine expression. "Hey, I need the rink. You're the one who has to come back later."

"Why would you—" I stopped talking as realization hit me.

I never got the chance to meet with Coach Warner and tell him I didn't need any of his players, and that they all needed to focus on their season.

"Basil?" Case asked as he inched closer and reached out with his hand. I moved before he was able to touch me because that was the last thing I needed. My brain would turn to goo and I'd lose my train of thought. "You okay?"

"Why are you here, Case?" I asked, needing to hear him say it. Or say something else. Maybe he was here to meet someone for an interview—because athletes do interviews all the time. Maybe he reserved the rink for some solo practice, and Mrs. Johnson was too caught up in her work to tell me. The ringing in my ears may not subside with his answer, but I needed one nonetheless.

Case looked me over, and realization seemed to hit him too. Because the crease between his brows softened, and a smile painted his face. "Wait." His gaze dropped to my skates and slowly roamed up before it landed on my whistle. "You're Coach Andrews?"

I opened my mouth to say…*something*. I wasn't sure if I was trying to start an argument and was going to tell him to leave or plead with him that I didn't need him here. But the doors opened, and the thundering sound of the kids' footsteps had us turning. I swallowed, thick and heavy, before I turned back to Case. Before I could say anything, though, he placed gentle hands on my hips, and steadied me before he leaned in and said, "Come on, Coach, practice is starting."

Case skated past me, toward the eager parents, and past the kids coming onto the ice.

"Who's that?" Matthew asked as he pulled on my sleeve.

"Yeah. He looks super weird," Michael mumbled.

I let out a soft chuckle when I saw he was squinting. "Michael, where are your glasses?"

"They broke, but don't worry, Coach. My dad let me borrow his superpowers so I can see. They just need time to start working." He rubbed his eyes. "Any second now."

I laughed and kneeled, so I was at Michael's level. "Just promise you'll be careful until those powers start working, okay?"

"You got it, Coach!" He grinned. It was wide and displayed the space where a loose tooth had once sat. When I stood, all the kids were still talking and were oblivious that the subject of their conversation was skating toward them.

Aiden spoke louder as he threw his hands out. "How do you not know who he is? Do you live under a rock?"

"Aiden. That's not a kind way to speak to your teammate." My voice was firm, and he turned to face me.

"But Coach, he's like the most famous hockey captain in history. It's not my fault Matt doesn't know this, 'cause you know," he shrugged, "rock."

Case skated past the kids and settled to my right, and I crossed my arms to prevent any accidental touches. "Who's a rock?" he asked as placed his hands on his hips with a grin.

I sighed and dropped my head before I looked at the kids, most of whom were standing there slack-jawed and wide-eyed as they stared at Case.

"Everyone, this is Mr. Whitlock." I glanced over at Case and took in a steadying breath before I continued talking. "He's going to be helping me out for a bit, okay?"

"Why do you need help, Coach?" Michael asked, and I froze. I obviously couldn't tell them Aiden's dad was out to get me and had gone behind my back to get Case here. Maybe I could make something up—yeah. As I formulated a good enough excuse a group of eight-year-olds would believe, Case spoke up. Which surprised me.

"Actually, I'm the one that needs the help."

The kids and I all looked at him as we waited for him to continue.

"You see, I was sent here because my coach heard she's really great at her job. And that you guys are the best team there is. He wants me to work with Coach Andrews and tell him what I've learned here." Case looked at me then, and his green eyes locked onto mine. I smiled. Case's expression changed into something I couldn't quite place, but I pushed past the strange feeling in my chest and cleared my throat.

"Okay, everyone!" I clapped and gained everyone's attention. "Coach Whitlock has set out the cones for today's practice. What did you have in mind?" I asked as I faced him. Case stood straighter and his demeanor changed into something more…commanding. Was this how he was as captain?

"We're playing a game today, split into groups of two. You guys are team captains." He pointed to Matthew and Joshua, who both looked equally excited to be chosen.

"What are we playing, Coach?" I asked.

Case smiled and winked before speaking. "Sharks and minnows."

CHAPTER 6

case

Whoever suggested Basil needed help with coaching needed to remove their head from their ass. Because in the entire hour since practice started, I hadn't done much of anything except help someone tie their skates because they couldn't reach them with all their gear on. Other than that, I was useless.

While the kids winded down and collected the cones to bring to Basil, I skated toward her. "You've done an amazing job." My comment seemed to hit a soft spot, and a soft blush crossed her cheeks. "Really, I wasn't expecting these kids to have such a solid foundation of the basics. They barely needed any help."

Basil lifted her chin, and my eyes traced over the soft bump on her nose, and the her full lips. When she opened her mouth to speak, my gaze snapped back to her eyes, hoping to get another glimpse of the freckled green and brown. Her eyes were so dark when we first met, I hadn't realized they were so colorful.

"Is he giving you a hard time, Coach?" Michael asked as he placed himself between Basil and me with his arms crossed. I chuckled and shook my head. I watched as Michael squinted his eyes and kneeled to talk to him.

"I was just telling Coach Andrews how awesome you guys are. I have a lot to learn from her."

"Hm, let me know if he bothers you again, okay, Coach?" Michael said before he skated off. I sat there, shocked, as we watched him join the other kids.

Basil watched them with her arms crossed as I stood up. She was biting her lip as she tried to contain a smile when she looked at me. "I was not expecting that." She took a deep breath before yelling, "Okay, everyone, bring it in!"

The kids skated over, and I took the cones from them before they form a semi-circle around us. Basil clasped her hands together before showing a prideful smile. "You guys were great today. Go home and get some rest and we'll see you on Saturday, okay?"

When Basil turned to grab the cones from me, I pulled them from her reach and smiled.

"What?"

"You said 'we.'" I pulled my brows in and curiosity filled my next words. "Why aren't you trying to get rid of me?"

She scoffed and reached for the cones again, but instead of pulling them away, I skated toward the side-board. Basil caught up with ease, and I saw the tension filling her shoulders as she huffed. "Is there any point? The only way I can get rid of you is if you decide to leave. But someone on your team will just replace you."

I stopped skating as a tightness landed in my chest with the brutal reality of her situation. Basil kept going until she realized how far ahead she was, then she skated back. I looked over her soft features and noticed the small signs of stress and what I could only assume was lack of sleep evident in the bags under her eyes.

She knew someone would show up. She just didn't know it would be me.

Had this been stressing her out that much?

While I was a bit reluctant to be here—already busy with obligations for the Peaks—I just accepted it was something I had to do. Now, was I surprised to see Basil was the Coach I was helping? Of course, but now guilt filled me knowing she didn't have any say in this. I didn't know Basil outside of this building. But I knew the woman who stood toe-to-toe with me and poked me in the chest deserved to have a say in everything in her life.

"Do you want me to leave?"

Basil snapped her head toward me, her eyes widened, and whatever defenses she had up dropped. She opened her mouth to speak, but a booming voice interrupted her.

"Mr. Whitlock!"

We both looked over and saw an older gentleman walking toward us. I closed the small distance and noticed how Basil kept her distance as she followed me. As recognized him as I skated closer, pristine suit, well-groomed hair, and thick glasses. He was the man that was talking down to Basil last week in the hallway.

I put on my blade protectors and stepped onto the green carpet. Then I stood straighter before I took his outstretched hand.

"How was your first day, son?" he asked.

Basil had stepped up behind me, put her blade protectors on, and walked toward the benches behind the man. He didn't so much as glance at her, and my grip tightened around his hand. He pulled away but showed no sign he noticed any change in my demeanor.

"I'm sorry. Who are you again? I don't believe we've properly met," I said before I walked past him and sat next to Basil. I placed the cones on the bench before I started working on my laces. She glanced at me briefly before she set her skates to the side and grabbed her shoes.

The man cleared his throat and smirked. "Theodore Clein, perhaps you've heard of me?"

Shit.

Of course, I'd heard of him. He was responsible for nearly half my team *being* on the team. Basil spoke up then when the silence between us turned tense. "He did great, better than I expected, really." Her voice was nonchalant as she continued to put her shoes on.

Mr. Clein clicked his tongue and waved a hand. "Oh, don't listen to her. She's just trying to humble you. I mean," he rolled his eyes, "why wouldn't a hockey captain be a great coach? You'll be teaching her all the tips and tricks she needs to be—hm—competent."

I watched as Basil flinched when his words landed on her, and I wanted to leave. Take her away and fill whatever crater his words and judgments left in her mind with kinder words.

"Anyhow, it was great seeing you. I'll be sure to see you at the game this weekend." He moved to pat my shoulder, but I stood and grabbed Basil's skates before he touched me. He quickly recovered and called Aiden over.

They left and once the door clicked shut, I asked Basil, "Has he always been an asshole?"

"To me, or in general? Cause I only have experience with one of those," she said before she stood and reached for her skates.

I held them away. "That's not funny."

"I'm not laughing. Now, give me my skates."

She held my hard stare as I let her grab her things. When she went for the cones, though, I grabbed them and turned. I walked over to the door and held it open, a silent command for her to go first. With a sigh, Basil walked through and waited for me before we headed to the equipment locker together. I hated the tense silence between us, but as much as I wanted to make things better, I wasn't sure what Basil wanted.

I gave Basil the cones and let her put them back. "You never got the chance to answer my question earlier," I stated as I watched her maneuver an old net.

"What question was that again?"

I watched as her eyes skated over me when I crossed my arms and inclined my head. "Do you want me to leave? I can talk with Coach Warner, tell him you've got this team handled and none of us will bother you."

Basil opened her mouth a few times before biting the inside of her cheek. I moved closer, ready to tell her it would be okay. I didn't know how I was going to deal with Mr. Clein, but I would, so she didn't have to be on the receiving end of his complaints. Now, I wouldn't lie and say I wanted her to tell me to talk to Warner. Because I *wanted* to stay.

This was the only opportunity I had to see Basil, and I didn't want to let it go.

"What are you doing later?" she asked.

I blinked. "What?"

Basil shook her head and walked past me, toward the locker rooms. "I asked what you were doing later. I'm getting dinner with my roommate if you want to come along."

"Uhh—"

We walked down the hallway, and I couldn't help but notice how little the walls were decorated on this side of the facility. The athletic wing had pictures of famous athletes lining the walls and trophy cases inside the locker rooms. These walls though—were pretty boring.

"Look." Basil turned around and held her skates in front of her. She took a steadying breath before looking at me, and I saw how her brows creased. "If we're going to be co-workers, then we should at least figure out if we get along. Be friends, maybe?"

I felt myself smile, an involuntary reaction I think, whenever I looked at Basil. She wanted to be friends. A blush crept across her cheeks as she shifted her weight. Her features tightened as she winced.

"Do you have any pain medicine?" I asked, wanting to reach out and offer some support, but Basil shook her head.

"I have some in my car. You gonna come eat or what?"

I looked down at her, determined to grab onto this chance at friendship and never let go.

"Can I invite some friends?"

———

First Basil wrongfully accused me of a crime, then she committed one herself.

"I'm pretty sure that would earn you jail time in some countries," I stated, before taking a bite of my pizza. The sauce was rich and perfectly acidic, like they used the freshest tomatoes they could find. It was one reason why this was my favorite pizza spot. It had live music, friendly people, and an aroma that made you feel like you weren't in downtown Denver. This place was perfect—until now. Seeing how Basil ruined her food with condiments might put me off pizza forever.

Basil rolled her eyes as a smile tugged on her lips. "Have you even tried it?" she asked.

I felt my face morph into something I hoped expressed disgust, but Scottie answered for me, dipping his pizza into the bowl.

"Don't mind him, Basil. He likes ranch on everything except pizza."

Basil raised a brow. "Is that so?"

"Yes, ranch dressing is reserved for things like chicken nuggets, vegetables, and popcorn." I watched as Basil made a face that matched my own.

Her nose scrunched. "Ranch popcorn? That's—ew."

I shook my head and pointed to her food. "No, that's ew."

"You just don't have good taste," she said, teasing as she dipped her pizza once again. My eyes quickly gave her a once-over before I took a sip of my drink.

I beg to differ.

With a blush on her cheeks, Basil turned her attention toward Scottie and smiled. And I was jealous for a second. She smiled at me once, earlier, and it wasn't enough. The way she seemed to warm with the expression–like she radiated sunlight. I wanted them all for myself.

"So, how long have you been on the team again?"

Scottie finished his food and cleared his throat before answering her. "Since the end of last season."

"Ah, a rookie then," Hollis said, finishing off her food and leaning back in the booth. She placed her head on Basil and continued with a smile. "How old are you? Because you clearly didn't get drafted right out of high school. Unless," Hollis leaned in and dropped her voice to a whisper, "did you take steroids?"

Scottie chuckled and crossed his arms. "No, I've never touched that stuff. I'm twenty-two. I played in college and was drafted my senior year. I signed right after graduation."

"He's a great addition to the team," I said, giving him a solid pat on the back. When I invited him after leaving practice with Basil, Scottie jumped at the chance to come. I guess he and Hollis had been meaning to meet up, but they couldn't figure out their schedules. Townes was invited too, but he had Hayley and it was a school night, and he didn't want to break her routine.

I turned to Hollis and asked, "So, Hollis, are you excited to be a homeowner?"

She perked up and straightened, placing her hands on the table as she leaned back. "Words can't describe how excited I am. I'm still in escrow right now, and a lot can change between now and closing, so I'm just hoping it's smooth sailing until I sign those papers."

"You've worked really hard to get it, Hol," Basil said, a soft smile on her face as she looked at her friend.

"Don't look at me like that or I'll cry," Hollis said, tears already forming.

Basil looked at me, that smile still on her face before it melted into a yawn. "Well, despite all the fun, I think we need to get going."

The warm feeling in my chest—that had been there all evening—cooled. But I kept a smile on my face. I wanted to stay here and watch Basil light up around her friend, but it was getting late. I grabbed the check from Basil's hands and ignored her protesting stare as I slid my card in. "You ladies should head out. We got this."

"You sure? I can send you our portion of the check," Basil said reaching into her purse.

"Basil, let me buy you the damn food, okay?"

Hollis and Basil looked at each other for a moment before Basil huffed. Her eyes glanced between us before her focus landed on me.

"Thank you." She looked back at Hollis, who nudged her with her elbow. "We don't have practice the rest of the week, so I'll see you on Saturday. Oh, here." She handed me her phone, and when I didn't take it, she rolled her eyes. "Your number, in case something comes up with the meet."

I quickly put in my number and handed her phone back to her. When her hand brushed over mine, a soft blush crept over her cheeks.

I smiled. "See you Saturday."

basil

"Want me to run back out and get you a coffee?" I asked, wondering if the dark circles under Case's eyes were from exhaustion, or the result of a couple of well-landed punches from his game last night. Not that *I* put the game on or anything. I was scrolling through the channels and it was the only thing on that was interesting. That was it.

My intrigue in watching his game had nothing to do with dinner the other night, and how I realized Case was a nice guy. I was overreacting toward him being at practice earlier this week and I projected my problems onto him. That wasn't fair.

Our game today was at a smaller community ice rink, and I met Case outside a few minutes ago, waiting for me. We walked inside and, after saying our 'good mornings' to the coaches of the opposing team, we set up our area on the bench.

The wood was worn, and the carpet was pulled up around the base of the bench. The arena smelled of cleaning products, and it was colder than our rink. I pulled my jacket tighter to my body before I set down our team's duffel bags, which were full of extra equipment. They took up an entire corner of the small area we were in and didn't leave much room for Case and me. I let him take the bench while I stood in front of him.

When Case didn't respond, and instead leaned his head on the Plexiglas with closed eyes, I clicked my tongue. "Here." I held out my untouched coffee.

Case shook his head with forced, lazy effort. "No, I'm fine. Just need to rest my eyes for a minute."

I shook my hand slightly—as if he would notice. "Take it. I'll run out and get some more. It's fine. We don't need you falling asleep during the game."

His brows pulled in together. "I won't," he grumbled.

I smiled and rolled my eyes. "I know you won't, because you're going to take this and let the caffeine do its job."

Case peeked through long eyelashes, and those tired, green eyes seemed brighter against his dark sweater. His eyes met mine and I couldn't help but notice how slightly blood-shot they were. I stepped closer to where he was sitting and set the coffee next to him. My body warmed as he tracked my movements, but I kept my gaze down as I grabbed my purse. When I turned around, I was met with Mr. Clein's hard stare, and the flimsy bag almost slipped from my shoulder.

"Going somewhere before the game starts?" he asked with a raised brow. The gray hairs seemed more prominent under the different lighting.

"Just to get some more coffee. Shouldn't be an issue, seeing there's still plenty of time before we have to start," I said, glancing at the spot on my wrist where a watch would sit. Case stood behind me and moved closer. His spiced scent hit my nose, and I wished I had more time to figure out exactly what it was.

"I'll go get it. You stay here to greet the kids," Case said from beside me. He flashed a smile and held up the coffee cup I had set down. "Besides, I need to move around. Get this coffee flowing."

I nodded and watched as Mr. Clein followed Case when he walked away. Case tossed his head back. "Text me your order!"

As soon as they were out of sight, I directed my attention to Aiden and his mom. She was adjusting his jersey before he ran toward the bench. I smiled in greeting as she walked over.

"Aiden is super excited to play today. He's been talking about it since the last practice."

I had always liked Elise. Where her husband was sharp and demeaning, she was soft and welcoming. Despite how Mr. Clein may treat me, he seemed to be head over heels for his wife. He was always smiling at her, and it made it hard to not like him sometimes.

"He's been working hard to improve his behavior."

"My dad said I'm back in the game because of him," Aiden beamed from the bench. My mouth opened before Elise beat me to words I wasn't sure I was going to say.

"You're starting because of *you*, sweetie." She rubbed the space between her brows before she shot me an apologetic look. "His father says the strangest things sometimes." The words were mumbled, and a smile replaced the slight scowl marring her pristine face. "Well, I'll leave you to it." Then she walked to find a seat. My phone buzzed in my pocket just as a few other kids arrived.

CASE

What kind of coffee do you drink?

Hm? Where are you?

Rhonda's.

Just ask them for my usual.

Case returned shortly after, two coffees in hand. I eagerly grabbed mine and sighed when the cool pumpkin cream coated my tongue.

"Are the kids ready?" he asked, watching as both teams on the ice stretched in their respective corners.

I nodded as I kept my focus on everyone. "This should be an easy win. The Meese haven't been doing so well this season."

"I'm sorry. Did you say their team name is Meese?"

I heard the smile that came with his tone's inflection, and I couldn't help but tilt my head up to look at him. "One of the kids had gone to Alaska before the season started. Guess she convinced everyone how cool Moose are and that's the name they decided on."

"Is Meese even accurate?"

"Not at all, but you try explaining the linguistics behind the word Moose to a group of eight-year-olds."

Case hummed and took another sip of his drink. "You've got a point. So," he shuffled closer and the hairs on my neck stood in response to his proximity, "did you have a good time at dinner?"

The tightness in his voice stuck out to me. Was he nervous? I kept my eyes forward on the other team as they wrangled their gear. I shifted my weight on the carpet and smiled. "I had a great time, did you?"

"Yeah, yeah. I mean, watching you eat your pizza with ranch kinda threw me for a loop. But once I got over your bad taste in food, everything was fine."

I turned to face him and my hand connected with his bicep with a solid *thwack*. I kept thoughts of how hard his body was at bay and opened my mouth in protest. "I do *not* have bad taste in food."

I was raised by a chef, for crying out loud. Just because I couldn't cook to save my life didn't mean my taste was bad. My cheeks heated as I peered up at Case and found his eyes were locked on mine, and I knew I should back down. Pull away and keep my distance. Because I was uncomfortable with how my stomach flipped and what it meant. Case's dimple made itself known when he smiled, and my stomach flipped again.

"If you say so, sunshine."

Sunshine?

The ring of the buzzer suddenly tore me away from whatever was going on in the small space between us and back to reality. I watched as the kids got into their positions on the ice and I set aside the warm fuzzy feeling that was crawling into my chest.

With Case at my side, and that nickname stuck in my head, we watched as the game began. The other team took possession of the puck by a new player. He was a bit bigger than the other kids, and much faster. Aiden and Matthew did well to keep him away from the goal, but they couldn't seem to take possession of the puck. All of a sudden, the kid faked out Aiden and skated straight toward the goal. He pulled the stick back and hit the puck—*hard*—it flew right past Michael into the goal.

"That's okay!" I yelled, clapping as our team rearranged themselves for the next play.

The rest of the first half wasn't any better. Case and I watched as Michael struggled to block the pucks, and it wasn't until Aiden skated by and said something to him that had me turning and scanning the crowd. The buzzer rang, and I turned just in time to see Michael's sodden face when he removed the goalie mask.

"Damn it."

"Everything okay?" Case asked. His mouth was tight as his eyes scanned over me. I nodded.

"I need to talk to Michael."

I moved to walk past Case, but he put a hand out to stop me. I opened my mouth to protest, but was caught off guard by the sudden, confident wink. "I'll talk to him."

Case sauntered right up to Michael before he kneeled in front of him and placed a hand on his shoulder. I watched as Michael wiped his nose before he and Case walked over to a less crowded corner. I turned around to the other kids who were ravaging their food.

"We suck Coach Andrews," Kyle said around an orange slice. His remark earned groans from the other kids before they joined in.

"Yeah, they're so much better."

"Can we just go home?"

I kneeled in front of the bench the kids were sitting on and clasped my hands together before I slowly made eye contact with each of them. Once they were all quiet and I had their attention, I shook my head. "Since when do we act like sore losers?"

Some of the boys slouched in their seats, but I continued, "What do we talk about every practice?" I asked, looking for a volunteer to answer the simple question. "Aiden. What do we say?"

He sat a little straighter and held my stern gaze. "It's okay if things are hard."

I glanced at the others. "Do we just give up when things aren't going how we want?" They shook their heads. "Look, you guys have done amazing so far this season. But I think it's a good thing you're struggling today. How else are you going to get better if every game is an easy win?"

The kids all nodded and continued eating their snacks, finishing just in time when the buzzer rang again. I looked around as they filed onto the ice, looking for Case and Michael. I almost called in another kid to take over for goalie when Michael came running by, and his goalie mask hit the sideboard. "Don't worry, Coach! I won't let you down!"

"What did you tell him?" I asked Case, as he took his spot next to me. He shrugged his shoulders and smiled.

"Just gave him a little encouragement, is all. He said his dad wasn't here?" His brows tensed, and I let out a sigh.

"He works a lot, is all." That was all I could give him because I didn't know more than that. What I did know was when his dad *did* show up, Michael wore the warmest smile. I always encouraged the parents to show up for games, because it meant so much to the kids. Case nodded, and a comfortable silence fell between us as we watched the rest of the game, each of us only speaking to encourage the kids.

They played great in the second half—stealing the puck and scoring with ease. They caught up easily, and with Michael blocking the other team's last attempt at scoring, we won. The kids cheered and gathered on the ice to celebrate, and I was too busy watching them to notice Case move. His arm wrapped around my shoulder before he pulled me into his side. My skin tingled at the warm pressure of his body, but I still froze, realizing it was kind of… nice.

"That was a close one." That too familiar voice sounded from behind us, and the excitement in my chest morphed into dread as the feeling fell to my stomach. I stepped away from Case and we turned around to face Mr. Clein.

"It was, but they did great that second half."

"Hm. Well, maybe if things were different, they would have done great the entire game."

I held in the rising anger and smiled through my teeth. "If you'd be so kind, Mr. Clein, to wait with the other parents by the benches? Case and I have to talk with the kids before they're released for the weekend."

Case shifted closer to me, and I didn't have to look to know he was leveling Mr. Clein with a stare. If I had any doubts, though, the way the older man nervously adjusted his cuff links gave it away. "Make it quick. We all have places to be."

"Basil—" Case said once Mr. Clein was out of earshot, but I turned around to greet the kids coming onto the bench.

"Amazing. I'm so proud of you guys. That was an amazing comeback. I hope we all learned something from today's game," I said to the kids, watching their proud smiles take up their little faces. "Go ahead and find your parents when you've changed out your skates and I'll see you next week."

I smiled at their eagerness to change and watched them run to their parents. My phone buzzed in my pocket, and I pulled it out to three new text messages.

MOM

Just put dinner in the oven, should be done when you get here.

But if you're going to cancel again, just tell me asap, okay?

HOLLIS

Good luck with your mom. Love you, B.

I groaned and shoved my phone back into my pocket before turning around, ready to get the equipment and get out of here, but Case beat me to it. He slung the duffel over his shoulder and handed me my bag and the coffee I didn't finish.

"So, do you normally celebrate wins on your own? Or are we going to start a new tradition?" he asked with a smile. I wanted it to last forever so I could stare at his dimple and question how it made my mood better.

If only time was on my side. I grabbed stuff from his

hands before telling him, "As fun as that sounds, I have dinner with my mom tonight."

"Is that a bad thing?"

Shoot. I didn't want him to hear the hint of disappointment in my voice, but I promised her I wouldn't cancel again.

"It is because it means I can't hang out with you," I said with a smile, and it wasn't until I got into my car that I realized how true that was.

basil

When I pulled into the driveway and shut the car, I took a minute to admire my childhood home. I used to look at the blue wood paneling and large white windows in awe. This home was built with so much love, and I was sad I only got to experience it for a short while.

With a steadying breath, I got out of the car and made my way to the door. The sun had dropped low in the sky and took its warmth with it. I shivered against the slight breeze and crossed my arms. The leaves Mom hadn't bothered to rake up crunched under my shoes.

I was overwhelmed by the smell of roasted lamb when I opened the door, but my attention was quickly pulled from the food to the obese black lab running up to me. His tail hit my shins hard enough to leave bruises, but I didn't care. I wiped my feet on the green entryway rug and bent down.

"Hi Socks," I told him with a solid pat on the side of his stomach. He licked my hand before running back to his dog bed, where I noticed the half-eaten dog bone. I stood and walked through the minimally designed house. Mom didn't have any decorations on her walls, instead, she had one picture hanging. It was the family pictures we had taken right before I left for college, and it hung just below the gigantic clock she spent too much money on a few years ago. I passed the front room and rounded the corner.

"Hi Mom," I said as I entered the kitchen, where I found her taking dinner out of the oven. The marble counters were free of any clutter, and it smelled even better in here.

"Hi honey," she said with a smile before wiping her hands on her black apron. "Do you mind getting the table settings?"

I nodded and headed straight for the cabinet, where I grabbed the plates and cups. As I laid them out, Mom followed behind me with the utensils, she sat them down before she retreated into the kitchen. She came back out with our dinner, and my mouth watered at the sight.

"There's some roasted vegetables still in the kitchen, mind grabbing them?" she asked.

I nodded and grabbed them from the counter. When I reached the light gray table, I placed the oval dish next to the lamb before taking a seat. Socks waddled up and nudged my hand, begging for food.

"No, no Socks. Come on, outside." Mom snapped her fingers. Socks waddled to the back door, his tail tucked in exaggeration to being denied food. I chuckled and started serving my plate.

"He acts like you never feed him."

"The vet put him on a diet, so to him, I don't," Mom said, filling her plate with food.

I pushed away the heavy feeling in my stomach and took a bite. "This is good."

Mom smiled and sat straighter. There was nothing my mother loved more than to be complimented on her cooking. She finished her bite of carrots and looked at me. "I'm just happy you didn't cancel at the last minute again."

The jab hit my chest, but my smile held firm. I poked the vegetables on my plate. "Yeah, sorry about that."

"You never gave me a reason, sweetie. Was everything okay?"

While letting my mother into the affairs of my personal life was not something I enjoyed doing, I knew she wouldn't drop the subject. My mother was not the kind of person to live and forget. She wanted to remember everything, so she could throw it back in your face when the time came. I cleared my throat and leveled her with a soft gaze. "I was just having a really bad day, and it slipped my mind. Sorry, Mom."

"What happened? You're usually more put together than that, Basil."

I looked at her and tried to remember when she changed, or if she ever did. Maybe my mother had always been this rough and her words had always felt like a branding iron. I had become so accustomed to her edges that I didn't realize soft things existed until I left.

My foot tapped on the hardwood floors as I took another breath. "I had gotten some news at work that made me upset. That's it. I'm sure the same thing happens to you sometimes."

"Well, sure. But I don't mope about it," she bit out and my gaze dropped to the table. "What news did you get?"

Whatever opinions she had—I could handle it.

"That I was getting an assistant coach," I said.

She laughed, and my skin prickled with the sound. It was too fake, too forced, and it made me feel small. "Why did that upset you? You shouldn't be turning down help." Her fork made a loud screech when she dragged it across her plate and I winced. I knew she had never been supportive of my decision to be involved in sports. Sure, she'd show up to my volleyball games sometimes. But we both knew she didn't want to be there. Growing up, she'd boast to her friends and colleagues she was raising the next best chef. She put her dreams and goals onto my little shoulders, even when I continued to fail.

Still, hearing those words from your mother stung.

"I don't need help. That's the problem, Mom. One of the parents thinks otherwise, though, but it's only because we don't exactly see eye to eye when it comes to disciplinary action."

"Well, clearly someone thinks you could use the help. Discipline is very important in your field. You shouldn't think you're above anyone just because you're the coach," she said with a shrug of her shoulders. "Just accept it and move on. You've always been sensitive when things don't go your way."

I had forgotten the food on my plate and sat straighter as I told her. "I've already accepted the help. I even invited him to dinner with me and Hollis so we could get to know each other better." I watched as she raised a blonde brow and lowered her fork. As she stared at me, I took note of all the ways we were different. Jean Brown had always been a refined woman, with long blonde hair and deep blue eyes. Her complexion was much fairer than mine. We shared a nose, but everything else was from my father.

"Him?" Her words were cold and edged with concern. I watched the warning land on her tongue before she even took her next breath.

I sank into my chair. I was tired, and this was the last conversation I wanted to have. "Don't worry. Nothing is going on, and that won't change."

I blamed my parent's divorce for Mom being so cynical toward relationships. And seeing how heartbroken she was when Dad left, well, it made me cynical, too. At least at first, until she became responsible for that feeling. At some point, she tried dating again, but those relationships never lasted. It only fueled her resentment until she decided she was better off alone. And that I was too. What was the point of love when it just ended in someone getting hurt?

She hummed under her breath and turned her attention back to her plate. I took a moment to gather myself, my nerves wrung out from the tension she created. It was silent for a few minutes before she tapped the table with her finger, the only indication she was about to say something that made her uncomfortable. "Have you talked to your dad lately?"

"Not in a while. Why?"

I hadn't spoken to my father in months. Our relationship never seemed to survive his split from Mom. Not that I wanted one with him to begin with. He cheated on her and then decided not to talk to me for the better part of ten years. Hard to *want* to get to know him when he forgot about me.

Mom sighed and leaned back, her finger still tapping on the table. "He's apparently decided to get married. Call him please so he can invite you himself. I'm not doing it for him."

That was all either of us said the rest of the night outside of casual small talk. Mom told me about a new restaurant she was going to be working at, and I told her about our winning game today. When our plates were empty, I helped her clean the kitchen and let Socks back inside, saving him from the late October cold.

After everything was clean, she walked me to the door and embraced me in a cold hug. "Get home safe sweetie and don't forget our next dinner night, okay? You live on the other side of town, but I never see you enough," she said, rubbing my shoulders before she pulled away and pinned me with a smile. I nodded, not trusting myself to promise her I'd be back for her monthly planned dinner nights.

After another small hug, I got in my car and headed

home. One nice thing about these dinners with Mom was how long they lasted. Once I was home, Hollis—completely oblivious to my presence—walked into the kitchen. Wearing nothing but disheveled hair and a bed sheet. I cleared my throat from the small entryway and she whirled around, her eyes going wide.

"B! I, uh—didn't expect you to be home so soon."

I smirked and shook my head. "Don't tell him I'm here, okay? Get what you need and go back and enjoy your night."

Hollis nodded and grabbed a glass of juice before scurrying back to her room, where I knew Ryan was getting dressed and making an excuse to leave. As I walked through the small apartment to the kitchen, I couldn't help but compare it to my mom's house. Hollis and I had papers littered along the countertop; clean dishes laid out on a towel because we both thought hand washing was easier. Bathroom carts were strategically placed in different corners to hold books, snacks, medicine, and other small items.

Mom would have a heart attack if she saw our kitchen. Where hers was pristine—everything had a place—ours was chaotically organized. I loved to collect mugs, and Hollis liked to buy new kitchen appliances. The air fryer and expensive coffee machine were shoved against one wall and the small decor she bought at a thrift store took up the rest of the space.

Anytime we cooked, we had to use the small counter and move all the papers. It wasn't much, but it was ours.

I grabbed a bottle of water from the fridge and started for my room, my head pounding from the night. I laid in bed, and stared at the ceiling as I went over dinner.

I never should have gone tonight. I should have waited a bit longer, so the sting of her disappointment wouldn't have hurt so much. My phone dinged on the bedside table,

I rolled over to grab it, and my mood brightened at the name on the screen. Which was...odd. I ignored that feeling and opened the text thread.

CASE

Hope you had a good night with your mom. How bout we start a new tradition next weekend?

It went...as expected. And I already have a tradition. Come home and nap...you want to do something else?

We're friends now right? How bout lunch before practice?

You aren't too busy?

Nah. My schedule is a lot lighter since I'm helping you now. So you get me an extra hour before practice.

That sounds great.

CHAPTER 9

case

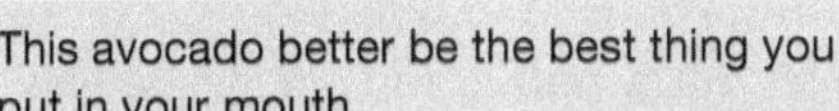

I shoved my phone back into my pocket just as Rhonda put my order on the counter, a strong smile overpowering her soft features. "See you next week, Case," she said as put something wrapped in parchment into the bag and winked. "A little something for Basil."

I thanked her and grabbed the bag from the counter before starting my walk back to the training center. Once outside, my phone rang. I glanced at the caller ID before answering.

"Hey, what's up?"

"You skipped out on our lunch last week." Aubrey's voice was hard, and I wished I had a free hand to run through my hair. I sighed and looked up at the cloudless sky. The past month had been busier than usual, and a lot of that was thanks to coaching. Between practice for the Peaks and helping Basil, I hadn't had much time for anything else.

Explaining that to Aubrey wasn't going to be fun, but I prepared myself anyway. "Yeah. Look, Aubs, you know I wouldn't do it on purpose."

"But you did it, anyway. You didn't even call."

"I know."

I had every intention of calling her, but I crashed after my shower from pure exhaustion. The team had a game Thursday, then I had practice with Basil, and then the Rockets had their game. Between recovering from a hangover and being responsible for a bunch of kids, I didn't sleep. But those were all excuses preventing me from doing what I needed to do—this thing with Aubrey needed to end.

"Aubrey, we need to talk."

She let out a huff, and I knew she was pouting. I could see how she crossed her arms over her middle, and I knew she had shifted her weight to her left leg. "We can talk when you make it up to me. Case, we have an image to uphold. You know how important that is." Her voice softened. "Besides, I miss hanging out with you."

I opened the door to the training center and waved to Daniel. Lunch with Aubrey was the last thing I wanted to do, but I relented. "I'll see what day works and text you when we can get together. I gotta get going, okay?"

"Yeah. Bye Case."

She hung up, and I continued walking to the glass doors that separated the athletic space from the rest of eye gym. The scanner on the door blinked green, and I hauled it open and made my way to the glorified cafeteria. Square tables filled the center of the room, and a long counter lined the far-right corner where athletes got their pre-made meals. The opposite side of the room was decorated with colorful couches and loveseats. They were placed in front of the massive windows that make up the front of the building. I started walking toward Basil's and I's usual spot, but my legs stopped when my eyes landed on her.

Like they often did.

Slowly, my eyes traced over her—she was sitting on the green velvet sofa she claimed she hated. Basil's deep brown hair cascaded over her shoulders as she kept her attention on the book in her lap. I wondered if the contents inside were responsible for her flushed cheeks. As I looked closer and watched as she bit the inside of her cheek, I got my answer.

I wanted nothing more than to sit next to her, pull her into my lap, and run my fingers through her hair while she continued reading.

This entire month, since she agreed to have lunch with me, I had been trying to determine if this feeling I got when I was around her was real. What started as a spark—when she jabbed me in the chest—had turned into a small, steady flame. It burned soft and warmed the cracks of my heart I didn't realize existed. And that flame continued to grow. Every time she walked into a room, each time she laughed at a bad joke, and when she smiled.

God, that smile.

Basil lifted her head, rolled it back, and made eye contact with me. She smiled, full, bright, and teasing. "Are you going to stand there, or are you going to feed me?" she asked.

The image of me doing just that flashed through my mind, making me warm.

I cleared my throat and continued my path toward her, unaware of how long I was standing there. Her eyes followed me and her head straightened when I sat across from her in the red leather loveseat. I placed the bag on the mahogany coffee table that separated us and started grabbing our food. Basil placed the book under her thigh and watched as I placed her food in front of her.

The sound she made when she took a bite of her sandwich was obscene, and my pants felt a fraction tighter. I cleared my throat. "What's the game plan for this weekend?"

"I'm still waiting on details from Hol. She said Scottie is helping her move things out on Saturday before they go pick up her new furniture. So, everything should be good to go when we show up on Sunday."

I nodded, and the sudden rumble of the air conditioning had me noticing the slight shiver that ran through Basil.

"Cold?" I asked.

She wasn't wearing anything particularly warm, a thin long-sleeved shirt and jeans. I didn't see a jacket anywhere. Basil tried to brush it off with a shrug, but the way she shoved her free hand under her thigh wasn't discrete. "I'm fine."

I raised a brow and watched as she tried to keep from shivering. As if I had no control of my body, I stood and removed my hoodie. A soft kiss of air touched my skin when I pulled the material over my head. I hurried and yanked the hoodie off and adjusted my undershirt before handing it to Basil. She sat there, eyes wide as her gaze darted between me, and the dark fabric bunched in my hand. I watched as she worked through a thick swallow and I cleared my throat.

"Here."

"Won't you be cold?" she asked without moving.

I shrugged. "I'll be fine; besides, you need it more than I do."

She opened her mouth, but I held out my hand, stopping whatever she was about to say. "Come on, stand up. Please?" I asked, holding out the hoodie. She eyed me skeptically before she rose to her feet. I rounded the coffee table before I gripped the fabric between both hands and held it out. I placed it over her head and helped her work her arms into the sleeves.

Once the hoodie was settled over her, my hands rested just above where the hemline settled past her hips. I smiled down at her and asked, "Better?"

Her cheeks were tinged a soft pink when she nodded.

I gave her a soft squeeze before I pulled away and sat down to eat my lunch. Basil stood where I left her, with her brows pulled together.

"What's wrong?" I asked around the bite of my sandwich.

She regarded me for a moment before letting out a small huff. "Have you ever taken a love language test?"

"A what?"

Basil sat on the sofa and pulled out her phone, taking a sip of her smoothie as she typed. "A love language test." She placed her phone in my hand and leaned back. "It pretty much tells you how you show love and how you like to receive it."

I started answering the questions on the screen as Basil continued talking. "For example, I scored highest on acts of service. So, I show love by doing things for other people, and feel loved when people do things for me."

She shifted in her seat, and the motion sent an uncomfortable wave through me. I kept my focus on finishing the test until the results popped up. Basil shifted closer, leaning over the coffee table to look at the phone.

She hummed, "I'm not surprised."

"You're not?"

"No. You're the most touchy-feely person I know," she said as she leaned back to look at me. Her cheeks were still flushed, but something was off. I didn't like it. I scrolled through the results: physical touch was the first one, followed by quality time, gift-giving, acts of service, and words of affirmation came last.

My brows pulled together as I asked Basil, "Which one did you get last? That's what you like the least, right?"

She sank back into the sofa and mumbled something, making me lean in so I could hear her. "What?"

"Physical touch. That's the one I like the least," she said, keeping her voice level.

A cold wave washed over me. The instances I had touched her in the past ran through my mind. Had I realized she was uncomfortable, I never would have done any of it. But I didn't understand why she never said anything.

"Shit Basil. I'm sorry."

"It's fine," she said as a flush crawled over her cheeks. But she kept her focus on the empty food wrapper in her hands.

"Why didn't you tell me?" I asked.

I swore, her pink flush deepened to a scarlet. When she opened her mouth to answer, she stopped. It made me feel bad for putting her in an uncomfortable position. So, while she mulled over her thoughts, I reached for the bag. Discreetly, I pulled out Rhonda's surprise and thought of how I was going to divert her attention. Pull her mind from her wandering thoughts to something more enjoyable.

"Hey, question." I waited until she looked at me before continuing. "How come you haven't been to any of our games?"

"You noticed?"

I smiled. "Of course, you're the first person I try to find when we get onto the ice." I resisted the urge to reach out and touch her when she looked away. The need to touch her was as normal as breathing, but she didn't like it. So, I rubbed my hands on my knees instead and tried to grab her gaze. "What's wrong?"

She cleared her throat before looking back at me, and I saw the smallest hint of embarrassment in those golden eyes. "I can't afford the tickets. That's why I haven't been to your games."

I clicked my tongue and pulled out my phone. Basil eyed the movements and waited patiently for me to say something. When I got the text back from Warner, I put my phone away and smiled at her. "You can come now," I said, before finishing off my sandwich.

"What?" she asked, surprise crossing her face.

I put the empty wrapper in the bag and shrugged. "There's going to be two tickets waiting for you at the ticket booth. Walk up and give them your name, and you'll be good to go."

She opened her mouth, but I cut her off. "If you argue with me, then you don't get your surprise." I pulled out the dessert and held it to my side; Basil's eyes widened as she looked between me and the brownie.

"They had some?"

"It was the last one," I said with a teasing smile.

I thought Basil was exaggerating when she told me about the brownies and the old lady who tried to push me out of the way to get one was being dramatic. But after I took a bite of the one I got before practice two weeks ago —I was a changed man. I never go to Rhonda's expecting to get one, but when I saw her put the brownie into the bag earlier, my chest warmed. The fact she made sure Basil got one solidified why Rhonda's was now my favorite food spot.

Although, I wasn't expecting to use the treat as leverage against a beautiful woman today. I had unwrapped the brownie halfway when Basil leveled me with a stare.

"Give me the brownie, Case." She reached for it, her knee rested on the small table and her fingers grazed the parchment before I held it out of her reach. Right above my head.

"Not until you accept those tickets without arguing with me," I argued.

She tilted her head and sighed, "You buying me lunch is one thing, Case. Those tickets are expensive. I feel bad."

I shrugged. "You know how much money I make. Does it really upset you that much?"

Basil pursed her lips, and her eyes held mine as that pink returned to her cheeks. She glanced at the brownie before letting out a heavy sigh. Her voice was low when she spoke. "I don't want your perception of me to change because I can't afford certain things. Or think I'm taking advantage of you because you have money."

Of all the ridiculous…

"Basil, that's absurd."

"You're the one that asked. Now, give it," she commanded.

Basil backed away and walked around the coffee table to stand in front of me, reaching out an arm to grab the brownie from my grip. I stood before she got too close, and watched as she raised her chin to match my gaze, determination filling those hazel eyes of hers. The golden flecks in her left eye were so clear from this proximity. I gave into my urge to touch her, and gently grabbed her outstretched arm, lowering it. Basil took an involuntary step closer, and I took a steady breath as my skin burned at the contact.

"Listen, Basil," I watched her swallow, a thick, slow

movement. "You shouldn't be concerned about what I think of you. Because I promise you, any assumptions you think I have about you are wrong." She sucked in a breath and I set the brownie in her hand before I let her go. Basil stood there, a dazed look on her face as her eyes shifted between me and the brownie. I took a bite of mine and watched Basil's cheeks flush.

"I'll come."

"What?" I asked.

I saw a smile tug on her lips when she scoffed and rolled her eyes. "I said I'll come to your game."

I took another, bigger, bite of the brownie and tried to keep my smile under control.

CHAPTER 10

case

I hit the snooze button on my alarm four times before I gave in to my responsibilities.

After breakfast and a quick shower, I texted Basil, letting her know what time I would be over to pick her up. I watched the screen and waited for her to see the text, but gave up after a few minutes. Basil was usually great at responding pretty quickly, but it was still early.

I was sure she would see it.

I set my coffee mug in the sink and sent off a text in the group chat Scottie made.

You and Hollis get everything handled okay
yesterday?

SCOTTIE

Oh yeah. Everything is packed and ready.
Just be careful with the moving truck. Some
stuff isn't steady and might fall out when
you open it.

TOWNES

I have straps you could have borrowed.

SCOTTIE

Thanks, man. But this isn't the time for that
kind of conversation.

TOWNES

You fucking know what I mean.

SCOTTIE

Do I?

Okay. Be careful when we open the truck,
got it.

TOWNES

Basil's coming too, right?

Me: Yup, just about to leave and get her.

SCOTTIE

She isn't driving herself?

Nah, figured we could save gas and
carpool.

SCOTTIE

Case and Basil sitting in a tree....

TOWNES

I swear...you're worse than Hayley.

I shoved my phone into my pocket before grabbing the
car keys. Basil still hadn't seen my text, so I called when I

was on my way over. I started to worry when my calls kept going to voicemail. Had Basil gotten sick? I tried calling her again before I allowed other worse-case scenarios to creep into my mind.

She answered on the second to last ring, and her voice was groggy and sleep-filled. My pulse slowed, and I took a calming breath.

"Mm?" she mumbled.

"Morning sleepy head. Guess what time it is?" I asked. There was a rustling on the other end, followed by a faint curse from Basil. I smiled and waited.

"I'm sorry Case, give me a few minutes and I'll meet you outside—" She was cut off by a thump, and I sat straighter in my seat. I pulled the phone away and saw the call was still connected.

My brows creased in confusion. "Basil?"

There was a faint echo on the other end, then I heard her. "Um, Case—can you hear me?"

"Yeah, I can. Is everything okay?" I asked as I pulled into the parking lot of her apartment complex.

"No. My phone fell behind my dresser and I, uh—it's super heavy."

I chuckled and turned off the car. "I'll be right there."

When I knocked on the door, I didn't know what state I was expecting Basil to be in. I assumed she'd be wearing her pajamas and would have a cup of coffee in hand. I wasn't expecting her to answer the door with hardly anything on, though. That possibility never crossed my mind.

She stood in front of me, wearing shorts and a cropped tank that exposed deliciously tanned skin. Her hair fell loose from its braid and framed those molten green and brown eyes that were still tired from sleep.

I almost lost it.

When I walked past her, I made sure to keep all body

parts to myself. I couldn't risk touching her by mistake and having my focus go out the window. I was here to move her dresser; we had somewhere to be. I couldn't let myself get distracted.

I could admire her later.

"You okay?" she asked, glancing over at me.

It was only when I nodded that she turned around and started leading me back to where her phone fell. Now, I know I should keep my thoughts appropriate. Basil and I were friends after all, and I didn't want to be rude. But it was hard to think of friendly thoughts when all I could focus on was where her shorts hugged her waist. My eyes danced over the Halloween-themed design before they moved down her legs. When she stopped walking I cleared my throat and snapped my attention up.

"I'm fine," I said, but it was too late. Basil was staring over her shoulder and realization flashed over her face before her cheeks flushed.

"Uh—sorry. Dresser's right there—I'll be right back." She grabbed a few pieces of fabric strewn from the end of her bed and ran out, leaving me standing in front of the oak dresser.

I took a couple of deep breaths before placing a hand on the top and one on the backside. It wasn't as heavy as I was expecting. I pulled it away from the wall with minimal effort and grabbed her phone. By the time the dresser was back against the wall, Basil was out of the bathroom. Now wearing pants and a Rockies Training Center sweatshirt, her hair had been brushed through and fell down her back.

She avoided looking at me as she walked up and grabbed her phone. "I'm sorry, Case. I didn't mean to do that."

I reached out but stopped myself from grabbing her hand at the last second. Instead, I tapped her hand with my finger, earning her attention. "It's fine Basil. Now, how about we grab coffee and some food?"

She smiled and I pulled my hand away. I must have imagined the way she moved to catch my fingers. Because she just made it clear, she didn't like to be touched. Basil brushed past me and started gathering the last few things she needed. Then, we left together.

———

"Guys, I said watch the corner!" Hollis yelled from the other side of the door. Yet another reminder to be careful moving the furniture into the old 1920s style home. Townes, Basil, and I had been here since ten this morning. It was now half-past two, and we were still one man short. According to Hollis, her boyfriend had an emergency work meeting right before he was supposed to meet us here. Which was fine, but when he texted Hollis an hour ago saying he wasn't coming—well—Townes and I weren't happy.

Neither of us had taken a break, wanting to get everything into the house in one visit. Which, in hindsight, was a bad idea. We were going to have to be mindful of how we recovered when we were done. So at practice tomorrow, we weren't completely useless.

Once everything was in the house, Townes and I planted ourselves on Hollis's new couch. Basil was kind enough to give each of us a beer before she and Hollis continued unpacking the boxes in the kitchen. I watched as Basil removed a set of bedsheets from a box and turned to Hollis, her brows pulled together.

"I literally gave you a detailed list of how you should pack, Hol. Why are these packed with your grandmother's China?"

Hollis grabbed the sheets and placed them into a

different box. "I didn't feel like buying bubble wrap. Sue me."

I took a swig of the ice-cold beer before resting my head back on the couch. Basil walked back into the room a few minutes later, waving her phone in her hand.

"I just ordered some food, but it's going to take a while before it gets here. Do you guys mind helping unpack some boxes?"

"Where do you want us?" Townes asked, finishing off his beer.

Basil pointed back to the kitchen. "You can help Hollis finish in there. Case, you and I are going to start on the boxes in the guest room."

We both nodded and stood. Townes walked into the kitchen and right up to Hollis, who had been struggling to place her nice plates on a high shelf. I looked at Basil, who watched as Hollis smiled when Townes took them from her and put them where she pointed.

"Guest room, you say?" I asked, pulling her attention back to me.

"Yeah, that's where we stuck most of the smaller boxes. So, fair warning, we might be there a while."

I followed her into the room and stopped in the doorway. "You know there's a whole house you guys could have utilized," I stated.

Boxes were stacked along the walls, some sat on the queen-sized bed, and I was positive this was where eighty percent of the boxes were. If not more. The house was a modest size, with original wood flooring and wallpaper that was peeling off. So the girls had plenty of room to put the boxes—I didn't know why they seemed to all be in here.

"Hollis wanted them in here because it would have stressed her out if they were all over the house."

"She's not going to forget about them, is she?" I asked as I started on the smallest box that sat on the bed.

Basil shrugged. "Whatever we don't get done tonight will get done by the end of the week. I told her if she doesn't finish unpacking, then she can't be my plus one to your game."

I smiled to myself before we fell into a comfortable silence. I liked knowing she was still coming, and couldn't wait to see her in the crowd. Basil and I created separate piles; one of Hollis's things, and the other of bubble wrap. The longer we sat and sorted, the hungrier I became, and I had to stop looking at the time. Basil promised multiple times the food would be here soon.

When my stomach growled for the third time in ten minutes, I turned around to face her. Except, her focus was on the box between her legs, which was weird because I didn't notice any new piles. She'd been over there for a while too.

What was she doing?

"Hey," I said as I moved closer to where she sat on the floor.

As I sat down, Basil shifted her body away, and that was when I heard it. The indisputable crunch of food. I pulled on her shoulder so she was facing me. Her mouth was full of *something* and all thoughts of asking when the food would arrive disappeared from my mind.

"What's that?"

"Whas wha?" she asked around whatever she was eating. The faintest smell of mint hit me, and her eyes dropped in shame as I pointed to her mouth. Slowly, she pulled a container of Thin Mints out of the box she was supposed to be working on, and it hit me.

"You're over here eating cookies while you're making me work without food?" I kept my voice low; I wasn't sure where Hollis and Townes were, and I didn't think Basil would appreciate it if she had to share.

I held out my hand and flexed my fingers. "Give me one."

She shook her head and stood. "No, they're mine," she said, before shoving another cookie in her mouth. I smirked, and something about it must have spooked her. Because, before I could stop her, she ran to the other side of the room. Jumping over the large piles on the floor I'd carefully organized, she hid the box behind her back and cornered herself between the wall and closet.

"Please Basil, just one."

"Get your own cookies, Whitlock," she said before putting another one in her mouth.

I smiled and stood before covering the distance between us in a few short strides. When she tried to get away again, I reached out. My arm wrapped around her waist, and I pulled her back into me. Her arms were outstretched to keep the box away—as if my arms weren't twice as long as hers. Basil laughed as she kept moving the box to prevent me from grabbing it.

"Just one!" I chuckled, but she didn't relent. I leaned in closer, an honest attempt to grab the cookies, but when my nose brushed the shell of her ear, she froze. Her strawberry and mint smell overwhelmed me, and I closed my eyes.

"Basil," I said softly, squeezing my arm that was wrapped around her. I waited for the moment she'd pull away, get onto me for not respecting her preference for space. But when that moment passed, and she stayed, I spoke low. "If you don't give me one, I'll expose you. I don't know about Hollis, but Townes will be in here faster than you can blink to get his hands on these cookies."

She gasped and turned to face me, still entangled in my grip. "You wouldn't."

Her eyes were wide and as mine roamed over her face, I spotted a few chocolate crumbs on the side of her lip. I reached up–testing my luck–and wiped it away, making sure not to focus too much on how perfect she felt under me. How soft her lips felt when my thumb grazed over them. I leaned in and challenged her.

"Try me."

With a scowl, she pushed herself away from me and begrudgingly pulled two cookies from the box and placed them in my outstretched hand.

"You're an ass Case," Basil teased, pulling the box to her chest when I was far enough away from her. Basil reached for buzzing her phone, and I laughed before putting one cookie in my mouth.

"You're the one who was withholding food from a starving man."

Basil rolled her eyes and smirked. "You're dramatic too, huh? Come on, food's here. Let's go eat."

basil

Mom was in a weird mood. She was—joyous. Ecstatic. Elated.

I hadn't seen her like that in years, so I kept my distance. I scratched Socks behind his ears and giggled as his leg thumped into the carpet.

"What's with her, hm?" I asked him, placing my hands on either side of his face and pulling forward. His face scrunched and I let out another laugh before he licked my cheek.

"Honey, can you set the table? Oh, and put the dog outside."

I gave Socks a solid pat on his side. "Come on, fatty," I said before leading him to the sliding door. Once he waddled into his doghouse, I shut the door and headed for the kitchen. Mom gave me a quick smile, and I paused before I grabbed the plates.

"What's got you in such a good mood?" I asked with a soft chuckle. Mom whirled around and pointed to the table with her wooden spoon.

"I'll tell you in a bit, now chop chop. Table isn't going to set itself."

Without hesitation, I left the kitchen and set the table. I laid out the last fork just as Mom carried in the pot of pasta. We sat down and she looked at me with excitement in her eyes as I filled my bowl. My brows furrowed as I stared at her.

"You're kind of freaking me out, mom."

"I don't mean to, sweetie. I'm just," she clapped her hands and sighed, "so excited for you."

"Okay, now you're just being cryptic, please. What's got you so excited?" I kept my voice light, but it was to distract myself from the heaviness pooling in my stomach. The last time Mom was this excited was when she told me I had been accepted into culinary school.

Yes, my mother opened my mail.

I only applied to appease her, but I never intended on going.

My brows furrowed even more. I was starting to get a headache. "What happened?" I asked as I twirled the pasta around my fork.

Mom took in a deep breath and folded her hands together over the table. "My coworker has a son."

"Good for him," I stated as I shoved food into my mouth.

Mom tsked, but her smile didn't waiver. "And I've set you up on a date with him."

My fork clanged on the plate when it fell from my hand in surprise. I stared at Mom in shock, and my mouth dropped open. Her face transformed back into that cold, judgmental stare I was so used to. "Close your mouth, Basil. You'll attract flies," she stated as she started on her food, disappointment evident on her face.

"Why?" I asked. Aside from my mother being the most cynical person I knew when it came to relationships, she was also the most judgmental. The one and only serious boyfriend I had during my freshman year of college, Mom, tore him apart when they met. Told him his dreams and aspirations weren't good enough for me and to stop wasting my time. She then proceeded to tell me that men only led to disappointment, and they wouldn't ever be good enough.

So, either this guy was blackmailing her, or he was the second coming of Christ.

"You'll like him, honey. He's my co-worker's son. Very ambitious and very handsome," she said with a shimmy of her shoulders.

I blinked and turned my attention to the food. "I'm confused," I confessed, with my gaze down. Mom shifted in her chair and set her hands on the stem of her wineglass.

"Look at me, Basil."

I did, and I was stunned by what I saw. Mom looked—remorseful.

She took in a steadying breath as her finger tapped away. "Listen, I know in the past I've been a bit harsh. But after a lot of thinking, I realized that I've pushed a lot of my feelings onto you and that's not fair. Just because my marriage failed doesn't mean you shouldn't believe in love or be scared to find it. So, I'm giving you my blessing to find someone who makes you happy."

"I don't need your blessing to date, Mom." The words flew out of my mouth before I could think of the implications they'd have.

Mom stiffened in her chair, and her hand tightened on the glass. "Well, considering you haven't brought anyone home, I wasn't sure if that was the reason or not. Thanks for clarifying."

I opened my mouth just to close it again, unsure of what to say to make things better. If I even wanted to.

Mom finished her wine and stood from the table. "I'll get the dishes, you go and head home. It's late." Then, without another word, she took my plate and stacked it with hers. As she walked to the kitchen, I groaned quietly and looked at the ceiling. If I left now, she was going to use this to guilt trip me about something later.

I stood from my seat and walked to the backdoor to let Socks inside. Then I headed into the kitchen and found her furiously scrubbing the dishes. "Mom."

"Hm? I'm fine Basil, I don't want you getting home too late."

I rubbed my hands over my face before taking a deep breath. "I'm sorry. I was caught off guard by the sudden change of mind. It was kinda abrupt, but I'll go on the date." I tried my best to smile when she whirled around to face me. Her smile was so genuine, a stark contrast to mine.

"Oh, yay!" she said, clapping her hands together. "I'll let James know the date is on." I let her wrap me in a hug, which still lacked warmth, before I stepped back.

My brows pulled together as I considered her. "I'll see you later, okay? Work is pretty busy, and I've got some other things going on. But I'll text you."

Mom kissed my cheek before turning back to the dishes. "Sounds good hon, let me know when you get home, okay?"

I scratched Socks' favorite spot as I passed him on my way to the door.

After a pit stop to grab some wine, I was home, and I didn't realize how empty the apartment was now that Hollis had moved out. My bag dropped to the floor where the shoe rack used to be, and I scanned the living room. Most of the decor was still there, but Hollis's big, ugly, yellow throw pillow was gone. As well as the coffee table. The countertop was empty, and she took the bathroom cart closest to the pantry. I missed her already. With a heavy sigh, I wandered to the kitchen to put the wine in the fridge. Then I got ready for bed.

Despite what Mom said, it wasn't late. It was seven fifteen, and I had the whole night to myself. Hollis was still unpacking. But when I called on my way home and offered to help, she assured me Ryan was there and encouraged me to enjoy my first night by myself.

After I changed into something more comfortable, I poured the chilled wine into a glass and settled myself on the couch. I didn't know what to do with the quiet, and the movie I had put on didn't help very much. I was so used to hearing Hollis talk to herself while she graded papers, that I was hallucinating her voice. With a groan, I tilted my head back on the couch.

I needed to do something, but going out was out of the question now that I had already changed. I could invite people over. Yeah, that sounded doable. I covered myself with the white blanket and picked up my phone, but my finger hovered over the only person I thought of.

He had a game tomorrow—he was too busy.

I also hadn't gotten over how it felt when Case pulled me against him the other night. My back was still tingling. Growing up, I hated being touched and would always wiggle away from people who got too close. Until Case. When he helped me up after I fell—it took me three days to realize I liked it.

My finger hit the call button before I could think better of it.

He answered on the second ring. "Hey, how was your mom's?"

I took a large sip of wine before I answered. "You want an honest answer, or what a good daughter should say?"

There was a slight pause on his end, and his voice was soft when he spoke. "Want to talk about it?"

"Maybe another night when you don't have a game to

worry about. What are you up to, anyway? Am I interrupting your bedtime routine?"

Case let out a booming laugh, and I smiled. "Just so you know, my bedtime isn't for another twenty minutes. I'm relaxing right now," he said.

I took another sip of wine and sighed. "That sounds nice."

"What about you?" Did his voice suddenly get deeper? Maybe he lied about when he was going to bed. I'm totally interrupting.

"I'm trying to enjoy the quiet, but I don't like it. It's why I called." The last part came out as a whisper, as if I was embarrassed to admit it.

Case shuffled again, and his voice was filled with hesitation. "Do you want me to come over?"

"Case, you have a game tomorrow."

"And you don't like being by yourself."

I didn't know how long I let the silence hang between us, but Case broke it with a sigh. "I don't mind. Just say the word and I'll be there."

I was tempted, so tempted, to say yes. He would come over, we would watch a movie, then I would offer him my couch when I forced him to go to bed. I let my answer sit on my tongue for a minute. Weighing the pros and cons.

"I'll be okay, big guy."

There was another heavy silence. "Okay. Now, what movie are you watching? I can hear voices in the background, but not much else," he asked.

I chuckled and walked into the kitchen to get another drink. "Iron Man."

"Good choice. Although Thor is significantly better."

I sat back on the couch and paused. "Did you really just say that?"

"Are we going to argue about this? Cause I promise

you, you won't win." I heard the challenge in his voice, and I would have. If we had more time.

So, like the adult I was, I took a deep breath and calmly told him. "Not tonight. We'll discuss your poor choices in superheroes another day, when I have more time to elaborate all my points," I said before yawning.

Case yawned, too. "I'm looking forward to it. Now, I think it's time *you* get to bed." I set my drink on the floor and laid down, humming in agreement.

"Sounds like a plan. See you tomorrow."

"Looking forward to it, sunshine."

I pulled my brows in at the nickname, and the question flew out of my mouth before I thought better of it. "Why do you call me that?"

Sleep thickened his answer, "Have you ever seen yourself smile? It's radiant." It was silent for a few seconds before he continued, "Good night, Basil." He hung up, and I stared at the ceiling with a spinning mind and a fluttering heart.

basil

I went over that text three times to make sure I knew how to read.

"You coming, B?" Hollis asked. She held the front door open, waiting for me to stop obsessing over the text.

"Yeah, let's go," I said before I shoved the phone into my pocket and stood.

Since our first week in college, Hollis and I had dedicated Fridays to girls' night. Where our microwaved ramen, pirated movies, and bags of smarties had evolved into more sophisticated things. Now we at takeout and made charcuterie boards, but the movies were still pirated —for nostalgia purposes. It was a tradition we didn't deviate from unless it couldn't be helped, like tonight. It was the first professional hockey game Hollis and I were going to, and my heart fluttered rapidly in my chest.

Case and I were friends. That was it.

We found decent parking before we headed inside to the ticket booth, earning a few displeased looks from various Peaks fans as we walked past them into the arena. The inside was decked out in the Peaks colors; green and gray lined the walls, and a sea of jerseys surrounded us. Once we got the tickets, Hollis and I split. She made a B-Line for the concession stands, and I continued to the arena to secure our seats.

I had to double-check the tickets a few times to make sure I was in the right spot. Case had gotten us seats behind the goalie net, a little off to the side, giving us the perfect view of the rink. Hollis came up beside me, her arms full of beer and popcorn.

"Can you pass along a message, B?"

"What message?" I asked as I helped free her hands.

"That Case should cover the food and not the tickets. I could hear my bank account cry in pain when the lady swiped my card."

"I'll be sure to tell him that," I said around a sip of beer.

"You gonna tell him anything else?" she asked, wiggling her brows while she shoved a handful of popcorn into her mouth. My eyes narrowed at her. I could already tell where this conversation was headed.

I shrugged and looked ahead. "I don't know what you're talking about."

She tilted her head and raised her brows in amusement. "Oh please. Did you see how he looked at you the other night? Or just, in general? He's got it bad and so do you."

"Do you know what you're talking about?" I kept my expression neutral as I took another sip.

"Always, and you're being silly, B. Trust me."

I rested my feet on the sideboard and sank into my seat. "I'm not being silly," I mumbled, keeping my focus forward. Hollis shifted in her seat and placed her feet next to mine. I heard the fondness in her voice when she spoke.

"It's nice. Seeing how you are with him."

I hadn't had enough alcohol yet to be comfortable with my growing feelings for the hockey captain. So, I took a huge swig of the overpriced beer and tried to focus on the men skating onto the ice. "What number is Case again?" Hollis asked.

"Uh, I think he's number ten," I said, scanning the players as they warmed up. When I didn't see Case right away, my shoulders fell, but thankfully Hollis didn't notice my disappointment.

"What are they doing?" she asked, bewilderment filling her voice.

"Stretching."

She pointed at some of the men who were doing a hip-thrusting motion on the ice, and her eyes widened. "That's stretching? Are you sure?"

I laughed at her astonishment, but it died when a dirty-looking man-child showed up and placed a kiss on Hollis's head. "Hey, baby."

"Ryan!" Hollis contorted her body in the seat to face him.

"Ryan? I didn't know you liked hockey. Or had a ticket?" I raised a brow at Hollis, who leaned in.

"I might have asked Scottie for an extra one. But I didn't know if he'd show up."

Ryan sneered at me and puffed out his chest. "Yeah, 'cause some of us are busy with work," he said as he started to step over an empty seat.

"I think that's taken," I said. Ryan made a show of looking around for anyone who looked like they were going to tell him to move before he shrugged.

"It's fine."

I gave him a mocking smile before turning my attention back to the ice. I promised Hollis I would keep my opinions to myself when it came to her boyfriend unless she asked—which she never did. However, she couldn't keep me from speaking my mind whenever he was around, which wasn't often.

Hollis laid her head on his shoulder and smiled.

"What were you ladies talking about?" he asked as he threw an arm around her shoulders.

"About the stretches they're doing." Hollis pointed at a group of men on the other side of the rink.

Ryan snorted, earning a side-eye look from me. "Seriously? Why does it have to be so provocative?"

"Groin injuries are really common in hockey. If you find it so erotic, then look away," I said, before noticing how he glared at me. So, just to get under his skin, I added. "Or don't. Maybe you could learn a thing or two by watching them."

Ryan huffed out in annoyance before he stole Hollis away in quiet conversation. I watched the hockey players continue to stretch and do a practice shot into the goal before the announcer's voice filled the arena. The crowd cheered, but I didn't hear whatever it was he said. Because my eyes snagged on Case, who was doing those provocative —yet necessary—groin stretches. It was as if there was some sort of invisible tether connecting us because Case lifted his head and looked right where I was sitting.

He smiled and stood effortlessly before skating toward us. I ignored the smirk on Hollis's face and the way Ryan seemed to shift in his seat. For a guy who didn't watch sports, he sure seemed jealous of me talking to one of the players.

People around us gasped in surprise as Case skated closer. He tapped the Plexiglas—as if he didn't already have my undivided attention. "You're here," he said.

I scooted forward so he could hear me better. "Yeah.

One of my friends is playing tonight. I came to support him." A warmth settled in my stomach as I watched him smile at my words. "If you lose, though, I'll be upset. Don't waste the tickets you gave us."

"Us? Lose? Never," Case said with a wink.

Then, he skated away, and toward his team huddled by the bench. I leaned back as I watched him and shoved more popcorn into my mouth. The people behind us, a group of women our age, whispered amongst themselves. I didn't know if they were gossiping about the random girl who knew the captain, or something else. But I smiled to myself, anyway.

When the game started, I did my best to watch everyone else. Townes was an amazing goalie, and the team made a great choice picking Scottie to join them. But no matter how hard I tried to focus on our other friends, my eyes kept snapping back to the man who wore the number ten.

———

There was one night in college when Hollis and I attended a Taylor Swift concert. We were supposed to present a project in our Communications class but had to reschedule because we yelled so much we lost our voices. This game rivaled that concert.

I knew professional games could get intense, but oddly enough, it was much more tame than I expected. Or maybe I was so desensitized to crazy because I dealt with overly competitive parents cheering their kids on at hockey games every other weekend.

Hollis, Ryan, and I waited until the area was almost empty before we headed out to the parking lot. Case said he'd find us when he was done with his post-game routine. We were huddled against Hollis's car, holding onto the expired hand warmers she found in her backseat. Excitement still flowed through us as we waited, and Hollis bounced on her heels, her blue eyes wide. "I can't believe it's *that* brutal."

"Yeah, it's pretty neat," I said as I tried to coax the rest of the heat from the hand warmer.

Hollis had seen videos of hockey players getting into fights on the ice, but everything was more intense when you saw it in person. The entire game, we were on the edge of our seats, completely focused on the game. Ryan, however, was content being on his phone the whole time. He rolled his eyes beside Hollis and let out an unamused huff.

"It was fine."

Now, I was good for the entire game. I ignored the unnecessary jabs he made when Scottie made a mistake, or when Townes missed the only goal the opposing team made. With each comment, I bit my tongue harder and harder, not wanting to upset Hollis when she was having such a great time. Ryan, though, just had to keep talking.

"And I don't know who voted on their captain, but he played the worst of all of them," he said as he shook his head. "They're supposed to be one of the best teams in the nation? What a joke."

"Hey Ryan?" I asked, waiting until he pulled his attention away from his phone.

His brown eyes darkened as he looked at me. "What?"

The way he spat that word angered me even more. Sure, he showed up to the game, probably because Hollis had to beg him, but he ignored her the entire time. The only things he did to gain her attention were buy her more popcorn—not even the refillable kind—and toss his arm over her chair before going back to his phone. I didn't understand why Hollis put up with his behavior, but I was over it. Hollis would forgive me eventually, but right now I had to give her boyfriend a piece of my mind.

My mouth opened, words ready to lash out, when a familiar deep voice carried from somewhere across the parking lot. I whipped my head around and found three tall figures walking toward us. The guys were all freshly showered and had their duffel bags slung over their shoulders. I didn't remember what I was going to tell Ryan.

My eyes landed on Case, and I smiled.

"Hey," Case said with a bright smile as he walked up to us and threw his arm over my shoulders. I was overly aware of how good he smelled and settled into the crook of his body. Making it a point to not make it obvious—I could feel Hollis' "I told you so" burning into my side.

Case looked at Hollis and Ryan. "Did you guys enjoy the game?"

"It was amazing! You guys played great!" Hollis seemed more excited now, and I realized I underestimated how much fun she had.

Case chuckled, and I settled in closer—he was warm, and I seemed to be getting colder. "I'm glad to hear you enjoyed yourself, Hol. Oh, sorry man," he reached a free hand to Ryan, "I'm Case."

"Ryan. Hollis' boyfriend," he said, not bothering to take Case's hand.

A tense silence fell between the group as he and Case stared at each other. I noticed the way Townes and Scottie shared a look before starting their own quiet conversation. Case sighed after a minute of silence and looked between the guys and me. "Well, let's get going. Can't miss our own party."

"Wow. You guys are so sure you'll win every game that you just plan these parties in advance?" Ryan asked as he wrapped his arm over Hollis, mirroring Case. He tensed next to me, but it wasn't enough for anyone else to notice if they weren't paying attention.

But Townes noticed, and he surprised me when he spoke up. "We always have a party after the last home game of the week. Win or lose, it's our chance to let loose and have some fun."

With his tattooed arms crossed, and dark hair pushed back, he leveled Ryan with a frown so deep I was afraid he'd hurt himself. Ryan rolled his eyes and scoffed. "Whatever, I guess we can go."

"Or you can go home. You won't be missed, I promise," I told him. Hollis opened her mouth to defend him, but he whispered something in her ear. She looked at me, her eyes promising to have a conversation with me about this later.

Scottie placed an audible tap on Townes's shoulder and grinned. "Come on, guys. We can all argue after we get some food."

Townes grumbled and started walking with Scottie toward wherever they parked. Case removed his arm from around me and I pretended not to notice how his hand dragged down and brushed against my fingertips. I suppressed the urge to reach out. "We'll meet you guys there, then. Basil, want to drive with us?" he asked.

When I looked at Hollis, she nodded and started unlocking her door.

Case and I started for the large, black SUV that I could only assume belonged to Townes. Before Case opened the door, I asked, "We *are* getting food, right?"

CHAPTER 13

case

They took all my sweet and sour sauce.

I tried to keep my focus on what Townes was saying, but it was hard when Basil was dipping her fries into the last of the sauce I held in my hand. She raised a brow when I stared at her.

"What?" she asked.

"You know what," I said as my eyes narrowed.

"I don't, though. Care to elaborate?" she asked as she reached another fry toward my sauce, but I pulled it back to my chest. I wanted the rest for myself before there was nothing left.

I pointed at her. "That. You should have asked for your own."

Basil rolled her eyes and smirked before reaching again. "You have like three more in the bag. Come on, big guy."

Something unfamiliar settled in my chest at those words, and I didn't like it. Scottie turned around then, his own sweet and sour sauce, packet in hand, and two empty ones sitting on the center console. I shook my head as his eyes darted to the mess.

"Sorry," he muttered before he turned back around.

My brows creased, and I pulled the sauce farther from Basil as she continued after it. "You guys know McDonald's has *so* many sauces, right? You each could have asked for some."

"I didn't think I wanted any," Basil said with a defeated huff before she munched on her sauceless fry.

I raised a brow. "You get chicken nuggets, but no sauce?"

"Sue me, Whitlock."

Townes cleared his throat from the driver's seat and Basil and I's attention snapped to him. "Like I was saying. Can you both help me with Hayley's birthday party?"

I dipped my last fry into the sauce and handed Basil the rest. "It's right after Thanksgiving, right?"

Townes nodded, "Yeah. I need you guys to help decorate while I have her out for the day."

"I'd love to help!" Basil said as she tossed her trash into the discarded food bag at my feet. "Is she your girlfriend or something?"

Sometimes I forgot just how much Basil didn't know about the team. Townes's niece had always been a sensitive subject, and he tried to keep her out of the public eye as much as he could.

I leaned in until her hair tickled the tip of my nose and told her. "Hayley's his niece. She's lived with him for a few years now."

Her face flushed, and she pulled her bottom lip between her teeth. I wanted to reach out and touch her. Like I did that night at Hollis's, Basil was so soft then. Was she always soft like that?

"You okay?" I asked her, nudging her arm with mine.

Basil peered up, and the lights from outside the car danced across her face. She kept her voice low. "I didn't mean to assume," her voice lowered, "and I don't want to be rude and ask."

I opened my mouth to reassure her that everything was fine. But Townes beat me to it.

"You'd be surprised how many times I get asked that, actually," Townes said as he pulled into a crowded driveway. He put the car in park and turned to face Basil. "It's okay."

The way Basil's concern morphed into something brighter made my chest feel lighter. She glanced outside, then unbuckled herself and ran out. I watched as she walked right up to Hollis, with her boyfriend right beside her. Some words were exchanged between them before the girls left Ryan and walked inside. I followed Townes and Scottie as they got out of the car and started for the front door. People congratulated us as we walked, giving us pats on the back, and some—mostly women—gave promises of a good time later in the night.

We walked through the arched doorway and were overwhelmed with music. The wood floors were slightly sticky, and Scottie let a busty redhead loop her arm through his before they walked past me. "Where are you heading first?" Scottie asked.

"To get a drink," I said as my eyes scanned the crowd for Basil, already wanting to be around her again. The woman, Cameron, smiled and leaned over Scottie to talk to me. I kept my eyes on hers, not wanting them to dip and see just exactly how low-cut her shirt was.

"Someone's here for you, Case," she said.

My brows tugged together. "Who?"

I didn't usually have anyone waiting for me at these kinds of parties. Cameron pulled back and tossed her hair behind her shoulder.

"Your girlfriend," she said before pulling Scottie into the crowd. I watched as she dragged him to where people danced in the living room before I left to find Aubrey.

She didn't come to these parties, ever, so the fact she decided to show up had dread pooling in my stomach. I looked for her as I made my way through the house, but there were so many blondes, and the light was so dim it was hard to make anyone out. I turned into the kitchen and stared between two women. One of them was Basil. She stood in the corner by another doorway, talking to Riley—one of the team's defensemen. The other woman was Aubrey.

"Hey, handsome," she said as she walked up—her hips moving in exaggeration—and attempted to place a kiss on my cheek. But I stepped away and gave her my best fake boyfriend smile.

"Aubrey, what are you doing here?" My shoulders relaxed when I saw Basil make her way out of the kitchen.

Aubrey clicked her tongue before taking a sip of her drink. "Well, since you can't seem to plan any dates, I figured I'd show up. Great game, by the way," she said with a wink.

So, this was why she was here. I had been too busy to uphold a public image. The edge in her voice was easily masked by her pristine smile and the glint in her baby-blue eyes. I furrowed my brows and leaned back. The music seemed louder, and people crowded around us. "You know how busy I am. We've talked about this."

"Yeah, but you should still find time for your girlfriend."

The words landed in the middle of my chest, and I couldn't help but scoff. "Fake girlfriend."

I was tired of this. Over the course of the year we had been doing this, Aubrey had demanded more. More dates, more mentions in interviews. I had given everything to her and hadn't gotten anything back. I agreed to help her because I wanted my friend to succeed, but this arrangement wasn't good for either of us anymore.

Aubrey looked at me in shock, and I straightened. "I'm not doing this anymore, Aubrey. We agreed on a year, that's it."

"But—"

I held up a hand to stop her. "No. Look, we need some time apart. I'll get with Jasmine, and she'll help us navigate whatever happens next. I'm done, Aubrey."

Saying those words lifted something in my chest, and that fire Basil's been unknowingly fueling filled the space. I pushed past Aubrey toward the counter where various drinks filled the space. I grabbed the first beer I touched and left to go find something to do. I needed to get my mind off Aubrey—and how I was officially on the market again. Jesus, I could finally have sex again without worrying about the repercussions.

I eventually found myself in the den. I saw Connor and his wife laughing on the couch while people played Beer Pong in the middle of the room. A large flat screen hung on the far wall, and a few people mingled in the far right corner.

The defenseman looked up and fist-bumped my hand before gesturing to the empty loveseat. "Glad you came, man."

"Yeah, well, thanks for hosting."

Connor and Joanna had two kids and rarely joined in the post-win celebrations. So, when they had an available babysitter, they dropped off their kids and hosted the best parties.

I sipped on the beer after I settled into the leather seat. "Who's watching the kids?"

"My Mom," Joanna spoke up. Her short lilac hair was pinned at the sides. "Everyone else was busy, and she had the night off. It was fate."

Connor smiled at his wife and placed a hand on her leg. "It wasn't fate if we planned this a week ago, honey."

Joanna poked his side and stood. "Want anything to drink?" she asked us both, even though I already had a beer.

I shook my head while Connor told her what he wanted. When she left the room, he threw an arm across the back of the couch and looked me over. I braced myself for his incoming question. "You see, Aubrey?" Connor asked.

Now, it wasn't a secret that the guys on the team didn't like her. Except Scottie, but that was because he hadn't been around her long enough to see her bad side. The guys were the first ones to see just how miserable I was anytime she and I hung out, but I assured them I had everything handled. It was a lie, of course, until now at least.

I took another sip of beer and looked at him. "I called it off."

"Really?" he asked as his brows raised in shock. "Wow man, good for you."

I nodded, not knowing what else to say, and hoped he didn't pry. Connor and I had a decent relationship outside of being teammates. When I first joined the team, he was the one I looked up to. He helped me navigate fame when things were stressful. He was also the first one to vote for me as captain. We had a lot of respect for each other, and I was going to miss him when he left. This was his last season before he retired.

"What are you gonna do now?" he asked, and when I gave him a questioning look, he leaned in. Keeping his voice low, he said, "You need to celebrate your freedom, dude. There're plenty of ladies here who've been waiting to have some fun." He winked before Joanna held a beer between us.

"What are you two talking about?" Joanna asked as she

took her seat, drinks in hand. Connor took the outstretched beer and took a drink.

I shook my head. "He's just giving me advice I'm not going to take."

While I appreciated what he was saying, I couldn't. Not when there was one woman who'd been on my mind every day since I met her. When I lifted my beer for another sip, I was met with an empty bottle. But before I could excuse myself, Joanna handed me another one. When I raised a brow, she winked.

"I notice things," she said plainly. I didn't have time to decipher her words, because Cameron placed herself in front of me and pointed to my lap.

"My heels are killing me. Do you mind if I sit?"

I patted my thigh. "Where's Scottie?" I asked as Cameron settled on the edge of my leg. She removed her heels and tossed them onto the side of the loveseat.

"Taking shots. I would join him, but I have stuff to do tomorrow, and a hangover doesn't sound fun."

I liked Cameron. She was one of the team's social media managers. At work, she was all business and took things very seriously. So, it was nice seeing her get comfortable and let loose on nights like this. She settled into casual conversation with Connor and Joanna while my mind wandered. I thought of how I was going to bring up Aubrey and I's 'break-up' to the team's PR manager. Then I shifted my gaze to the door right as Basil and Hollis walked into the room.

basil

I saw the redhead sitting in Case's lap and forced myself to be interested in something else.

Hollis walked over to the wall, and I followed, sipping on my beer as I settled next to the guy I talked to earlier. Riley. He was nice and asked if I was the coach Case kept talking about. I was glad the house was dark enough he couldn't see the blush that crawled up my neck. Case had talked about me, and the information made something in my stomach flutter.

That lasted until I walked into the room and saw the woman in his lap. Which was for the best. There was no sense in those feelings when you were just friends with someone.

"Basil, you wanna play?" Scottie asked as he handed me a ping-pong ball. I shifted on my feet and ignored the way my shoes stuck to the dark laminate as some guys set up a new round of Beer Pong.

I shook my head, but Hollis interjected before I could make up an excuse. "Hell yeah, she does!" She turned to me; determination set on her face. "Show 'em who's boss, girlie." She smacked my ass and grabbed the ball from Scottie.

Did I often play drinking games? No, and it was for one simple reason–I was horrible at them. It was why Hollis felt the need to hype me up so much, well, that and because she hoped it would psych out my opponents. It had never worked before, but that didn't stop her from doing it.

Scottie stood behind me and placed his hands on my shoulders. He spoke encouraging words into my ears as we walked to the table. I had to keep from pulling away as he spoke.

"Okay, the really tall guy, Riley? Drunk off his ass and can't aim for shit even when he's sober. You've got this." He gave me a solid pat on my back before he pulled away.

I ignored the odd sensation on the back of my neck as I lined up my shot. Hollis leaned as I readied my shot and whispered in my ear, "Case is watching you."

I fumbled and my ball landed nowhere near where I was aiming. Scottie and I looked at Hollis, bewildered, as Riley lined up his shot. "Why'd you do that, Hol?"

"What? I just thought you'd like to know. Pretty sure he was staring at your ass." She winked.

I took her drink and downed it before I pinned Scottie with a stare. "She's cut off."

Hollis huffed and crossed her arms. "That's not fair."

I turned around in time to see the small ball land in one of my cups. The two guys on the other end cheered and bumped chests as I downed the drink. I welcomed the burning sensation as they looked at me with teasing smiles.

"You're going down," Riley said with a crooked smile.

"In more ways than one, if you're up for it," the other said with a wink. He was leaner than the other guys around. His hair looked as if it hadn't been washed in a couple of days, and his neck tattoo looked poorly done.

I opened my mouth to say something, but Scottie beat me to it. He placed himself in front of me and pointed at the man. "Shut your fucking mouth, Cormack. Either play the game or go somewhere else."

I was stunned at his outburst and watched as the guy eyed Scottie before taking a step back.

Scottie leaned down and kept his voice low. "Your turn."

He handed me the ball, and I lined up my next shot. We went back and forth like that, with Riley leading. I was down to two cups, and he still had five in front of him. My vision turned fuzzy as I tried to aim, drunken determination filled me as I let the ball fly. When it landed in one of Riley's cups, Scottie and everyone around cheered as he downed his drink.

When we were down to our last cups, Scottie placed his hands on my shoulder again, and the excitement in his voice vibrated through me. "You've got this."

"You said he had horrible aim," I whispered.

Scottie whirled me toward him and bent over so our eyes could meet. How did I just realize how much taller he was than me? Were all hockey players giants?

"I was trying to motivate you. Now, you've both got one cup left. You got this Herb," he said. And when he smiled down at me, I felt a burning sensation on my back.

Case was staring. I didn't know how I knew—but I did.

I ignored the way the way my body burned under his stare and nodded at Scottie. I grabbed the ball and took a deep breath as I aimed. "I got this."

The ball flew and landed in Riley's cup. People around the table cheered, and Scottie picked me up from behind. He spun me a few times before he set me down, then kept his hands on my hips to keep me steady.

"That's some damn good motivation I gave you. Riley hardly loses Beer Pong," he said as he dropped his hands. Hollis ran up and embraced me in a hug of her own.

She squeezed before she pulled away and asked, "When did you get good at drinking games?"

Scottie threw an arm around my shoulders, and without thinking, my eyes darted to Case. He was still sitting on the loveseat, but the woman was gone and there was something heated in his eyes. Butterflies took flight again in my stomach, but I reminded myself it wasn't because of him. I was buzzed, and everything was supposed to feel warm and tingly. Case had nothing to do with how I was feeling, nor was he the cause of it.

Besides, that heated look I saw was probably the result of his own drinking. I looked away from his hands as they worked the paper off the beer bottle and shrugged at Hollis. "Maybe I've been holding out on you."

"For four years? I don't think so." Her smile widened as she grabbed my hand. "Come on. Help me find Ryan so he can take me home."

Right before she hauled me out of the room, a spiced scent overcame me and I turned around. Case stood there, and seeing him made my already unsteady knees even weaker.

"Hey," he said with that dimpled smile.

"Hey Case!" Hollis yelled from beside me. "B was just about to help me find Ryan, but don't worry, I'll give her back when I'm done."

Case chuckled as Hollis dragged me past him and into the living room. When I was sure he wasn't around to hear us, I smacked her shoulder. "Why do you say stuff like that, Hol? Just how drunk are you?"

"Oh, please B. I'm drunk, not blind. He hasn't been able to keep his eyes off you since we walked in there. And when Scottie picked you up? I've never seen something so hot. The man was feral," she said with a wink before she turned, refocusing on her mission to find Ryan.

I wasn't sure when it happened, but we eventually split up to cover more ground because this house was huge, but we still couldn't find him. Hollis resorted to asking some people at the party if they had seen him, to which they all gave us different directions that they saw him go.

After fifteen minutes, my shoes were disgusting, and we still hadn't found him. Hollis finally grabbed her phone and held it to her ear. But the deepening worry lines told me he wasn't answering. Despite this, she tried to call him three more times. Eventually, Hollis held her phone in her hands, and I could see she was trying to keep her frustration in check. Her knuckles clenched the phone, and she started to shake.

"How did you guys get split up, anyway?" I asked, trying to distract her. They came into the kitchen with me, but when Riley pulled me into a conversation, I lost them.

"He told me he had to step out and take a work call, that he'd find me." Her disappointment was radiating off her, and I reached out for her hands.

"I'm sorry, Hol. Come on, let's get you home."

Neither of us could drive, so I took her back, and we looked for Case. We would order a car service, but I wasn't going to leave without saying goodbye. We found him still in the living room, and much to my relief, there weren't any women in his lap this time. Not that it was any of my business to care. Case chatted with the same burly guy from earlier. His hair was cut short on the sides and he looked like he ate raw eggs for breakfast. The woman next to him, with lilac hair, had her hand on his thigh and a fondness in her features as she stared at him. As if Case sensed us, his head shot up and our eyes locked. My cheeks heated as I watched him stand.

He walked over to us, and his demeanor softened when

he was close enough to see how upset Hollis was. "Everything okay?"

"Yeah, uh, I just wanted to let you know we're leaving. We can't find Ryan and Hollis wants to leave."

Case looked at her for a second before giving me a sharp nod. "Okay, let's go, I'll drive." He walked past us and scanned the living room while Hollis and I followed after him.

"Are you okay to drive?" I asked.

"I started drinking water when you started playing Beer Pong. Just in case, you know? Oh! Townes!" Case walked away and left me and Hollis standing next to a couple making out on a loveseat. Not that we were paying attention to them, but I couldn't find it in myself to move right now. I couldn't tell what this feeling in my chest was, but all I knew was that his words put it there. I watched as Case found Townes and they talked. Townes nodded a few times before he turned and headed toward us.

When he reached us, he held out a tattooed hand and curled his fingers inward. "Keys."

Hollis promptly reached into her purse that was slung over her shoulder and handed them to Townes.

"Come on," he said and turned without another word. As Hollis started to follow him, Case planted himself by my side, his keys in hand.

"You're coming too?" I asked as the warmth traveled to my lower stomach.

"How else is Townes going to get back? Unless you have an extra bed that can fit him?" he teased. When I didn't say anything, he put a gentle hand on my lower back and led me through the crowd of bodies.

CHAPTER 15

case

"Can we get some food before you drop me off?" Basil asked from the passenger seat while Townes got in the car.

Once the door clicked shut, I pulled away from the sidewalk and headed toward Basil's apartment. "Where do you want to go?"

"You didn't eat anything?" Townes raised a brow. "And drank on an empty stomach?"

I chuckled and flipped the blinker on. "Calm down, *dad*. We're going to get food now. Basil?"

She bit her bottom lip, and I focused my attention on the road. I may not be drunk on alcohol like she was, but looking at her too long may have the same effect.

Basil sighed, "I need a burger. A good one too."

"There's a good spot up the road. It's Hayley's favorite," Townes chimed in.

"So, is it good, or have you acquired the taste of a child?" Basil asked, turning in her seat to face a stunned Townes.

I laughed at his reaction and switched lanes. "He has great taste in food, actually. He likes to show us the best places to eat. How else do you think we get all this muscle?"

"By eating anything and everything," she quipped.

Townes huffed and crossed his arms. "I don't eat garbage."

I pulled into the pothole-filled parking lot of the small burger place Hayley had forced us to bring her too many times, and my stomach grumbled.

"Are chocolate chip cookies the only exception, then?" I asked as I unbuckled my seatbelt. "Or does Hayley force those on you like all the other junk food you keep in your house?"

"Let's go," Townes grumbled as he opened the door. He stalked inside without us. Basil giggled as she exited the car. She swayed slightly when her feet hit the ground. I reached for her, placing one hand on her low back, and the other on her arm.

"You good?" I asked.

She looked up and with a cute, drunken smile said, "I'm perfect. Come on, I don't want Townes to get lonely."

She untangled herself from my arms and walked to the door. I forced my eyes on her back while I followed behind her. It wasn't right to ogle her when she was inebriated. Even though it was all I wanted to do lately. I reached above her head and opened the door. She walked under my arm, and I didn't miss the faint blush painting her cheeks.

We spotted Townes quickly in the small retro-themed diner. Red booths lined each of the walls and the floor was laid in a checkered pattern. Aside from us, another small group of people sat on the opposite side of the diner, chatting and laughing over their food.

Basil slid into the booth across from Townes and patted the space next to her. I raised a brow before sitting. "You're in an exceptionally good mood."

"Well, now that Hol is at home, I feel like I can relax," she said with a soft smile before looking at the menu, prompting Townes and me to do the same.

Once the waitress came by, her apron covered in a hard day's work, we put in our orders. "We've got a deal on milkshakes. Want any?" Her voice was hoarse, worn from either too many cigarettes or exhaustion. Her hair was falling out of its ponytail and the bags under her eyes were dark. I wondered when the next person was coming in—if anyone was. This diner was open twenty-four-seven, and I hoped for her sake she wasn't responsible for the night shift.

Basil looked at me and pointed to the menu, forcing my attention to the picture of the milkshake. "Want to share one with me? I can't finish a whole one."

I nodded and Basil told the woman the one she wanted, and the waitress walked toward the other table.

Music filled the diner, and I looked at Basil. "Did you have a good night?" I asked.

She nodded and rested her head against the booth. "I did. It's been a while since I've been out like that, but winning that game was the best part, I think. I haven't won a drinking game since college. And that was the only one."

"Well, you played great. Riley was practically crying when he lost," I said as I glanced between her eyes. Her lids were heavy, and the small smile she gave me was full of drunken tiredness.

The waitress came back with our drinks and placed Basil's milkshake between us. I looked at the vanilla and graham crackers in it and leaned in. "What did you get?"

"It's a cherry cheesecake milkshake," she stated as she unwrapped the straw and plunged it into the thick drink.

I watched as she drank it and made a satisfying sound as she closed her eyes. It was a simple, reasonable reaction any drunk person would have to something that tasted good. But I couldn't stop my mind from wandering to places it had no business being. I didn't know where to look, but looking at Townes was the wrong thing to do. Because he raised an eyebrow and let out an exasperated sigh before he took a sip of his water.

Basil pushed the tall, thin glass to me and smiled. "You want to try it? It's really good."

I took a sip while Basil ran her hand along the chrome detailing of the table, and she was right. It was good, but I couldn't help but think of something better.

NO.

Maybe I drank more than I thought, and my attempt to sober up did nothing.

I started coughing and took a few sips of my water. Townes stared at me with an unconcerned brow. Basil patted my back, concern marking her soft features. "Are you okay?"

She continued patting my back and kept looking at me with those pretty eyes—I was overwhelmed by that warmth in my chest.

I ignored it and nodded. "I'm fine, promise," I said between coughs.

Once Basil and Townes were sure I wasn't going to drop dead at the table, our waitress came back with our food. Basil took a bite and did a small dance, her fist to her chest while she moved side to side.

"You like it?" I asked before taking a sip of the milkshake.

"Mhm." She glanced at Townes. "I'm sorry about what I said. About you having a kid's taste." Basil sat her burger down and grabbed the milkshake from my hands.

She took three large gulps and turned to me. "Can you move? I gotta run to the bathroom."

I moved and let her out of the booth. When I sat back

down and glanced up, I noticed Townes—whose scowl was deep enough to reach his brain.

"What?" I asked.

"Did you tell her about Aubrey?" he asked, his voice low and rough.

I shrugged. "She hasn't come up in conversation. Why? Do I need to tell her right now?"

Townes rubbed the scruff on his jawline and sat back in the booth. "It would be better if she finds out about your little pretend relationship from you than anywhere else."

"I don't see the big deal. I broke up with her at the party. She's just another ex now. Why do I have to tell Basil right now?" I bit out the question as I dipped a fry into the ranch dressing on my plate. Frustration radiated off Townes now, and I didn't understand it. I wasn't wrong.

"Do you think Aubrey is going to let this go? You know how she is. She's going to make your life suck. And how do you think Basil is going to feel when she finds out? You've been looking at her with puppy dog eyes this whole time when you had a girlfriend."

"Fake girlfriend," I reminded him around my fry.

Townes wasn't wrong. But I wasn't going to explain to Basil the details of my fake relationship when she was drunk. I'd do it later, after I talked with our coach, to try to get ahead of whatever the media was going to say. Because he was right about one thing, Aubrey was going to make my life suck. He glanced behind me as Basil came to my side.

"Scooch," she commanded.

I maneuvered myself close to the photo-covered wall and switched our plates as Basil sat down. She took another sip of the milkshake and bit into a fry and asked, "So, what's the plan for this week?"

With how often we traveled for games, Basil tried to ask

as early as possible so she could plan out practice for the kids.

"We're traveling this week, so I won't make it to any practices," I said. Basil nodded in understanding and glanced at the milkshake.

I hated seeing the glimmer of disappointment on her face and asked, "Want to do something when we get back? I think we're getting back early on Thursday, so maybe we can grab dinner or something." I looked at Townes before Basil could respond. "You down?"

As he nodded his head, Basil took the milkshake and bit the straw. She sighed, "Can't. I've got a date."

Now, I understood that Basil and I were friends. Nothing more. However, the news that she had a date hit me square in the chest. And I hid whatever feeling that landed in my stomach—it *wasn't* disappointment—and smiled. "Oh, I didn't know you were talking to anyone," I said as I took the milkshake from her.

Townes scowled again and leveled me with a stare while Basil finished off her food. "I'm not. It's a blind date, and I promised I'd go."

That didn't make me feel any better.

"Oh okay, no problem. We can always hang out another time," I said as I handed her back the drink, but she waved it off.

"What else do you guys have going on other than games? Townes? Anything exciting in your life?"

I was glad when she changed the subject because I didn't want to keep wondering about her dating life. Come to think of it, I didn't know if she had one—at least that she had told me of. Not that I was entitled to that information, but I wanted to know. Basil was the most self-sufficient woman I'd ever met. Other than my mother, I mean. Maybe dating just wasn't on her radar.

Townes put his napkin on his empty tray and leaned back. "Aside from Haybug's birthday? Nothing really."

"I can't wait to decorate," Basil said with another smile as she put her trash onto the tray.

Townes answered with a hum under his breath before shooting me a glance. I cleared my throat and leaned in close to Basil. "Wanna go home?"

Basil nodded and looked at me. Her eyes were even more sleep-filled than they were earlier. Townes shifted out of his seat and stretched. "I'll get the bill. You guys get the car started." He walked to our waitress, who was chugging coffee from a thermos a second before she noticed him. I watched their interaction as I waited for Basil to get out of the booth, and then we walked outside.

I opened the passenger door and waited until she buckled. Then, I walked around and started the car.

"Are you excited about your game?" she asked. When I looked over, she was sitting with her eyes closed and her arms crossed. I chuckled and watched as Townes paid through the window.

"Yeah, I'm excited. But I'm kind of bummed that I won't be at practice this week."

"Oh, don't be. The kids will be fine without you," she said, opening her eyes slightly to look at me. I pinned her with a stare and scoffed gently before looking forward.

"They aren't the reason I'm bummed, sunshine."

basil

I wiped my hands on my pants before checking my phone —again.

Beau had texted me twenty minutes ago, letting me know he was on his way. Since then, my palms had gotten sweaty five times, and I paced the entryway enough times to wear down the cheap laminate. I should have canceled when Case texted me last night after his plane landed. He'd been gone all week, and I was surprised to realize I missed his company more than I thought I would.

But I didn't cancel. So here I was, stressed about how this date was going to go.

I wasn't a stranger to blind dates. Hollis was notorious for setting them up for me in college, but they never ended well. Maybe because I spent those dates trying to figure out if the guy was a serial killer, not because of a lack of connection. Both were true, so I was never upset when they didn't call again.

The rapid knock on the door sent my heart reeling. I glanced in the mirror to make sure any flyways were slicked back before I opened the door. Beau stood there with a smile that made my skin crawl. He dropped the small bouquet of purple flowers and let his eyes roam over me. Beau was handsome by societal standards. He was tall, had dark hair, and dressed well. As I looked closer, I noticed something was off. Maybe it was the smirk he wore, the heat in his blue eyes, or the way he seemed to hold himself above me.

I didn't know. But my stomach turned, and I knew he wouldn't hit any bases tonight.

"Hey," his voice sounded like he was forcing it into a lower register. But maybe that was how he sounded all the time. I hoped my smile didn't give away my nerves when I took the flowers.

"Hi, Beau," I said as I set the flowers down on the entry table.

"Damn. Basil, you look really nice, ready to go?" He glanced over my body again and held out a hand. His eyes darted to the lock at my side and an unsettling feeling landed in my stomach. I ignored it and pulled the door shut as I stepped through the doorway. I could catch an Uber if things didn't go well. He took my hand, and I let him lead me down the stairwell. I offered a kind smile when he opened the passenger door.

I suppressed a jolt when the engine roared to life, surprised by the muffler's backfire. Then my anxiety spiked when Beau started driving. Once on the main road, he weaved in and out of traffic, and I kept my hand on the door.

"Where are we going?" I asked, trying to keep my voice level while I watched a minivan swerve back into its lane when we drove past.

"Mystic," he grinned as we pulled up to a stoplight.

"Oh, that's uh, fancy." I wanted to be excited, but I was underdressed for the upscale restaurant he was taking me to. When the light turned green, Beau started off again. But when he cut off yet another car, I placed my hands on the dash and glared at him. "You need to slow down."

"Ah, come on, babe. You don't like going fast?" he asked with a boyish smirk.

I bristled at the unwelcomed pet name but kept the annoyance from my voice as I moved my hair behind my shoulder. "Fast is fine when there's no traffic." I looked at him and tried to add humor to my next words. "And I'd like to get to dinner alive."

"Don't worry babe, I got you," Beau said as he reached over to take my hand. Goosebumps peppered my skin at the contact.

His hands were too soft, too hot, and I didn't like it. When I tried to slide my hand away, he tightened his grip. So, I was stuck. Forced into physical contact until we got to the restaurant—when he only let go because he had to hand the keys to the valet. Once I was out of the car, he gestured to the tall double glass doors. We walked into the low- lit restaurant, and he placed a hand on my lower back. He checked into our reservation with the blonde hostess, and she took us to a secluded table in the back. Beau pulled out my chair and helped push it in after I sat down.

I didn't like how the faux leather felt under my hands when I pulled my chair the rest of the way in. I smiled anyway. "Thanks," I said as I reached for the thin drink menu. "Do you come here often?"

Beau smirked and picked up the menu from his plate. I knew from my mom that his dad was a successful pastry chef and, like her, was well respected in the industry. So, it wouldn't surprise me if Beau was a regular here, or at any other upscale restaurant like this one. But I wasn't one to assume.

Our waitress, a pretty brunette, came by and offered a smile. "Hi, guys. Can I get you started with any drinks?"

"A Moscow mule please, Van," Beau stated, and I couldn't help but notice the eye roll from the waitress as she turned to me.

"And for you?"

"Just water for now, please."

She walked off, and Beau cleared his throat. I looked at him when he shrugged. "I come often enough."

I peered over the menu. "Lots of dates, then?" I asked, trying to lighten the mood. But he didn't find anything funny about my words. I saw the tick in his jaw and back-tracked. "I mean—this place is expensive. You must do well for yourself if you can afford to be a regular."

Damn, I needed to find an excuse to leave. This date wasn't going to end well.

Beau leaned back in his seat and crossed his legs. "I'm a software engineer, actually, and my uncle owns the place."

I nodded and waited for a follow-up question from him, but our waitress came back with our drinks before he got the chance.

"Are we ready to order?"

Beau shifted in his seat, and I suddenly realized he never looked at the menu; he just set it aside. "The wagyu for me. Medium rare with the Caesar salad."

The woman nodded and turned toward me. When I opened my mouth to order, Beau cut me off.

"She'll have the Caesar as well, along with the scallops. Thanks, Van." Beau winked at her and ignored her scoff as she walked away. I sat there, mortified, staring at him while he rolled up his sleeves.

"So, what do you do for work?"

Frustration bubbled in my chest. "Beau, I can't have scallops."

His brows pulled together, and he asked, "What?"

I took a deep breath, my last attempt at containing my

frustration. "I can't have scallops, I'm allergic. That was incredibly rude of you to order for me without checking."

Beau rolled his eyes and scoffed. "You're the only one who's ever complained. Just change it when she brings it out. Now, again, what do you do for work?"

I kept staring at him, but I couldn't find myself to be surprised by his behavior. I crossed my arms and leaned back. "I coach youth sports."

"Hm. Interesting."

"What is?" I asked.

Beau shrugged and took a drink. "I was told you worked in the sports industry, but I thought you did something more important."

I blinked. "More important? What's more important than coaching kids? How do you think any of these professional athletes out there learned if they didn't play sports growing up? If it weren't for people like me, then people like you wouldn't even have sports to watch."

I loved my job more than anything. Growing up, I knew I wanted to work with kids, but I didn't have the patience to be a teacher. Then, I joined the volleyball team. My coaches encouraged me in ways no one else could, and that's when I knew where I was meant to be.

Beau chuckled and leaned over the table, keeping his voice low. "I mean, it's a good job. I guess. But don't you have a degree? Why not use that education to do something better?" His eyes darkened as he dragged them over me. "Besides, with your looks, you could become *very* successful, *very* quickly."

I'd had it.

"If you'll excuse me." I pushed my seat back from the table and, without a backward glance, walked toward the bathroom. Screw calling an Uber. I didn't have time to download the app, and I needed someone here now. Once inside, I pulled my phone from my purse and tried to call

Hollis. But my calls kept going to voicemail. I took a deep breath and called the only other person I could think of.

Case.

"Hey, what are you up to?" I heard the joy in his voice, and I let out a heavy sigh of relief. His next words were tense when he noticed. "What's wrong?"

I tried to smile when I talked, to mask how upset and uncomfortable I was. "Remember that date I told you about?"

"Yeah." His voice was clipped. Was he bothered I went on a date? Why? I cleared my throat and messed with a frayed thread on my purse.

"Well, I need you to come get me. If you're not busy."

I heard the sound of his jingling keys over the phone and the frustration that bubbled over died. Case's voice was a touch softer when he spoke. "I'm never too busy for you. Where are you?"

The sound of a car engine broke through the line, and I sucked in a breath. "I'm at Mystic. I'll meet you outside."

"Okay, I'll be there soon, Basil."

I checked myself in the large gold-framed mirror after I hung up, making sure I looked as put together as I did when Beau brought me here. I pushed down the uneasiness in my stomach and walked back to the table. When I reached Beau, he was cutting his steak, and he gestured to the empty seat across from him.

"I changed your order for you. Next time, you should tell people you have allergies when you meet them. It'll save everyone the trouble," he said with a smirk. But it fell and his face tightened when I started going through my purse.

"I'm leaving, Beau." I placed a few twenties on the table. "This should cover whatever you were going to get me." I wasn't going to address his other comment, because I knew it wasn't worth it.

I turned around and started for the door, giving soft smiles to the waitresses as I passed them. I was almost outside when I heard footsteps behind me, but I only walked faster. The cool air hit my burning cheeks when I stepped outside, and Beau was right behind me. He grabbed onto my wrist and whirled me around. Panic filled me when I faced him and saw the anger that marred his features. I tried my best to pull away from his grip, but he tightened his hand and leaned in.

I scanned the area, and my panic intensified when I realized we were alone.

"Our date isn't over," he bit out, keeping his voice low. I tried to pull my hand away again, but he yanked me closer. "Stop it." His words made me pause. "You don't get to walk out like that and make me look like a fool. You're going to go back inside, eat whatever I fucking got you, then I get to take you home. Understand that, *babe*?"

Pressure built behind my eyes, but I couldn't give him the satisfaction of seeing me cry. I had to hold out until Case got here. I never should have agreed to this stupid date.

I planted my foot behind me, ready to drive it straight between his legs when the wind carried a welcoming, familiar spiced scent toward me. I glanced behind Beau and saw Case walking furiously toward us.

He got here quicker than I thought he would.

His hand reached out and met Beau's shoulder before he pulled him off me. Case stepped around Beau and placed himself between us, shielding me.

Beau stood straighter as he looked up at Case, and it was hilarious to see, considering Case had at least four inches on the asshole. "What's your fucking problem, pal?"

"My problem?" Case's voice was low, and it sent a shiver through me. "Is that you had your hand on my girl."

case

The man's gaze darted to Basil, but I moved to block his view. He pinned me with a glare and scoffed, throwing up his hands.

"This is ridiculous. You're not worth all this bullshit." His face morphed out of anger and smirked. He shook his head before he looked at me. "I don't even know why I'm getting so worked up." He patted a hand on my shoulder and moved to walk past us.

"She's probably not a decent fuck, anyway. You can have her, man. No bitch is worth this much drama."

I pulled my arm out of Basil's grasp and grabbed the man's shoulder before my fist landed on his nose. His head snapped back as he scrambled to reach his face. Blood dripped down onto his white shirt. A couple had opened the door to leave the restaurant and stopped. Their attention darted between us before the man ushered the woman away. I grabbed Basil's hand and turned us around. We walked back to my car and ignored the stream of curses that sounded behind us. I helped Basil in, and she sat quietly as I buckled her. After I started the car, I asked, "Are you okay?"

"Yeah," she said, her voice quiet. "Are you?"

I nodded and started driving. "Did you Uber, or did he pick you up from your place?"

"Uh, he picked me up."

We drove in silence as I willed the anxiety in my chest to dissipate. When we passed the street that led to her apartment, she looked at me with creased brows. "You missed the turn."

"Can't miss it if that's not our destination. We're going to my place. I'm not leaving you alone after what happened. For all we know, that asshat could show up later."

"I'm sure I'd be fine, Case."

"And I'm not taking that chance, sunshine. This is just as much about your safety as it is about my peace of mind."

I kept my focus on the road but felt Basil's small smile from beside me. The anxiety in my chest loosened and changed into something I hadn't felt in a long time—jealousy. It sparked when she told me about her date, and it settled into my bones where it had lingered since. I hadn't been able to think much of anything else all week. I didn't let it affect how I played on the ice, and our winning game was proof of that. But whenever I sat in the hotel room or was at dinner with the team, my mind strayed to her.

Basil was free to see whoever she wanted, to do whatever she wanted, but I was jealous anyway.

She sank back into the seat and kept her eyes on the window. "Thank you, Case, for coming to get me."

I hoped she didn't hate me for what I was about to do. I didn't think about it—it was instinctual. I reached for her hand and rubbed my thumb over her soft skin. But she didn't pull away like I was sure she'd do. Instead, she faced me, and I knew what I would see if I looked at her.

I'd see her soft, curled hair that cascaded over her shoulders, and I'd see her flushed cheeks. She'd think I couldn't tell because the dim light softened everything about her, but that wasn't true. Everything about Basil was ingrained in my mind. I'd never not notice her beauty.

I squeezed her hand and looked over at her. "Don't thank me for being there for you, Basil."

Her lips parted on a soft inhale, and I turned my attention back to the road. I had thought about that mouth too many times while we were away, and temptation tugged on my willpower. We drove the rest of the way in comfortable silence, and I let her hand go as we pulled into the driveway. Maybe the dip in her smile was my imagination, because why would someone who didn't like being touched be upset if I pulled away? She had a bad night, and I wanted to change that.

Once in my garage, I parked and walked around to open her door. She smiled up, and my chest tightened at the sight. I cleared my throat and gestured to the door.

"So, what do you want to do?" I asked as I followed behind her.

Inside, Basil placed her purse on the small entry table and turned around. "Do you mind if I change into something?"

She wore jeans that hugged her frame, and a sweater so tight it left nothing to the imagination. I noticed it when I picked her up, and had done a good job of keeping my eyes on her face until now. I cleared my throat and pointed to the wide stairs behind her. "Second door on the right is the bathroom. My room is at the end of the hallway. Feel free to find something that fits. I'm going to get a movie going while you change, okay?"

She nodded and walked past me. I headed into the kitchen and grabbed some popcorn from the pantry. While

I let the popcorn do its thing, I wandered into the living room and got everything ready. After I picked a movie and put the popcorn into a bowl, I grabbed some blankets and waited for Basil. I was busy adjusting the blankets on the beige couch when I heard Basil behind me.

"Can we order Chinese?"

I finished smoothing out a wrinkle on the black duvet. "What, you didn't eat anything on your—" Words died on my lips when I turned and looked at her.

This woman was trying to kill me.

Of all the comfortable sweats and hoodies I kept in my closet, Basil just had to pick the hoodie that had my jersey number across the back. She walked past me, and in a moment of weakness, I glanced down to where the hemline sat on her mid-thigh.

It didn't look like she found any shorts to wear.

Once Basil settled under the duvet, she shrugged, oblivious to the heated thoughts running through my head. "No, I probably would have if he let me order my own food."

"He ordered for you?" I asked while I handed Basil my phone, my favorite Chinese spot already pulled up.

She busied herself with picking out what she wanted before she spoke. "Annoying, right? And of all the things he could have gotten me, he ordered scallops."

I took my phone and put in my order. I looked at Basil with a raised brow. "You didn't tell him about your allergy?"

She leaned forward, causing the blanket on her lap to shift down and expose the skin on her legs. "You know about it?"

I shrugged. "One time when I got lunch, there was a new girl behind the counter. Rhonda almost knocked her over to keep me from grabbing the bag. Apparently, the person who ordered before you had gotten something with shrimp. They cleaned everything and remade our food."

"That's the day you were running late?" Her brows pulled in, and I nodded quickly. I waved my phone, the order confirmation page shining.

"Food will be here soon. Want to start the movie?"

Basil stood from the couch and walked past me. "Can I get a drink first? Do you have wine?"

I followed her and gave in to temptation. I watched her hips sway as she walked to the oversized fridge and wondered exactly how they'd feel in my hands. *Jesus*, what was with me tonight?

I was self-aware enough to know how busy my life had been recently. Between ending things with Aubrey, traveling for games, and being forced out of my hotel room, I hadn't had any time to relieve stress in ways that I needed to. I shook my head and headed toward the dark cabinet where I kept the nice wine glasses my mom bought me for Christmas last year. I handed Basil the stemless glass, and she handed me a beer in return. Still standing, I leaned against the island and watched Basil pour her glass.

The Edison Bulbs dressed her in the warm light, and my eyes traced over her. Memorizing every dip and curve, while my hands begged to reach out for her. I was caught off guard when she looked up and noticed a crease had formed between her brows.

"Are you okay?" she asked before she placed the bottle back in the fridge and I nodded. Too afraid of what would come out of my mouth when it opened.

"Come on." I inclined my head back to the living room. Basil followed me this time, and I took her wine from her so she could settle back into her spot. She threw the blanket over her legs and I felt like I could breathe normally again.

We got just a few minutes into the movie when the doorbell rang. When I came back to the living room, Basil was sitting cross-legged, a hungry look in her pretty eyes as she held out her hands. "Say please," I teased as I settled back into my spot.

"You're gonna withhold my food? After all that I've been through tonight?"

There it was again. That tug somewhere between my sternum and my throat as she smiled at me. I raised a brow, and I placed her food in her outstretched hands. "I could never do that, but you looked ready to rip my arm off if I wasn't careful."

It was quiet again while we ate, but when the empty containers made it to the coffee table, Basil laid back on the couch. She threw her feet onto my lap and sighed. "I should have canceled that date."

I ignored the warmth in my stomach and threw my arm over the back of the couch before looking at her. "Why didn't you?"

Basil kept her gaze on the ceiling. "Because my mom set it up, and I didn't want to listen to her comments if I canceled." Her feet shifted in my lap and I couldn't escape the feel of her against me. I *really* needed to get laid. "Besides, hanging out with you sounded way more fun."

I chuckled. "Well, I'm glad you enjoy my company so much you didn't cancel your date." I pushed against her feet and she kicked gently before scowling.

"You know that's not what I meant."

I reached for her foot before she could kick me again and pressed into her arch. The sound she made went straight to my head, and I wanted to hear it again. When I looked over, Basil was sitting up. She rested against the throw pillows had discarded on the floor earlier, and her cheeks were flushed. Her eyes stayed where I gripped her foot.

"Is this okay?" I asked.

I waited until she nodded before continuing and did my best to contain my excitement that she was letting me touch her this way. Another breathy sound escaped her when I rubbed the side of her foot, and I wondered what else made her sound like that. My grip tightened slightly, and I had to say something to distract myself. To keep my mind from going farther than it already had.

"You said your mom set up your date?" I cleared my throat and kept my gaze on the movie.

"Yeah, he's her co-worker's son. I knew there was never going to be a second date, even if it had gone well. I really just did it for the free food."

"Food that you didn't get to eat," I stated, moving onto her other foot.

Basil tossed her head back with a laugh and I couldn't help but smile at the wonderful sound. "Yeah, you're right. Man, I knew that guy wasn't going to be a good kisser, but I didn't expect him to be that much of an asshole."

Something snapped in my chest, and I looked at her with a questioning smirk. "You think you can tell if someone's a good kisser?"

She scrunched her nose. "You can't? That's a shame. I bet you could have saved yourself from a lot of bad lip-locking experiences."

My movements on her foot slowed as I thought her words over. Then, with my eyes forward, I answered, "I can tell."

I needed to keep watching the movie. Because we were heading into dangerous territory.

"Case, look at me." I did and regretted it when I noticed a heat in her eyes that darkened when they darted to my mouth. She was beautiful. We had turned the lights off, and the only thing illuminating her face was the light from the TV—but I could see her perfectly. She licked her bottom lip, and my grip tightened on her foot. "I'm curious about something," she said, her voice dipping to a whisper.

Yeah. Dangerous territory here.

"What's that, sunshine?" My voice came out rough, and I hoped she didn't notice it.

"Do *you* think I'm a good kisser?" she asked with a tilt of her head. I moved her feet closer to my knees. Not wanting to accidentally give away how hard I was getting. Her words hit me and every scenario I had thought about played through my mind.

Me kissing her after practice before taking her into one of the utility closets.

Me surprising her after a winning game and coming back here instead of going to the after party.

How badly I wanted to rip Scottie off her the other night and take her over that Beer Pong table.

So, did I think she was a good kisser? Yes. *God*, yes.

We had to talk about something else. I poked her foot and hoped my smile was real enough. "I have a question for you."

She nodded. "Go for it."

"You said you don't like physical touch, right?" Her face flushed deeper and my smile turned real. "How come I can touch you like this and you're okay with it? Or are you really not? Because if you're not, Basil, and you haven't told me then—"

"I said it's fine." She cut me off.

I blinked, stunned and unsure of what she was saying. "What?"

Basil tossed her head back and sighed. I had to look away from her chest to maintain whatever control I thought I had. "That day we took the test? I told you it was fine. I meant that I'm fine with you touching me. I still don't like when other people do it, though."

I kept my face neutral as her words hit me. This whole

time, I could have touched her, reached for her hand, or pulled her into my arms. I had misunderstood her. Basil didn't wait for me to respond and instead leveled me with that same heated stare from before.

"Now answer my question, big guy. Do you think I'm a good kisser?"

basil

I missed him, and the sight of him punching Beau in the face did something to me.

Those were the only reasons I could think of to explain why I was flirting with him. It had nothing to do with anything else, like how he made me laugh or made me feel safe. I pushed *loved* from my mind before it could sink into my heart because that wasn't it. Case and I were friends. I just had to get this feeling out of my system. Give him a chance to show me he didn't think of me how I'd been thinking of him. It wasn't totally new, but I also didn't know when it started. Maybe the first time he bought lunch and ate my pickles when they ended up on my sandwich. Or maybe it started when we fought over those cookies and I couldn't get over how my skin tingled when he pulled away.

It could also be just now when he told me he knew about my allergy.

None of those reasons mattered, though, not when he didn't feel the same way. I needed him to be the one to change the conversation because I didn't trust myself to do it. He could even tell me I had made him uncomfortable, and I'd leave. I would shove these confusing feelings into a box and pretend they didn't exist.

I watched Case as his eyes darted to my mouth before his brows furrowed, and an almost pained expression crossed his face. Shit. Just how badly had I screwed things up with that question? I shook my head and tried to hide the embarrassment from my face.

"You can't tell, can you? That's fine. It was a silly question, anyway." I moved to pull my feet off him, but his grip tightened. My eyes widened as I looked at him. His breathing came in heavy, shallow movements. He looked so imposing in the dark, but I didn't feel uncomfortable.

He leaned as close as he could, and his voice dropped. "You're deflecting. Why? Do you not think *I'm* a good kisser?"

I tried not to focus on where his thumb sat just above my ankle, where my pulse beat rapidly. Instead, I followed his lead and smirked. "You're the one who said it. Though I had a feeling, you just have this look about you."

Case started moving this thumb in small circles, and my breath caught in my chest. His eyes moved to my throat as I swallowed and lingered for a moment. I watched his Adam's apple bob before he pinned me with that stare again. All I saw in those green eyes was a heat so heavy, they turned a shade of dark evergreen, and my entire body tightened.

"You couldn't be more wrong, sunshine." His voice came out rough and sent shivers down my spine, but I held firm.

I sat up and leaned toward Case, disappointed the space between us was still too much.

"You know, this entire time I thought you were a humble man, but you're so full of yourself, huh, Case?" I licked my bottom lip. "How can you be so sure you're a good kisser?"

"That sounds like a challenge, Basil," he said. The roughness in his voice was replaced by something hard, and I wanted him to keep talking. That sound was something I could become addicted to if I wasn't careful.

I shrugged again and looked at him through my lashes with a teasing smile. "Do you want it to be?"

I had never done this before, flirted this much. Hadn't ached to be wanted like this. Sure, I'd had sex before, so nothing would be new. But these feelings were the ones I had been conditioned to run away from. What would happen if I didn't run, and just–walked? Let them catch up to me and get to know them? I didn't know what the answer was, but I figured Case could help me figure it out.

Case shifted under me to kneel between my legs, keeping a hand on my ankle. The duvet bunched between us with his new position. His eyes, heavy and heated, bore into mine. "What do you want, Basil? Tell me to back off and I will." I could hear his uncertainty, like he was as unsure as I was. But he was ready to take the risk, anyway. "Ask me to kiss you and well," his grip softened before he dragged his hand up my leg, "I'll be at your mercy."

His hand landed on the back of my thigh as he finished talking. The words, filled with a silent promise, landed on my lips. Panic settled into my stomach when I realized he wasn't going to back down. Did this mean anything? I opened my mouth. Whether to ask him to kiss me or admit this was a mistake, I wasn't sure. But I didn't get the chance to say anything because his phone rang, diffusing the tension between us.

"Can we pin this for later?" he asked, kneading the tight muscles in the back of my leg. When I nodded, he pulled back and ran a hand over his face. He reached for his phone on the coffee table and kept his hand on my leg when he answered.

"What's up?" He kept his focus on me as he spoke, and

I diverted my gaze to the soft material of the blanket. The voice that answered sounded angry. I assumed it was Townes. "Are you serious?" Case's words came out clipped as he sat up straighter. "Yeah, give me a few minutes and I'll come over."

I finally looked at him, and the worry between his brows filled my chest with anxiety. "Everything okay?"

Wordlessly, Case set my legs aside and stood from the couch. He turned to face me and held his hands outward in silent command. I placed my hands in his and let his warmth move through me as he pulled me to stand. He smiled, but it wasn't the warm and bright smile I knew. This one was filled with worry and agitation. "It will be. But I have to go see Townes."

Oh, he was leaving.

"You're more than welcome to stay here because I still don't feel comfortable with you being by yourself at your apartment tonight. Or I can take you to Hollis's place."

I—we—needed space. Whatever just happened between us held a promise for more, and I wasn't in the best headspace to process what that meant. I pretended to think about my options.

"Let me give Hollis a call." I grabbed my phone from where it sat on the couch and Case let out a small groan. I looked behind me to see him holding his fingers on the bridge of his nose, his nostrils flared.

"Are you okay?"

Case looked up and made it obvious he had no intention of dropping his gaze. "I'm going to go find your pants." He stalked out of the living room before I could respond.

———

"I never should have said anything," I said as I watched Hollis skip around her dining room table.

"You should have told me sooner!" she giggled.

I leaned into the chair and watched her with a sigh. "I wasn't going to gossip about Case in his own home. Now, are you going to sit down and help me figure this out? Or are you going to continue wearing down your floors?"

Hollis stopped jumping and cleared her throat. She ran a hand over her purple robe, wiping away creases that never existed. It was her way of showing she was capable of being serious in my time of need. "What is there to figure out?" she asked, keeping her voice as neutral as possible while she took the seat next to me.

I saw her fight a smile and poked her side. "Stop it."

"I'm not doing anything." Another giggle escaped her, and she clasped her hands over her mouth. "Okay, sorry. Just help me understand why you're freaking out."

Her demeanor softened as she put a hand over mine. I opened that box of feelings and tried to sort through them. But it was hard when images of Case and me on his couch, not even an hour ago, were added to the mix. I didn't know what to do with the butterflies in my stomach, and it confused me more.

I looked at Hollis, and she must have seen the conflicting emotions on my face. Her smile dropped. "Come on, B. Help me understand."

"I don't know how," I started, focusing on the direction of the wood grain of the dark table. "He just came back from his games, and I just missed him. I don't know what came over me."

She furrowed her brows. "Have you missed him before?"

"Sure I have, but it's never been like this." My voice was soft as I recalled the other times he'd come home. The first time I texted him a thumbs up, and the second I asked to meet for lunch. Since then, our conversations had graduated to phone calls that lasted until one of us fell asleep. Now, I was letting myself become overwhelmed by some silly feelings when he got back.

Hollis could see my thoughts racing and pursed her lips. "You know what I think, B?"

"That I embarrassed myself and I need to buy him one of those fruit gift baskets to say sorry?"

She blinked. "No."

I groaned and threw my head back. She tugged on my hand, a silent request to look at her. Hollis's blue eyes were soft as she looked at me.

"I think you like him." I opened my mouth to protest, but she cut me off. "I think, before, you didn't know him well enough to miss him. So every time he came back, it didn't impact your day. But now that you've known him longer? Your feelings have changed."

"But how do I know what I'm feeling isn't just some fluke?" I asked, keeping my voice low.

Hollis smiled. "Because, B. You're the only person I know who doesn't shy away from their feelings. You accept them for what they are. Now, whether or not you act on them is different, but I've never met anyone who cares as fiercely as you do."

I kept my mouth shut. How could I argue with what she was saying when she was right? I did feel everything. My anger, sadness, hope, and even that new warm feeling I couldn't name yet. It wasn't a misplaced emotion either, how I felt about Case. I think that was why I was so freaked out, because so much could go wrong and I could lose him. Like earlier tonight. What would have happened if he regretted kissing me? If we went too far beyond whatever boundaries of our friendship we had in place?

I couldn't risk making a mistake and losing him. Nothing like that could ever happen again.

"Talk to me, B," Hollis said as she tugged on my arm again with a smile.

"I don't want things to change between us. And this is not me saying I like him, okay? But if I did, I'm happy with what we are."

Her lips dropped into a tight line, and her stare filled with concern. "Is that something you're really okay with?"

I nodded and let the heavy feeling of denial sit on my shoulders. I was happy being friends with Case. Nothing needed to change. With a yawn, I glanced at the clock on the wall and tore my hand away from Hollis to stretch.

"Enough about me. How have you been?" I had to steer the conversation elsewhere.

Hollis threw her head into her hands and groaned. "Physically? Fine, I guess. Mentally? I'm drained, B. The school is pulling me in so many directions, I don't even know my left from my right anymore."

"How many classes have you had to cover?"

"Too many. I do my lesson planning at home now, and that's if I have the energy to do it. They've asked me to take over two after-school activities because people keep quitting."

My mouth opened in shock. "That's horrible. I hope Ryan is helping you out, since you're so tired."

When she didn't say anything, I raised a brow and leaned closer. "He *is* helping you, right, Hol? You know, being the supportive boyfriend, you've boasted about these last two years?"

Hollis looked down and picked at the skin of her thumb. "He's been really busy, too."

Sensing her hesitation to further that particular conversation, I scooted the chair back and stood. I moved my arms over my head in a much-needed stretch and yawned again. "It's late and I've got a long day tomorrow."

"Oh yeah, you've got that birthday thing, right? For Townes's niece?"

I nodded and stifled a yawn. "Yeah. Case is going to pick me up in the morning and take me back to my place so I can get ready. Are you not helping? I thought Townes asked." If I remembered correctly, Case volunteered Hollis to help plan the outing they're going on tomorrow. Townes couldn't figure out what Hayley would have liked because she had given him conflicting answers.

Hollis's cheeks flushed, and she looked away. "Actually, something came up and I can't help. Everything is planned, though. Townes just has to follow through with it."

My tired eyes looked her over, but she deflected my concern with a smile. "Now go, the sooner you get to bed, the sooner you get to see Case," she said with a wink. So I walked into the guest bedroom and noticed the set of pajamas Hollis had laid out.

I ignored them and fell asleep wearing the hoodie Case didn't bother to ask for back.

case

Townes was right about Aubrey pulling something. I had hoped it wasn't that bad, but when he showed me the article, that hope quickly died.

WHO IS SHE? CASE WHITLOCK SIGHTED WITH MYSTERY WOMAN AMONGST CHEATING RUMORS WITH MODEL GIRLFRIEND.

I'd sent Jasmine an insane amount of emails asking her to get on top of this. I didn't care how she did it, but those articles needed to be pulled. Not for my sake, but for Basil's. She never asked to be included in the parts of my world that everyone else seemed to envy. But if this didn't get resolved soon, then I'd have to tell Basil, and I was worried what her reaction would be. My phone dinged in my pocket, and I reached for it, only to be disappointed with a text from Townes.

TOWNES

Make sure you get plenty of balloons.

And a helium machine.

I sighed and looked up as Basil tossed a purple table runner into the cart. It slid off the packs of balloons we'd already gotten, and I reached out to grab it. After putting the table runner where it was safe, I smiled at Basil, and my mood brightened when she did the same.

"Just a few more things then we can go," she said before turning back to the shelves. I moved to stand next to her and bent so we were both looking at the purple decorations. My shoulder brushed against her with the proximity, and it was nice to not be concerned about making her uncomfortable.

I leaned into her. "How many things did he put on that list? And does everything have to be purple, or are you using your best judgment?" She showed me the double-sided list, and my eyes widened. "That much for a birthday party?"

"Mhm. Townes said she wanted to 'go big or go home,'" she said with quotations. "And the purple is a judgment call. Who doesn't love purple?" I helped her grab the last few things we needed before walking to the register. The red cart squeaked as I pushed it, and I was glad we were done.

Basil's cheeks flushed as she talked. "I think this is something you'd do." She gestured to the full cart.

"What do you mean?"

She smiled. "I mean, you'd be the dad that filled up the cart with decorations for your kids' birthdays. Probably make multiple trips, too."

When I looked down at Basil, she had her attention forward, but the flush was still there. She was right. I would go out of my way to make every celebration special. But I knew I'd be extra with my kids.

"One day."

"Yeah, one day. You've got plenty of time before you even need to consider settling down."

"Do you want kids?" I asked her, trying to sound casual as we started unloading the cart. I wasn't afraid to admit that I had thought about what our kids would look like if we had any.

They'd be the cutest kids ever.

"Two girls and a boy. I have names picked out and know what time I want to get pregnant, so they have optimal zodiac signs."

"Wow." I tossed the last package of napkins on the counter and crossed my arms. Basil shrugged, but the movement was heavy. I didn't understand it. Why would she have a future family planned out, and not seem to enjoy it? I hated it, seeing the tightness in her body, and the way her thoughts seemed to push out the happiness that was just there.

I poked her side. "So, are you keeping the theme of your name within the family? Going with names like Rosemary and Tarragon?"

She paused and blinked. I watched as that joy came back and brightened the green in her eyes. "You know what? I was going to keep the names simple, but I like how you think," she said it with a teasing smile before she faced the cashier.

We finished up at the store soon after and started for the large townhome Townes and Scottie shared. Basil and I talked about baby names until we pulled into the driveway. She got out to unlock the front door while I grabbed the mountain of bags from the trunk. Once I made it through the doorway, she tried to help take the bags, but I pushed past her and set them on the island.

"What time are they supposed to be here again?" she asked as she started opening the balloons.

I double-checked the text he sent me earlier and started opening the box of the helium machine. "He said around five."

I settled back into my spot between Basil's legs as Hayley did her best to convince Townes to watch another movie.

"You said I could do anything on my birthday. I wanna watch Moana. Please?" Hayley hit him with her perfected puppy dog stare and Townes caved almost immediately. After a victory dance, Hayley settled back into her pillow fort, stepping over her friends who had fallen asleep on the floor.

Townes looked at her as he scrolled through to find the movie, and I swore his scowl deepened. "Don't tell Nana."

She made a zipping motion over her mouth and threw away the pretend key before looking back at the TV. If she was a force to be reckoned with when she was six—then I couldn't wait to see what she'd do now that she was a year older.

Basil laughed behind me, and I tilted my head back, so it rested in her lap. When she smiled down at me—I couldn't think. My instincts itched to pull her down, to close the distance and kiss her. I could see in the way her soft eyes dipped to my lips—the brown, which deepened to a rich chocolate in the darkness of the living room—that the thought crossed her mind. We hadn't talked about last night, and I had planned on bringing it up this morning when I picked her up from Hollis's.

But then she walked out in the hoodie I forgot I let her borrow, and my brain was suddenly occupied with other things. Like how it sat perfectly over those hips I came close to grabbing last night.

Basil leaned down. "Can you get us more popcorn?"

I brought my hand up and grabbed the popcorn bowl from beside her and asked, "Can I put some ranch on it?"

"That seasoning stuff?" Her nose scrunched as she thought it over. "Sure."

I untangled myself from between her legs and walked to the kitchen. The counters were littered with party favors and decorations. When I flicked on the light to the walk-in pantry, I found Scottie with his hand deep in a package of chocolate chip cookies.

"Are those from the party or Townes's secret stash?" I asked him as I grabbed a popcorn bag and walked to put it in the microwave.

When I turned back to face him, I chuckled. His face paled, and he closed the package. "Don't tell him."

"He's going to find out man, I can't save you."

Scottie, in a panic, put the package back on the top shelf of the pantry, then hauled ass out of the kitchen. I peered around the corner that separated the two rooms and watched him find his seat on the couch. Then, my gaze drifted to Basil, who was talking with one of Hayley's friends.

The microwave beeped, and as I grabbed the seasoning, I remembered something. I separated the popcorn into two separate bowls and seasoned mine.

I planted myself in front of Basil before handing over her bowl, and I could hear the awe in her voice when she spoke. "You didn't put the ranch seasoning on?"

"Your nose scrunch told me you'd rather I didn't. And I remembered how you said you don't like it on popcorn, which is still crazy to me, by the way." I smiled up at her before focusing my attention on the movie. Basil laced her fingers through my hair as the movie played and I tossed some popcorn into my mouth. When a piece landed on my lap, I reached down and my hand bumped into the pouch on my hoodie. The sound of plastic caught my attention.

Oh, I forgot.

I took a quick look around to make sure none of the kids were looking my way before I reached into the pouch.

With the candy in hand, I stretched and dropped the item into Basil's lap.

Townes may have caved with the movie, but he held firm on his strict 'no sweets after seven' rule. If he saw what I had, he wouldn't be happy. Basil shifted as she moved the candy under her leg before she leaned over.

"How'd you know green was my favorite?"

I whispered, which made her lean in closer. "You always have candy when we get lunch, and it's always green. I had a hunch." She patted my shoulder and leaned back against the couch. The sound of a wrapper opening followed soon after, and we fell into comfortable silence.

I made it halfway through the movie when my neck started to ache, and I hadn't done a good job of hiding my discomfort because Basil leaned in again.

"You okay, big guy?" she asked.

I looked back at her and shook my head. "Just a sore neck. I'll live."

Basil surprised me. She placed her hands on either side of my head and forced me to look forward. Her hands started working the tender muscles in my neck, her thumbs moving in slow, steady circles. My body heated at the contact, but I couldn't help but lean into her touch. When her fingers traveled over a particularly sore spot, I tensed, and her movements paused.

"Shit, sorry," she said before she pulled back. I reached a hand behind me to stop her, my thumb brushed over the pulse in her wrist.

"Don't be sorry for my inability to stretch properly." I leaned back and smiled. "It feels good. You can keep going, but only if you want to." I pulled my hand away and rested it on my lap before eating a few more pieces of popcorn.

Basil hummed under her breath and I could hear the

smile in her voice when she leaned in. "Well, next time, do a better job. I don't mind rubbing your neck, just don't judge me too bad, okay? It probably won't be as good as the massage you gave me. But I'll try my best."

Her hands found their rhythm again, and I sat there. My mind wandered into dangerous territory, wondering what her hands would feel like running down–

I moved the popcorn into my lap when my pants tightened. With every ministration of her hands, my body wound tighter and tighter until I had to remind myself to breathe. I had to get away from her hands, even though this was the best neck massage I'd ever gotten. Before I could excuse myself to the bathroom, or kitchen, or anywhere I could get some air—the credits rolled on the movie. All the kids were asleep on the floor and Townes was putting a blanket over Hayley. Basil pulled away, and I stood up faster than I intended, which earned me a shocked look from everyone awake.

"You okay?" Scottie asked, wiggling a knowing brow.

"My ass hurts," I told him before I turned to take Basil's hands. Once she was on her feet, she yawned and stretched her hands over her head. I had to look away when the hoodie rode over her waist. "You ready to go?"

"Yeah, night Scottie," Basil smiled at the redhead who was gathering the blankets he brought down from his room.

"Night Herb." Scottie walked over and wrapped her in a hug, his blankets forgotten on the floor. Scottie must have seen something on my face because while his arms were around her, he winked.

I resisted the urge to tear him off her and throttle him.

Basil pulled away and waved to Townes. "Thanks for inviting me."

"Thanks for helping." He waved to her.

I placed my hand over her lower back and directed her to the front door, waving goodnight to the guys before we stepped outside. The ride to Basil's apartment was quiet. She rested her head against the window, and my hand rested on her leg. It might seem pathetic, but I couldn't seem to stop touching her. I felt like I had to make up for all the times I couldn't. It was purely platonic, of course. I'd put my hands on Scottie or Townes if they were okay with platonic physical intimacy. Women did it all the time.

I wasn't making excuses.

When we reached her apartment and got to her door, Basil fiddled with her keys. I grabbed them from her hands and picked the one she needed. When I handed it back, I found her staring, and I saw a question run through her mind before her mouth opened.

"Can you be my date to my dad's wedding?"

"What?" I asked, blinking, unsure if I heard her correctly.

Her brows furrowed. "My dad's wedding. I need a date and don't want to go with anyone else."

She wanted me to go with her?

I smiled down at her, nerves twisted in my stomach. "I'm flattered you want me to go with you. Do you want me to act like your boyfriend or something?" It was a joke, at least on the surface level. I had heard of people being hired to play the part of a significant other. Whether to save themselves from a lie they're caught up in or to keep their family from asking questions. Basil looked up at me, and my eyes caught the way redness spread across her face. God, she was beautiful.

"My relationship with my dad is complicated. So, I'd be more comfortable if you were there. Help keep me steady, ya know?" She had opened her door, and I stared after her as she walked inside. She started to close the door, and those hazel eyes met mine. The redness in her cheeks had deepened. "But if you want to act like my boyfriend, I'm not going to stop you."

She shut the door, leaving me on her doorstep, stunned by her honesty.

I was utterly fucked.

basil

He abandoned me.

Case had to leave and talk to his coach about something urgent—his words, not mine—and he left me with the kids. Now, on a normal day, it wouldn't bother me. But the kids saw him give me a hug and now they wouldn't stop with the questions.

"Is Coach Whitlock your boyfriend now?"

"How long have you been his girlfriend, Coach?"

"Are you guys getting married?"

That last one made me blush harder than I expected, but I was able to regain my composure before they noticed. Thankfully, the questions stopped once I split everyone into groups to run drills, and the hug was all but forgotten when practice ended. I waved goodbye to everyone before I skated around the rink to collect the cones, then I put the equipment away. I glanced at the ceiling and smiled at the change of decorations. Snowmen and snowflakes now hung where the fall garland had been, giving the facility a winter wonderland feel.

After I put everything away and grabbed my stuff from the locker, I headed toward the offices. Maybe I could catch Case on his way out and we could grab a bite to eat or spend some time together before he left tomorrow.

As I neared the hallway, I noticed all the doors were closed except for one. I walked closer and paused when a heated voice carried into the hallway. I stopped and glanced at the plaque on the wall just outside the door, and sucked in a breath when I read Donovan Warner written in black letters.

I kept enough distance between me and the door to ensure no one inside would see me.

"I don't see why it's such a big deal. I didn't do anything wrong," Case said. I leaned closer to peek inside, and I saw him sitting upright in a dark leather chair. This office was much more disorganized than Mrs. Johnson's. With papers scattered on the desk, and the trash bin over-flowing.

Coach Warner, a middle-aged man with blonde hair, pushed up his glasses and sighed. But it was the tall, pretty brunette next to him that spoke up.

"We know you didn't. But we felt it was necessary to let you know what was being said, and the implications it could have on you and those involved."

Questions ran through me as I listened. What was going on with Case? How bad was it that he needed to be hounded by his coach and whoever this woman was? And selfishly I wondered…why didn't he tell me?

"Well, fix it. I gave you a statement. Shouldn't that be enough?" Case said, and I held my breath. I had never heard him sound so flustered, angry.

The woman took a deep breath and pinched the bridge of her nose. The pink fabric of her blazer bunched around her elbows. "Clearly not if they're still running the story."

Case turned to his coach. "What's going to happen if it doesn't get fixed?"

Warner leaned back in his chair. "Your image and

everyone who's involved could be damaged. I don't think those kids's parents would appreciate one of their coaches being the center of something like this. But, I can't see anything else happening besides that. If nothing gets done, then your life might suck until this blows over."

Case was quiet then as his leg bounced, and he kept his gaze down. When he stood from the seat, I jumped back. I didn't want to make it obvious I was eavesdropping, so I leaned against the opposite wall and took my phone out. It wasn't much—but more believable than hiding behind a plant.

The woman walked out first and didn't even glance in my direction before she headed down the hallway and toward the front of the building. The click of her heels was faint by the time Case walked out, and my heart felt heavy at the look on his face. His brows were creased, and he kept his gaze down. I felt the urge to reach out to him. When I took a step forward, he lifted his head, but the tension didn't disappear. He did his best to smile, but the dimple stayed hidden.

"Hey big guy," I said, keeping my voice soft.

"Hi." I could hear defeat lacing his voice, so when Case reached for my hand, I didn't fight him. We walked toward the front doors, and my skin warmed under his. I hoped the feeling was as comforting to him as it was to me.

We stayed silent until we reached my car. Case pulled his hand away and smiled again. This one reached a little higher than the other one, but it still wasn't his. "How much did you hear?"

"Not enough for me to understand what's going on if that makes it better?" Worry rushed into my chest, and I wanted to demand answers. I wanted to help him.

"Oh." He nodded.

I tilted my head and kept my eyes locked on his. "Who was that lady?"

Case kicked a piece of ice before answering, "Jasmine. She handles all the public relations stuff for the team."

"Is everything okay? You sounded pretty upset in there, and right now, honestly. You know you can talk to me, right?" I tried to hide my disappointment when he pulled away from my hand.

He looked at me with furrowed brows, and I could feel the frustration that radiated off of him. It was suffocating. "I don't want to talk about it. We're friends, Basil, but that doesn't mean we need to know everything going on in each other's lives."

The words pierced my chest, and my heart wilted. My throat constricted when the threat of tears made themselves known. How could I be so—stupid? He was right. How did I not see it? I wasn't any more special than Scottie, Townes, or any of his other friends. I shouldn't expect or ask him for more of himself than what he gave to others. One almost kiss didn't change anything, and all those other moments—I'd clearly misread them. How could I be so blind?

As soon as the words left his lips, Case's features softened. The tension had disappeared, and he reached out. But I took a step back. "Basil that's not—"

"It's fine, Case. You're right, I don't need to know everything going on with you. I'm sorry for thinking we were better friends than that." I turned away before the first tear escaped and got in the car. I hated letting my emotions get the better of me, but I couldn't help it. Whether I liked it or not, Case was special to me. I couldn't understand, though, why his words hurt more than I expected. I was used to hearing them, from my mother at least. His harsh words shouldn't be any different. Hollis and I have had fights, big and small ones, but I never felt like this afterward. I wiped away another tear with the back of my hand and continued driving home.

Wine would make me feel better.

———

My ass wasn't on the couch for a full minute before there was a knock at the door.

"Damn salesmen." I shoved aside the fluffy white blanket to stand. I needed to invest in a sign, because these late night sales pitches were interrupting my self-care. With my feet in my slippers, I walked to the door and grabbed the handle. I was ready to kindly tell whoever was on the other side I wasn't interested in what they were selling and to not come by again. But words were forgotten when I opened the door.

Case stood on the other side, wearing a thick coat to keep warm, and he had a paper bag in his hands. I raised a brow and leaned on the doorframe, not caring I was letting the heat out.

"Can I come in?" Case asked with a soft smile.

I looked him over, my eyes locked on the paper bag for a moment before I met his gaze. "What's in the bag?"

"Let me in and I'll show you."

"What if I don't want to?" I challenged.

Case smirked and shook his head. His tongue poked the inside of his cheek as he looked at me. "Then I'll stand here and tell you how badly I fucked up. Then I'll lick my wounds at home while I hope you'll forgive me. But you'll never find out what I brought you." He held up the bag.

My eyes narrowed on him as I pretended to think it over. The reality was, I had already forgiven him. While it wasn't right of him to lash out at me, I knew I hadn't given him any time to think things over. We were both at fault, so I didn't blame him too much.

There was a good chance I would have reacted the

same way. The least I could do was hear him out. Besides, I wanted to know what he brought me.

I looked Case over one more time and clicked my tongue. "Come on, you can watch this movie with me while you grovel."

Case beamed as he followed me inside. He took off his shoes first as I settled myself on the couch, but when I looked at him after he removed his coat—my mouth felt like the desert. A black under-armor shirt outlined *every-thing*. I wasn't blind. I knew how built Case was—and everyone else on the team. Scottie and Townes were big guys too, but there was something about how the shirt hugged Case that made me heated.

Okay, I had too much wine. It had been one sip, but clearly, it was enough.

I cleared my throat and turned my attention to the beginning scene of Harry Potter as Case made his way to the couch. He placed the bag on the floor—because I still hadn't bought a coffee table—and looked at me.

"About earlier," he started as he found a comfortable spot.

"I'm listening," I said as I kept my focus on the movie. That was until Case paused it and placed his forefinger and thumb on my chin. He turned my face, so we looked at each other. His eyes darted between mine, and I took note of the darkness that shadowed the green in his.

"I'm sorry." His voice was as firm as the grip he had on me. "I never should have talked to you like that, Basil."

"It's okay." That was all I managed to say, because what else was there? I had already forgiven him, even though he didn't know it yet.

Case shook his head, and this time when he looked at me again, I saw it. The concern, the regret. "I was in a bad mood and took it out on you. So no, it's not okay."

I let my head rest in his grasp as I looked at him with a

soft smile. "Case, I could see you were in a bad mood. I should have respected that and left it alone. I should have waited to ask you any—"

"No. Don't do that." He pulled me in a fraction, causing my breath to catch in my throat. "You are not going to carry any of the blame. It was my fault for opening my mouth when I was upset and lashing out at you. You're special to me, Basil, and I'm kicking myself for letting my problems and reactions become more important than you. I promise it won't happen again."

I took that word–special–and tucked it into the shadows of my heart.

I placed my hand on his face and took in the way his stubble felt under my hand. "I like your beard."

He pulled away and looked at me with astonishment. "I'm over here trying to make you not hate me and you tell me you miss my beard?"

"I didn't say I missed it, just that I like it."

Case sighed and covered my hand with his. "Basil—"

"I forgive you Case, and if in the future I ask you something you don't feel like sharing, just tell me. Don't push me away. Deal?" I asked, and when Case nodded, I looked at the bag. "Now, what did you bring me?"

I reached for it, but Case was faster and pulled it out of my reach. He smiled. "You're not going to say please?"

I cocked a brow and opened my mouth. "No, no, no, you don't bring treats here, then deny me. Give me the bag, Case."

"Has anyone ever told you that you're bossy?"

"The kids, almost every practice. Now, gimme." I held out my hands and made grabbing motions. Case chuckled again and dug into the bag. My mouth dropped when I saw what was in his hands.

"Case Whitlock, care to explain how you got a brownie

from Rhoda's?" The dessert was wrapped in cling film, with Rhonda's sticker right in the middle.

Case made quick work of opening it and broke it in half. "Last time I stopped by, I got two. Figured this would come in handy."

"So you thought you could bribe me, huh?" I took the brownie half he handed me.

Case raised a brow as he pressed play on the remote. "Is it bribing if I give it to you after we fight?"

"You were practically waving the bag in my face when you got here, so yes," I said around a bite.

"True, but you didn't know what was inside. So, it wasn't a bribe."

We ate in silence for a few minutes as the movie played in the background. Then, when we were done, we settled onto the couch. I covered myself with the thick blanket while Case rested his arm behind me. My head rolled into the space between his shoulder and his chest, and I sighed.

"You know you didn't have to come all the way here, right?"

Case shrugged under me and his arm dropped, letting it rest on my side as his fingers played with the material of my hoodie. Well, not mine. The one I still hadn't given back yet. "We're traveling for the next few weeks. I didn't want to leave without clearing things up, and I didn't want to apologize over the phone."

I was glad he couldn't see my face because then he'd see the blush that crawled over my cheeks. "I'm going to miss you," I confessed, my voice coming out as a whisper.

Case's hand dipped under the material and caressed my hip. I couldn't help but shiver. "Well, you'll get me for two weeks when we get back. Bye-Week starts right after."

I snuggled more into his side to hide my smile. As much as it sucked, him being gone so long; I decided him leaving for two weeks was well worth the time I'd get with him when he got back.

case

Get off the plane.

Head home to shower.

Then, head to the grocery store so I could get ingredients for brownies.

It took some convincing, but after I explained how much of an ass I was to Basil, Rhonda gave me her brownie recipe. Then proceeded to lay out all the things that would happen if I gave it to anyone else. So, I committed the recipe to memory—after I wrote it down—and deleted the text message. Her secret was safe with me.

I followed Scottie to baggage claim and groaned when my phone rang *again*. Aubrey had been calling non-stop since we left town. Pleading for me to enter into our fake relationship again. Her threats of my career being ruined didn't phase me, but I was worried about Basil. She still didn't know, and I didn't know how to tell her. Once I fixed this, then I would explain everything and we could laugh about how ridiculous all this was.

Hopefully.

I yanked my phone from my pocket and had my carefully crafted argument ready for her. But, thank goodness, I checked the caller ID first.

"Sweetie, you really should change your door code every once in a while."

"See, you say that, Mom, but all I'm hearing is that you broke into my house," I said and smiled when Mom gasped over the line. Scottie and I grabbed our bags and started for the arrivals gate, where our team bus was waiting.

"I used your key to get in. Is this your way of telling me you *haven't* changed the code?"

"I plead the fifth."

"How long until you're home?" she asked, and the distinct sound of pots banging together sounded in the background. It was most likely Dad raiding my kitchen for a snack Mom didn't keep in the house.

When Scottie and I walked outside, we were met with the late December cold. Our breath fogged as we hurried to the bus, and Scottie almost kissed the sidewalk when he ran over a patch of ice. We filed onto the bus with the rest of the team and waited for Warner before leaving. "I'd say twenty minutes. When did you guys get into town?"

Mom yelled something at Dad before she spoke again. "We got in a few hours ago, but we've been enjoying the city. I can go into details when you get home."

"Okay Mom, I'll see you shortly."

After I hung up, I sent Dad a text to let him know where I kept the good cookies. I closed my eyes and rested my head back, exhausted from a whole day of traveling. It wasn't until Riley nudged my arm that I opened them again. "Hey, next Wednesday. What are you doing?" he asked.

"Isn't that the day after Christmas? Probably sleeping. Why?"

"A lot of the guys have talked about not going home

this year for the holidays because the weather is going to be pretty bad. So, I'm having a get-together at my place. You should come, and Basil too, if she's free."

I nodded. "I'll see what she's doing." When I grabbed my phone from my pocket, though, it didn't turn on. I didn't realize the battery was so low when Mom called. Oh, well—it would go on the charger first thing when I got home. The rest of the ride to the facility was quiet, and we all said our goodbyes in the parking lot before going our separate ways. I drove home in silence. The sounds of the busy airport still rattled my mind when I pulled into the driveway.

When I got to the door, I looked down and noticed how much cleaner the handle looked.

Mom and her thing about dirty handles.

I opened the door, ready to relax on the couch and catch up with Mom and Dad, but I smelled something burning. My bag fell from my shoulder and I raced toward the kitchen. When I rounded the corner, I found Dad holding a pan over the trash can, while Mom was busy opening the backdoor to let the smoke out. Neither of them noticed my presence, too busy with their respective tasks.

"What happened?" I asked as I watched a black, sticky substance fall from the pan.

Dad sighed and shook his head, and his eyes met mine. "Your mom wanted caramel, but then distracted me."

"Excuse me! The only thing I did was walk by you to get some water."

"Exactly. You know you can't walk by me without getting some type of action."

Now, I knew how fortunate I was that my parents were still together and very much in love. Especially after thirty years of marriage. But there was something about watching your dad hit on your mom—I still got the same reaction at twenty-eight as I did when I was seven.

Mom scoffed and pushed her way past Dad to wrap me in a tight hug. Her body radiated so much heat it was almost suffocating. I returned the gesture anyway, but only for a moment, and then I gave Dad the same embrace. He gave me a solid pat on the back before he took the pan to the sink and filled it with water. I noticed the clean dishes on the counter and wondered when Mom did them.

"So, Boston went well, huh?" Dad gave me the same flashy smile he passed down to me. We were a lot alike, both had stunning personalities and the same brown hair. Mom was responsible for the dimples and green eyes.

I grinned while I followed Mom to the couch and settled in the seat next to her. She threw a blanket over us both as I answered Dad. "Yeah, it wasn't what we expected, though. Their defense is normally a lot tighter than it was this game."

"Well, they did lose Williams to an injury a few weeks ago. And he's the only one keeping that team together," Dad said as he sat on the edge of the loveseat across from us. Why this man could never fully sit down, I would never know.

Mom shot her hand between us and held up her finger. She looked between the both of us as she spoke. "We're not talking hockey right now, boys. James, we're here to beat our son at Scrabble."

"Mom, it's getting pretty late. And as much as I love having you here, shouldn't you guys get to your hotel?"

"Nonsense! We can play one round," she said without looking at me, and I sent Dad a pleading look. Mom got super competitive when we played any sort of game, and I knew if we started playing now, then I wouldn't get any sleep. In the past, it hadn't been an issue. It'd been a tradition to play something when they got into town. Tonight, however, I needed to rest after being away for so long.

Dad must have seen the exhaustion on my face and stood to gain Mom's attention. "Amelia, let's get going. You've got the whole week to kick our asses with whatever games you want to play."

Mom looked at me with a softness in her eyes and smiled. "Case, sweetie?"

"Yeah, mom?"

She leaned in closer and gave me another tight hug. "I sure do love you. We'll see you tomorrow, okay?"

"Love you too, Mom."

I watched as they collected their bags, and we said our parting words for the night before I locked the door behind them. I picked up the forgotten duffel and walked upstairs. Once in my room, I plugged my phone in. It didn't take long to unpack my clothes and get a load started in the laundry before I hopped in the shower. My body ached from traveling all day, and from sleeping on a not-so-comfortable hotel mattress. Not that I was sleeping well, anyway.

My roommate, while we were away, was Scottie, who just so happened to be exceptional at bringing women back to the room. Of course, he would give me a heads-up so I could stay with Townes or someone else. It just meant that most of the time, I was crashing on a pull-out sofa.

I groaned when I stepped into the shower. The hot water ran down my body, soothing all of my aches and pains. I wasn't even upset with Scottie for putting me out, but there had been a tinge of jealousy that he was enjoying himself. It had been months since I'd invited anyone to share a bed with me, and it was all thanks to a pretty brunette with a smart mouth. Anytime women had approached me—at a game, or when I was out with the guys—I took one look and couldn't help but be disappointed. I won't deny how attractive those women were, but they weren't Basil.

My hand dropped to my hardening cock as my mind wandered back to that night when I had my hands on her. I had thought a lot over the past two weeks; about how she felt under my touch and wondered what sounds I could have dragged out of her. Every time I closed my eyes, I had been haunted by those pretty eyes rolling back as I whispered secret praises into her ear. It was new; the all-consuming feeling I'd get when she was close, the way I wanted to spend however long it took to find what made her tick.

It didn't take long for me to find release

Completely spent, I shut off the water and quickly dried off. I threw on whatever pair of clean underwear I could find and fell onto the bed. I didn't stay away long enough to care about the notifications lighting up my phone.

Those could wait until tomorrow.

CHAPTER 22

case

I never realized just how good strawberry and mint went well together until Basil, who smelled like it all the time. The first time I caught a whiff was when I helped her stand up after she fell on the ice. Now, it was my favorite combination and a reason I hadn't wanted to wash the hoodie she gave back to me. I needed to find a way for her to wear it again. Maybe, if I did it enough, then her scent would be so ingrained into the fibers that it would survive being bleached and still smell like her.

But, for some reason, it was stronger now.

I closed my eyes against the light that filled my room and turned my head into the silk pillow. The bed dipped, and I mumbled into the crook of my arm. "Five more minutes."

A beautiful giggle sounded from my side, and I turned my head to find Basil sitting there. "Your mother sent me up here, and I don't feel like relaying that message to her. She's making muffins and kind of scares me, so come on big guy. Time to get up."

I took my time to drag my eyes over her. She had a few strands of hair around her temples that curled and framed her cheeks. The soft morning light scattered through the curtains and danced across her face. She was beautiful. The freckles in her left eye, her cupid's bow, everything else I could see and everything I couldn't. But I couldn't imagine any piece I hadn't uncovered was less beautiful than the last. I turned over and sat up, not caring I hadn't bothered to put a shirt on last night before I passed out. Basil didn't seem to care either, not with the way her eyes roamed over me.

My body heated as she bit her lip, and I needed a distraction. I didn't think she'd mind if we didn't make it downstairs. But my parents would.

"My mom isn't scary, sunshine," I said.

Basil's eyes snapped back to mine. "Well, given how she treated me like a criminal when I showed up twenty minutes ago, I'd like to think otherwise."

I raised my brows as concern filled my chest. I reached a hand for her as she started for the door. "Wait, what happened?"

"Come down and I'll tell you." She winked before she shut the door. The soft click echoed in the empty room.

I rolled out of bed and threw on a pair of sweats and a shirt from the drawer before brushing my teeth. When I walked into the kitchen a few minutes later, I was hit with the delicious aroma of Mom's blackberry muffins. She and Basil were talking at the island as they sipped out of their coffee mugs. Mom was still wearing her apron—a pink one covered in flowers with white lace trim. She never left home without it.

Mom saw me first and raised a brow. "Well, good morning, sleepyhead."

"Hi, Mom." I reached for a muffin, and she slapped my hand away.

"They have to cool completely, you know that."

"But they look so good," I said as I inched my hand

toward them again. When she raised a brow and gave me the 'mom look,' I decided I wanted coffee instead. Basil snickered as I turned on the machine.

As I searched for a mug, I called over my shoulder. "Mom, Basil said you scared her this morning? What did you do?"

The garage door opened, and Dad answered for her as he kicked snow off his shoes. "Your mother threatened to call security on the poor girl. Thought she was some crazy fan or worse," he smirked, "a solicitor."

I barked out a laugh. "I don't even have security."

"Well, your mother thought the threat would work. But Basil showed us your promise to text her when you landed and never did. Your mother all but dragged her inside and forced her to bake after that."

I raised a brow at Mom as she sipped her coffee. "How do you go from threatening to call security, to dragging her inside without further questioning?"

Basil stood then and reached over to grab a muffin. I eyed the steam that came out of it when she tore it in half and noticed how Mom didn't care. "Actually, she interrogated me while I helped her bake. Don't know if that makes you feel better," she said around the muffin.

"And she is *such* a dear sweetie. You better keep her," Mom said, patting Basil's arm.

Basil's gaze shot to mine and I winked at her before turning around to finish making my coffee. I didn't need to correct Mom's statement and didn't care if she thought Basil and I were something more than friends. Because I wasn't letting her go.

I planned on keeping her as long as she let me.

Once my coffee was done, I took a seat on the barstool next to Basil. I reached past her for a muffin and narrowly avoided Mom's swatting hand. "Do you not want me to grow big and strong?" I raised a brow as I took a bite.

Mom scoffed and rolled her eyes. Like how she did when I was younger when I said something she couldn't argue with. "If you get any bigger, you won't fit in our home."

Dad had walked over then and pulled Mom into a quiet conversation. Something about Christmas decorations and other plans for the day, but I wasn't paying much attention.

I tugged on Basil's sleeve. "Hey." She swiveled in the chair and the sight made my chest expand. I cleared my throat and draped an arm over the back of her chair. I leaned in and grabbed a piece of her muffin. "Sorry, I didn't text you. My phone died, and I fell asleep before I could respond. I was exhausted. "

"Oh, it's okay. I figured with all the traveling, you would be."

I shifted in my seat and pushed out the scenarios that ran through my mind last night. "Yeah, the traveling. Thanks for understanding, and sorry about my mom."

"Case, your mom is wonderful. Don't apologize, okay? Want the rest?" she asked as she held up the rest of her food.

As I looked at her, I couldn't help but imagine how Basil would fit in my future. Next year, I would bring her home for Christmas. She and Mom would bake and set up the decorations inside while Dad and I cut down a tree. Then, that night after we decorated the tree with all the ornaments mom saved from my childhood, they'd go to bed first. Basil and I would sit in front of the old fireplace while we drank hot chocolate, while a movie played in the background.

If we were still friends, I'd spend the rest of the evening being torn between closing the distance to kiss her—and doing more.

Dad's gruff voice pulled me from my thoughts. I

blinked and the first thing that came into focus was Basil. Her eyes dipped to my mouth, but I shot my gaze to Dad when I noticed the keys in his hands.

"You ready?"

"For what?"

Shit. How long had I zoned out?

Mom stood from her seat and patted Dad on the chest with a loving smile before looking at me. "Shopping. Case, sweetie, you don't have a single decoration inside or outside this house. We need to fix that."

I chuckled and looked at Basil. "Are you going to come with us?"

"Do you want me to?" she asked, a smile tugged on her mouth. I kept myself from leaning in and instead rubbed my thumb on the spot between her shoulder blades. She sagged into the touch and that smile grew when I nodded.

"Well then, let's go."

———

Mom could make anything fit into an overstuffed cart.

She moved around a few boxes and shoved the smaller box of Christmas lights into the cart. Then she turned around and continued down the aisle to find more stuff. There were more than enough decorations in my cart alone. But she insisted it wasn't enough, and that I always needed extra. Basil was sent off a few minutes ago with Dad to get another cart so they could start on the outdoor decorations.

Growing up, Christmas was the one time a year we decorated. Dad would spend all weekend putting up the lights on the house while Mom directed me where to hang things from the ceiling. The house always smelled like peppermint or cinnamon, and Mom had Christmas music playing on repeat. Shopping with them again was nice.

The past few years, they've put up with me and the tiny tree I got when I moved away for college.

It was hard to want to decorate when there wasn't any guarantee you'd have the time off to see family.

Mom placed a tree topper in the cart and pretended to admire it while she asked in a casual voice. "So, how long have you and Basil been friends?"

I kept my eyes on the stuff in the cart, not wanting to give her the satisfaction of seeing how happy I got talking about my *friend*. "Since the start of the season."

"Oh, I see." I heard the smile in her voice and glanced up to find her looking at me.

Her eyes were lighter than mine, which made it easier for her emotions to shine. "She's special, sweetie. I hope you know that." The softness in her voice warmed my heart. It was the same tone she used when she told Dad she loved him. That's how I wanted to talk to Basil one day.

But I needed to get everything sorted out. Right after we left, an article was sent to my phone.

HOCKEY CAPTAIN CASE WHITLOCK SEEN AGAIN WITH MYSTERY WOMAN AT ROCKIES TRAINING CENTER. IS THIS A WORKPLACE ROMANCE SCANDAL?

I sent it to Jasmine, who assured me she was working diligently to get the article taken down. Normally, that kind of stuff wouldn't bother me. It was the comments I didn't like. People talked about Basil like she was some kind of home wrecker and blamed her for splitting up a 'power couple' like me and Aubrey.

Aubrey told me she'd stop talking to reporters if I took her back. But I couldn't, especially not after everything she had done.

The sound of a squeaky wheel from the next aisle over had me looking up.

Mom smiled at Dad when he rounded the corner. "You'd think they'd lubricate those damn wheels every once in a while," he said, pulling Mom into a hug. I walked away and found Basil wrangling an inflatable reindeer into the cart. I chuckled and walked over to help her. She was out of breath when she looked at me.

"For the record, it wasn't heavy, just awkward."

"If you say so," I told her as I grabbed onto the cart. It shook as I pushed it, and I stopped to raise a brow at Basil.

She shrugged. "It was the only one left."

Mom rounded the corner and waved at us. "Your father and I are going to grab some things for dinner. We'll meet you guys back at the house."

I looked at her, confused. "I thought I was paying for everything?"

"Just the decorations, sweetie." She pushed the other cart down the aisle and turned it so Basil could take it. "We'll take care of the food."

She waved before disappearing again. I chuckled and started walking toward the front of the store.

Basil walked next to me and kept one hand next to mine on the cart. "Your parents are great."

I smiled and looked at her. "Are you doing anything with your parents?"

"No, my mom doesn't like the holidays."

I hated how she seemed to get smaller when she talked about her mom. This beautiful woman who gave so much to everyone around her, who offered so much warmth, didn't deserve to feel anything less than what she was. Which was perfect. I moved my hand to grab hers as we continued walking.

She looked at me, her mouth parted, but my words came faster. "Well then, guess you're an honorary Whitlock this year. Come on, the faster we check out, the faster we can go home and finish those muffins."

Basil laughed, and the sound was as beautiful as ever. "What did your mom say about not fitting in her house if you kept eating?"

"Please, she's my mom. She'll find a way to make room for me."

basil

I couldn't remember the last time I had this much fun during the holidays. Mom usually cooked dinner, and I would send Dad a hesitant Merry Christmas text. I would always pretend he never responded because it was easier. But this year, I cooked with Amelia almost every day since they got here, and watched Case and his dad set up decorations.

It took them a few days to get everything done. But I never stopped reminding Case about the clause in his contract where it stated he couldn't put himself in danger. When he asked me if I read it, I told him 'no'. But I knew it was in there, anyway. Case laughed and pulled me into a hug before he climbed the ladder to the roof.

My body was still burning from the contact—something it always seemed to do whenever he touched me— but I had to pretend I was fine. Because Amelia was sitting across from me in the office while we wrapped gifts. I couldn't get over how huge Case's home was. It was at least five times the size of my apartment, but it was lived in. His kitchen was clean, but something was always out. The living room was full of blankets, pillows, and pieces of

Case. His keys would be on the end table, and a book he brought down from his room would be forgotten where he was reading on the floor. Even in his office, papers were scattered on the desk, and art supplies were shoved on the last shelf of the bookcase.

It was hard to see how comfortable his home was the last time I was here. Everything was dark, and I had other things on my mind.

The paper I was holding ripped as I tried to cut a perfect line.

"Shit," I muttered under my breath.

Amelia chuckled as she reached for the tape. "I was terrible when I was your age too, you know." She set aside the gift she wrapped to grab another one from the pile. "It wasn't until we had Case that I got any good. And that's only because he was much better than I was," she winked, "I wasn't about to be shown up by a six-year-old."

A laugh escaped me as I continued wrapping the slippers in front of me. "I'd be the same way."

We fell back into silence as we worked, and I couldn't help but compare Amelia to my mother. It didn't take long to place the emotion pressing on my chest when I saw her and Case together. It was jealousy, which led to so many questions.

Why couldn't my mom talk to me the way Amelia talked to Case? My mom was always so serious and made everything about her. It wasn't fair. I knew I should be grateful for everything she did for me as a single parent, but it was hard. It was hard when my memories consisted of being ripped apart because I wasn't living up to what she wanted me to be. It was hard to ask for love from someone who didn't know how to give it.

I think—because of Case—I realized I didn't have to ask him. Case gave himself freely with no expectations of anything in return. I didn't realize it at first until he started leaving and it felt like a part of me was missing. That night when he picked me up from that date—I thought it was a one-time thing. It didn't take long for me to see how wrong I was.

It terrified me. How I felt about him. Because what if he didn't feel the same? I didn't know how to differentiate between serious feelings and casual ones. Case showed affection through touch, but did the way he touched me mean more? How many women before me had he touched with such care, only for things to not end well? So many questions ran through my mind. But the scariest one wasn't what if he felt the same way, it was, what if things didn't work out?

Heartache wasn't something I could handle. It was easier to save myself from the possibility of it than to lose him. We were better off as friends, anyway.

Amelia cleared her throat, and I noticed I had been working on the same gift for the past ten minutes while my mind ran free.

"Ah, sorry," I said before I placed the gift on top of the pile.

She pulled her brows in and gave me a tight-lipped smile. "You know, when Case called me and told me about this assistant coaching position, I was worried."

"Why?"

She clicked her tongue as she thought for a moment. When she looked at me with those green eyes–lighter than Case's–I held my breath. Worried about what she'd confess.

"Because I know how hard he works to please every-one. Did he ever tell you how stressed out he was during his first year as captain? He called me one night in a panic, asking me to pick him up." She shook her head, fondness fueled the movement. "I told him to take a walk, get a good night's sleep, and think about it. He texted me three days later, apologizing."

"He never told me that," I said as I wrapped a ribbon around the gift I was going to give Case later. "He doesn't talk a lot about things that are bothering him."

Amelia pushed against my leg when I had turned my gaze down. Her smile was kind when I looked at her again. "That's because he's a man, sweetie. He may be a great communicator when he wants to be, but that doesn't mean he knows how to ask for help. And that's why I was worried. Because I knew he would do it, but I didn't want him to push himself too hard."

I nodded, taking in her words. "But that changed?" I asked, keeping my voice down as I placed the last gift on the pile.

She nodded, and her smile matched the softness in her gaze. "He called me after his first day and raved about the coach he got to work with. I wasn't worried after that." My face heated at whatever implication I picked up on, and looked away. Amelia stood and wiped her hands on her pants.

"Well, let's see what the boys are up to since we're done."

"Okay," I said as I got up and followed her into the living room. We found James flipping through the channels.

"Where's Case?" Amelia asked him.

"Cooking."

She placed her hands on her hips and tapped her foot. "And you're not helping because?"

James looked at his wife like he was about to get run over. He put his hands up in surrender. "He kicked me out. Promise. You know how your son gets in the kitchen." Amelia let out a huff and crossed her arms.

"Wonder where he gets it from," James mumbled under his breath.

I didn't stick around to see how Amelia was going to handle that comment. I quickly walked toward the kitchen, and let the wonderful aromas surround me as I made my way to the island. Case stood at the stove, working out of three different pots at once. He grabbed a wooden spoon and dipped it into a sauce from one of them. Then crossed his arms as he thought about something.

I moved and walked to stand at his side. I peered at the pans in front of us. "Whatcha making?"

Case hummed under his breath before he spoke. "Right now? The gravy, but it's missing something and I can't tell what it is?"

"Maybe you shouldn't have kicked your dad out of the kitchen," I said playfully, poking my elbow into his side. Case moved away and grabbed my hand. Then he placed our intertwined hands down at his side. When I looked up, he had an unamused brow raised.

"Last week I walked in on him after he burned caramel. Mom might have the patience for him, but I don't."

"You're so serious when you cook," I said, blinking up at him. Case smiled down at me, and my gaze darted to where it always did—to that dimple. I blinked and looked back down at the stove. "Which one is the gravy?" I asked as I reached into the drawer for a spoon.

Case pointed to the pot on the very back burner and I dipped the spoon in. When the sauce reached my mouth, I let out a small moan when the decadent flavors hit my tongue. This was better than anything my mom ever made. Case chuckled when I reached for seconds, but stopped me and took the spoon from my hands. "You have to wait like everyone else."

"Why?"

"Because I said so."

I scrunched my nose and stuck my tongue out at him. "And here I am, thinking you liked me better than that. I deserve another taste."

Case moved then. He caged me against the counter, his arms on either side of me as he leaned in close. The cool granite bit into my back, but I held firm. His eyes did a slow once-over of my body before they locked with mine. "How much do you think I like you, Basil? Be honest."

I couldn't speak. My body burned and my mind emptied. Case was overwhelming my body in the best way, but we didn't have time for games. Not when his parents were in the other room. So, I smiled and reached for the spoon. "Enough to let me have another taste?"

Case dropped his head for a second, and I watched as the muscles in his arms tightened around me. When he looked at me again, he was closer. But I didn't move away even when his breath caressed my cheek. "Get out of the kitchen, Basil. Let me finish up."

My mouth opened as he pushed off the counter. "You can't kick me out."

"I just did," he said with a smile as he pointed to the living room.

———

Dinner was amazing, both the food and the company.

Amelia and James spent most of the evening embarrassing Case by telling me his childhood stories. My heart swelled with each piece of information about Case they gave me, and I wanted more. I didn't think I could ever have enough. After dinner, Case sat with them at the table while I cleaned up. Despite the initial argument from him, he hadn't said anything to me, enjoying his parents' company before they had to go back home.

Once the kitchen was clean, I walked out and found everyone by the front door. Amelia was embracing Case in a hug only a mother could give, and I smiled. James caught my attention and gave a solid nod as Amelia let Case go. Then she headed straight for me and hugged me just as tight. After we said our final goodbyes, Case and I headed to the couch. We plopped down on the big sectional and let out tired sighs.

"That was fun," I said as I looked at Case. He had a sad smile on his face as he stared at the ceiling.

"Yeah."

I shifted closer to him. "Are you okay?"

"I wish they lived here, is all. I miss them."

Although I didn't understand the feeling, I nodded anyway. Case turned his head and his smile changed completely. I didn't know what was behind it, but it made me feel warm. "Did you have fun? I know it was a long two weeks and my mom can be, well, you've met her."

"Case, this was the most fun I've had during the holidays in years," I told him with a smile.

Silence fell between us again until Case stood from the couch and stretched. He turned to me before gesturing back to the TV. "Want to watch a movie? Or do you need to go home? I know it's getting late."

He rubbed the back of his neck and–wait–was he blushing?

I smiled and shook my head. "I don't have anything at home worth going back to. What movie do you want to watch?"

Case grinned and put on E.L.F. before he left the room. Only to come back a few minutes later with an armful of blankets. He threw them on the couch and helped me unfold one before he settled back down next to me. Before I could think better of it, I leaned into him. He moved his arm and draped it behind me without so much as a blink. Like this was normal, us cuddling on the couch.

Man, I was in for a world of hurt if I didn't do something soon.

I cleared my throat and untangled myself from him. I brought my knees up and wrapped my arms around them. Case questioned my movements with a raised brow, which I ignored. Neither of us said anything for a while, both of us were too much into the movie to feel the need to talk.

So I flinched in surprise when Case finally spoke. "I think I know the answer, but how busy are you the day after Christmas?" he asked, keeping his eyes straight.

I shrugged. "Not busy at all. Why?"

He tilted his head toward me and smirked. "Want to go to a party?"

CHAPTER 24

case

I thought this party was going to be fun. That I'd come and relax with the team before we had to start eating protein-packed food again, keep drinking to a minimum, and worry about traveling for games.

It started out that way. When Basil and I first showed up, we spent time talking with Connor. Then, Scottie appeared from nowhere and stole Basil. He dragged her to the kitchen while Connor and I stared in disbelief.

I wasn't having fun. Because Basil was standing between Scottie and Riley, covered in flour and frosting, and I couldn't do anything about it. It would be easy to walk over and lick up the side of her neck—so I could effectively reach the icing on her jaw—but I couldn't. Because then she'd be disqualified from this poor attempt of a cookie baking and decorating competition Scottie came up with.

"I don't think it needs any egg," I said to Basil as she reached for the carton. This was her third attempt at making the frosting, and she almost had it. I kept trying to direct her to the vanilla extract by process of elimination, but it wasn't working that well.

"Hey Whitlock! Give her another hint and I'm kicking you out of the kitchen!" Scottie was pointing a Christmas spatula at me when I looked at him.

I leaned over the counter at the same time he did and gave him a knowing smirk. "You never said anything about helping, just that I couldn't judge."

"Not helping should have been synonymous with not being able to judge." He threw his hands in the air.

I snorted before I took a handful of chocolate chips from the bowl beside me. "Those two things aren't remotely the same."

"Scottie, get your ass over here and help decorate!" Basil called as she mixed whatever was in her bowl.

Scottie pointed his fingers from his eyes to mine as he walked away. "Watch yourself, Whitlock." I watched him find his spot next to Basil before he took the piping bag she held out for him. They worked together to finish the cookies before the timer buzzed. When everything was done, they all took a step back as people filtered into the cluttered kitchen.

"Presentation could use some work." One of them mumbled.

"Hey, if you want to do dishes, then we can plate it again," Riley said from inside the fridge as he grabbed another beer. Scottie and Basil snickered as the judges walked around and taste-tested everything. It was clear that no one knew how to bake, even if they were sober. Because none of the judges made a face that showed otherwise. One of them spat out their bite while another left the kitchen entirely, and it wasn't likely he would come back.

They all gathered in the other room to deliberate, and I took the time to walk over and see how creative Basil was with her cookies. The Christmas-themed shapes were, to my surprise, perfect. At least on the outside, Basil came to my side as I looked over the stockings that were covered in red frosting.

"Do you like them?" she asked, leaning in.

"Yeah, you guys did a great job."

"Want to try one?"

Before I could decline, Basil had grabbed one and shoved it into my hands. She looked up at me with something in her eyes that made denying her anything impossible. Which wasn't too different from how I felt most of the time. Maybe all the alcohol she drank had amplified its effects. I gave her my most confident smile before I took a bite.

Now I knew why that one guy made the face he did. This cookie was all wrong, too dry around the edges, while not cooked all the way through.

"You like it?" she asked, but before I could answer, she reached for one and took a bite. I watched as her face morphed from excitement to disgust before she spit it out. "That's horrible! Why would you let me eat that?" She took small sips of her wine to down the horrible taste.

I spit out my piece too and grinned. "What do you mean? You're the one who grabbed it before I could warn you."

Her eyes narrowed, but I could still see amusement dancing there. "You and I both know that's a lie. You would have said it was the best thing you've ever tasted and would have taken the whole plate to keep me from trying any. I know you."

She was right, and I didn't know how to handle it. I wanted to wrap my arms around her waist, pull her in, and kiss her. Basil and I had spent so much time together these past two weeks, and it was getting hard to hold back. She's haunted my dreams so many times that without her, they were nightmares.

"You're a know-it-all, you know that?"

"I know most things, Case, not all. I'm still working on that."

I stared after her as she pulled away when the winners were announced. Connor and our equipment manager Miles celebrated their victory as Scottie came between Basil and me.

He threw his arms over our shoulders. "Who's up for a game of strip poker?"

———

The night hadn't gotten better, but I was glad Basil was having fun.

Or was—until now. She didn't seem to appreciate that she lost this last round of strip poker. Basil was bluffing the entire game, and I knew it wouldn't end well. She and I seem to do some mental math at the same time, taking note of how many chips she threw onto the table. I saw the panic set in her eyes as she glanced toward me, and I was trying to come up with something so she didn't have to go through with stripping.

Because I knew how uncomfortable that would make her. But also, if I saw her strip in front of all these people, I didn't know what I'd do.

She sat straighter in her chair and smirked at Riley— the winner of the game. Her hands slowly wrapped around the bottom of her shirt, and my blood rushed south, making my pants tighter. Basil didn't break her gaze away from Riley as she started to pull her shirt up. I only saw an inch of skin before I couldn't take it. My hands landed on the table with more force than I intended, which drew everyone's attention.

I faked a yawn. "Well, would you look at the time?"

I saw Connor smirk beside Basil before he checked his phone. "You heard the captain. It's getting pretty late."

Riley dragged his heated stare over Basil, and I clenched my hands. It didn't take a genius to realize how disappointed he was, but he didn't get to see Basil like that. None of them did. He blew out a breath and changed his expression to something more friendly. "You're more than welcome to stay in one of the extra rooms upstairs. Or I can call you an Uber."

I walked around the table and stood behind Basil. She tilted her head back, and I was caught up in the way her cheeks flushed as she smiled.

"Come on, I'll show you where everything is." I tapped the back of her neck and wondered if the redness had spread there too.

She stood and said goodnight before I led her upstairs. I showed her the room at the end of the hall she'd be staying in. It was between the one I'd be staying in and another guest room. Of all the guys on the team who owned nice houses, I liked Rileys the most. Because he had so much space and would force you to stay if he knew you couldn't drive. I opened the door and Basil walked straight for the four-poster bed.

She sat down and ran her fingers over the cream-colored duvet. "Where are you sleeping?" Her eyes were hooded when she looked at me.

I leaned against the doorframe with my arms crossed. "Next door. There are fresh clothes in the dresser, and extra toothbrushes in the bathroom. Come get me if you need anything, okay?"

She nodded, and I shut the door when I left the room. Hoping she'd go to bed, sleep off the alcohol, and she wouldn't have a hangover in the morning. As for me? I knew she'd plague my dreams—but that wasn't the hard part of sleeping anymore. It was waking up and realizing she and I were stuck in the same place, with no signs of moving forward.

basil

The thumping in the room next door woke me up. I tried to ignore it by shoving a pillow over my head and by turning over in bed. But the thumping started getting more intense. It wasn't until a muffled moan crawled through the drywall that I realized what was happening.

Someone was having a *great* time.

Suddenly, I realized how thirsty I was, so I got up and walked over to the dresser. When Case left, I passed out on the bed without changing. I was hot, sweaty, and in desperate need of a shower, but that could wait until the morning. Right now, I had to change into something more comfortable. It didn't take me long to find a pair of black sleep shorts and a gray shirt that hung off my shoulder, but I wasn't too worried. It wasn't like anyone was going to be in the kitchen this late at night. Once I was ready, I left the room and walked into the hallway. My eyes darted to the room Case was sleeping in.

I wasn't able to determine which room the sounds came from. Was it his room?

I bit my lip and headed down the stairs, making sure to

keep the lights off on my way down. I tiptoed my way around the Christmas decorations until I reached the kitchen, where I found the counters completely clean. I wondered who Riley got to do the dishes.

I turned on the light above the stove before I started opening the cabinets to find a cup. After finding one—a small thing decorated with a Christmas tree—I poured myself some water from the filtered jug Riley kept in the fridge. Then, I perched myself on one of the barstools. I wasn't in any hurry to get back to my room with what was happening next door. My only hope was they went to bed when they finished. As I sipped my water, jealousy coiled in my stomach.

I should have knocked. Dealing with the embarrassment seemed easier than not knowing what he was doing.

These past two weeks I had tried to convince myself the warmth that was growing in my chest—every time Case looked at me—was normal. That anytime he touched me, it didn't mean anything. Physical touch was how he showed affection, and I needed to keep reminding myself of that.

I sat there for a while and sipped my water. When I realized it was getting harder to keep my eyes open, I groaned. I didn't want to go back yet, not until I was sure it would be quiet when my head hit the pillow. Maybe I could close my eyes, just for a minu—

There was a thud. I turned in the stool, adrenaline fueling my racing heart. But when Case came into view, it started racing for a different reason. His hair was a mess, like someone ran their fingers through it. He was shirtless, but the thing that got my attention…

Were those goddamn sweatpants.

Gray ones.

"Can't sleep?" I asked as he made his way toward the cabinets.

The smile he gave me was filled with the same exhaustion I felt. It was soft and lazy, and I wondered what the reason for it was. My face heated under his tired gaze, so I took a sip of the water, hoping it was still cool enough to calm me down.

Case shook his head, and that smile never fell. "Not really. You?"

I tried my best to keep my eyes on his face, but it was hard when he was leaning against the counter and his arms were flexing. Have you ever had an unobstructed view of a shirtless hockey player? It was impossible not to appreciate their dedication to the sport. He could easily lift me and–

I caught Case looking at me when my gaze finally roamed back to his face. He raised a brow, and I realized I hadn't answered his question—or if I even understood what he asked.

"No," I said, hoping it was a sufficient answer.

"Why not?" Case asked, before bringing the glass to his mouth. When did he get a drink? I had to pretend I didn't notice how his Adam's apple bobbed as he took deep gulps of his water.

I cleared my throat and tore my gaze away before I answered. "Whoever was in the room next door had a uh —*guest.*"

Case nodded in understanding, and I waited for an apology, or for him to deny he had anything to do with the sound. "That would be Scottie. I should have told him that your room was next door so he would be more responsible with his activities. Sorry about that."

Relief rushed through me, and the tension in my shoulders disappeared. "You don't have to apologize. It's not like you were the one with the lady friend who woke me up."

I didn't know what it was about my words that made Case go rigid, but they did. I furrowed my brows and tilted my head. "Are you okay? Need to sit down?" I asked as I gestured to the empty barstool next to mine. Case cleared his throat and quickly hid whatever had happened with a smile before he walked over. Once he sat down, he spread his legs enough that his knee brushed against my thigh, and flutters erupted in my stomach. I pulled away slightly, and if Case noticed, he didn't bother to say anything. I tried to find words to fill the silence, but my eyes were heavy again. The only thing I could focus on was the counter under my hands. It was cool, like the pillow I was sleeping on.

"Sunshine?" Case nudged my leg with his, and I jumped in my seat.

When did I fall asleep?

"Come on, let's get you back to bed."

Case grabbed my glass and set it in the sink before he came back to help me out of the barstool, making sure I didn't trip in my sleepy state. He placed one hand on my inner arm, and the other on my waist. I leaned into his touch, and he chuckled under his breath. "Think you can make it? Or do I need to carry you?"

The mental image of Case carrying me upstairs to bed is what woke me up. I pulled away and looked at him with wide eyes. "You wouldn't."

"Try me," he said with a teasing smirk. Not wanting to call him on his bluff, I straightened and walked confidently to the steps before looking back at him.

"Are you coming?"

Case nodded and followed behind me. We made it to Scottie's door and waited, and it only took a minute before we both heard what woke me up. I groaned and walked over to my door with my head down. I looked back at Case with a tired look.

"You think Riley has any earplugs?" I asked. Case pulled his brows in as he looked between our three doors. He muttered a curse under his breath and grabbed my hand before leading us to his room.

"What are you—"

"You can crash in here until he's done. Hopefully, it won't be too much longer," he said as he led me into his room. The bed was a mess, with the comforter in a big pile at the bottom, and the pillows were arranged on top of each other. Looking at them made my neck hurt.

Case stood in front of me and ran his free hand through his hair. "Feel free to make yourself comfortable." He tore away from me and sat on the bed. He leaned against the headboard and patted the spot next to him. "I don't bite."

Maybe it was the dream I had before I woke up. It could have been how often I let my mind wander when we were apart. Or maybe it was a relief knowing he hadn't been responsible for the woman's moans. There were many possibilities, but I didn't know what caused me to say my next words.

"That's a shame."

Whatever confidence I had to say that had drained from me when I sat on the bed. Case kept his gaze on the ceiling as I sat next to him. We weren't touching, but the bed was small, which only left a couple of inches between our arms. I crossed mine as the tension between us built, and I couldn't help but chew the inside of my lip. I had blurred the lines again, and I didn't know why. It was always me starting things. Case hadn't gone farther than touching me, only after I encouraged it. If he was interested, then he'd make some kind of move, right?

"Case, I'm sorry. I don't know why I said that."

"Did you have fun tonight, Basil?" he asked almost immediately.

I blinked and sat on my knees as I faced him, and I wished he was looking at me to so I could see what emotion he wore. I thought of all the stolen glances between us, of how he held me after he ate that disgusting cookie. I nodded and kept my voice low. "Yeah, did you?"

He looked at me then, and even in the dark, I could see the way Case's eyes roamed over me. My body burned under his attention. His voice was rough when he spoke. "It could have been better."

"Why do you say that?" The tension between us grew thicker, and I so badly wanted to see where this line of questioning would lead. Was it all in my head? Did he feel it too? Was I just so starved for something I could call love that I was latching onto the first thing that felt like it?

I was so busy asking myself these questions that I didn't notice Case had shifted. He sat higher on the bed now, his arms still crossed, but he didn't look at me. "Everything was fine until that game of strip poker."

I swallowed hard as I watched his bare chest rise with deep, slow breaths, and it didn't go unnoticed how he tracked the movement. "Why?" The word escaped on a breath as I caught his gaze. "What about the game made your night not fine, Case?"

When did he get closer? Or was it me who moved?

Case reached up and threaded his fingers through the hair at the nape of my neck. He tightened his grip, and I held in a moan. I watched as his hooded eyes traced my exposed neck and said, "Because, Basil, when you lost, I realized something."

I licked my bottom lip, and his gaze shot up, eager to watch the movement. "And what was that?" The air was getting thicker, making my mouth dry as I tried to fill my lungs, but I couldn't. Not until he answered my question. I didn't know what I wanted to hear. I only cared that he hadn't pushed me away yet. Even if I started this, he clearly didn't mind continuing it.

"I realized that I'm a selfish man. And I don't want the

first time I see you strip your clothes to be in front of an audience."

What little air I managed to drag into my lungs escaped all at once. Case and I were so close now, and I glanced past him. I didn't know why. Maybe it was to escape the suffocating tension, but I had to collect myself. I was still scared of what could happen, but I knew he would keep me safe. My eyes shifted over the nightstand, and something caught my attention. I hovered over Case and reached for the small item.

I held it between us and let my eyes adjust in the dark. "What is this?"

"Mistletoe, shit. Riley probably put it in here for—whatever reason."

Maybe that was what led to Scottie's late-night activities. Thick, suffocating silence fell between Case and me as I twirled the small plant between my fingers. Case kept his hands at his side, clenching and unclenching them. Like he was holding himself back from reaching out, and I didn't know why. Of all the times he could touch me. Why was he choosing not to? I'd let him. I'd welcome his touch and whatever happened after his skin met mine.

Case sucked in a breath and closed his eyes. "We should sleep."

A few months ago, if we had been in this position, I would have relaxed and agreed with him. Even a few weeks ago, when I held the promise of a kiss in front of him, it would have been fine. But now, with my feelings overflowing from its box, I was disappointed. "Is that what you want to do?"

If he said yes, then we'd never talk about this again. The blurred lines of our friendship would turn solid, and I'd do my best to remember that. I'd stop trying to cross that line, and this heated moment would be forgotten. Case reached up, and his touch was soft as he moved a stray piece of hair behind my shoulder. I could see the conflict in his features, and I wanted to ease it.

Case's chest caved as he breathed out, but it did nothing to ease his discomfort. "Goodnight Basil."

He turned over and crossed his arms. I waited until he started snoring and set the mistletoe on the bed before I walked out of the room.

basil

It was the second practice after the holidays, and the kids were already fighting.

"Coach! Michael called me a butthead!" Aiden yelled from the other side of the rink.

Michael threw his hands up. "Did not!"

"Yes, you did."

This had been practice all afternoon, the kids bickering with each other instead of playing the game. Case chuckled from beside me and skated over to Aiden—the supposed butthead. I looked down at Michael and crossed my arms. "What happened?"

"He said my aim needed some work, which we all know isn't true," he said, crossing his arms and matching my stance. "So I called him a butthead 'cause he doesn't know what he's talking about."

I kneeled in front of him. "How would you feel if someone called you a mean name when you were trying to help them?" I asked.

The crease between Michael's brows softened, but his mouth stayed tight as he worked out his thoughts. When he spoke again, it was low, soft, and full of regret for what he said to his teammate. "I didn't need help, Coach."

"That might be true, but next time, talk to him instead of jumping to conclusions. Okay? Now, go apologize."

Michael skated off toward Aiden as Case made his way to my side. He crossed his arms, and we watched the kids talk. I shifted away from him and hoped he didn't notice.

"Crazy to think that used to be me," Case said, his voice full of fondness.

"What, being the one who got his feelings hurt?" I teased as I laced my hands behind my back.

Case laughed and faced me. "No, being the one calling everyone butt heads." I made the mistake of looking at him and was immediately caught up in him. The way his green eyes danced between mine, and how they dipped over me.

I couldn't look away, and his words echoed in my mind.

I realized that I'm a selfish man. And I don't want the first time I see you strip your clothes to be in front of an audience.

Things were confusing. If he said that, then why didn't he act? He knew I was more than willing to go farther. We needed to talk.

As I stared at Case, and my mind spiraled, I noticed the shift in his expression. Whatever he saw on my face, he didn't like it. Case opened his mouth to speak, but was interrupted by the program director.

"Mr. Whitlock!"

Case and I both turned to see Mrs. Johnson standing with Coach Warner, and they both wore serious expressions that made my chest tight with panic. Case placed his hand on my back and rubbed his thumb in the space between my shoulder blades. "I'm sure it's nothing. I'll see you tonight." He didn't wait for me to respond before he skated to the sideboard.

I was surprised when earlier this week, Case told me

he'd be at practice today. He had a game tonight, and I knew how seriously he took this time to relax and get in the right headspace. I was so busy watching the three of them leave the arena that I didn't notice Mathew had come up beside me.

"Is Coach Whitlock in trouble?" He asked.

I offered a confident smile and hid away the uneasiness that ran through me. "No, he's not in trouble. Come on, we still have a lot to do today."

The rest of practice went better than how it started, and I was happy when it was over. Because it meant I had time to think of how I was going to approach Case. About everything; his house, the Christmas party. Maybe then we would find common ground and go from there. I collected the cones as I thought of ways to bring it up, while the kids changed out of their skates and left with their parents. When I made it to the sideboard, Mr. Clein was waiting for me. His arms were crossed, and his scowl was harsher than usual. I put on my skate protectors and braced myself for whatever he thought I did wrong today.

I stepped up and asked, "Good afternoon, Mr. Clein. Did you guys enjoy the holiday break?"

"Are you happy with yourself?" He barked.

I stared at him and noticed some of the other parents had stuck around to watch whatever was happening. "Excuse me?" I was frozen, staring at him in disbelief. Mr. Clein being unhappy wasn't unusual, but this was the first time his anger got the best of him enough to cause an outburst.

He raised a finger as his face turned red. "You were the reason this team was destined to fail, and what do you do when I graciously help you? You ruin it. I hope you're happy with yourself, Ms. Andrews."

Mr. Clein stalked off as the other parents looked between us with confused expressions. I was glad I wasn't the only one who had no idea what that was about. We exchanged nervous smiles before we went our separate ways. I debated heading to the offices again to wait for Case, but my phone dinged with a message after I put my shoes on.

Worry ran through me as I read his message, but I tried not to focus on it. He said we'd talk about it later. Maybe then we could talk about other things too.

Now, if only later could get here sooner.

———

"Is Case okay?" Hollis asked as she kept her attention on the penalty box.

Case had been sitting there most of the night. The reason? Case decided tonight was a great time to start fights. The first punch he threw, I assumed someone said something that made him mad. Then he threw another punch, and I had no clue why. The team wasn't affected, but it didn't look good either.

I stared at him and willed him to glance in our direction. But he kept his swollen gaze forward as his coach talked to him. Ryan spoke at my side, and I wished he had canceled. "Look at your boy toy all you want, Basil, but it won't put him back in the game. He probably realized how much he sucks and is taking it out on everyone else."

I bit my tongue. This wasn't the first thing Ryan had said that got under my skin tonight, and it wasn't fair to

Hollis. Because even though Ryan sat between us, she was trying her best to stick up for me when he said something harsh. I looked at Ryan, exhausted from everything that had come out of his mouth.

I didn't even attempt to be nice. "Ryan, why do you come to these games? You're always negative and you're horrible to be around. I don't care if you stay and watch, but you need to find a different seat. Because you're really pissing me off."

"B," Hollis said under her breath.

Ryan's eyes darkened, but I held his stare. "What's your problem? If you don't like my commentary, then stop inviting me."

"I'm not the one inviting you. Hollis is because it's the only way she can see you for more than a few hours."

His face pulled tight in anger, and he stood from his seat. "I don't know why you're so sensitive. Jesus, come on, babe." He grabbed Hollis's hand and pulled her to her feet.

She looked between the two of us, and I waved a hand. "It's fine, Hol. I'll talk to you later, okay?"

She nodded and grabbed her things before following Ryan. I sat back in my seat and let out a heavy sigh as a pounding started behind my eyes. I did my best to pay attention to the rest of the game, but it was hard when worry consumed me.

Case was the most well-rounded, level-headed person I knew. What happened that made him act out like a child? Was this the adult version of calling people buttheads? Throwing fists and causing black eyes?

The last half of the game went by quickly. The Peaks won by one point, and the collective sigh of relief was obvious from both the crowd and the team. I waited until the arena was empty before I made my way to the waiting area that Case pointed out the last time I was here. He had left a visitor's badge up at the front with the tickets tonight, and I felt important as I passed by security. I filed into the small room and was surprised at just how many people were there. Most of them were the other players' wives and other family members. Small children ran around the room while the women talked amongst themselves. I made my way through the crowd and headed to wait on the back wall.

I was grateful that no one seemed to notice me, or if they did, they simply kept to themselves. It only took a few minutes of waiting before the players started to filter into the room. Some women grabbed their kids before meeting their partners, and some ran straight into their partner's arms. Congratulating them on their win and promising to celebrate later. I tuned those conversations out as I scanned the crowd for the one person I was here for.

I saw Townes first, but the look he gave me when our eyes met told me everything I already knew. Case wasn't in a great mood, and when Townes gestured toward the door, I left. I headed back to the ticket booth and saw Case waiting by the doors. My chest ached when I saw the solemn look on his face, accompanied by his swollen brow bone. It had been cleaned up and bandaged already.

"Hi," I said softly.

He did his best to smile, but it didn't quite reach his eyes like it normally did.

This time, I reached for him first, and interlocked our fingers before I led him to the parking lot. Once we reached his car, I moved to take his keys from his hands, but he pulled them out of my reach.

"What do you think you're doing?" he asked, amusement lacing his voice.

I raised a brow and pointed to his face. "You've got one good eye. I'm driving."

Case didn't fight me and handed me the keys before he

walked around to toss his bag into the backseat. As soon as he was in the passenger seat, I started for my apartment. The drive through the city was quiet, and every time I looked at Case, his eyes were closed. Whether exhausted from the game or from whatever was causing this sour attitude, I wasn't sure.

When we got to my apartment, Case got out of the car first. He walked around and opened my door before he took my hand in his. I knew I should pull back. We needed to figure out where we stood, but I didn't feel comfortable weaponizing affection. Especially when I hadn't told him about my inner turmoil. So, we walked hand-in-hand to my door. Case stood awkwardly at the entrance as I walked into the kitchen and gestured to the couch.

"Are you going to sit down? Or does your butt hurt from being in the penalty box all night? I promise, my couch is more comfortable than it loo–"

"I got let go as assistant coach."

Case blurted out the words. I sat my mug down as I stared at him and tried to make sense of what he said. "What?"

It was obvious how upset he was over this. If not for how poorly he played tonight, then because of how he was acting now. His shoulders were slumped over, and the air of confidence he carried was gone. Case ran a hand through his hair and glanced at the wall, as if he was still trying to make sense of it.

"They made the decision before Christmas. They waited to tell me so my holidays weren't ruined. But, yeah. That's why coach and Mrs. J wanted to talk to me."

"Did they say why?"

The kids were going to be devastated, and I was going to have to figure out how to tell them. Was this what Mr. Clein was yelling at me about? Believe it was my fault?

Case shook his head, but I saw the words he wasn't

saying. I wanted to press, demand the words he was keeping from me. But, I promised I wouldn't. I told him I would give him space and would be here when he was ready to talk to me. I just had to be patient.

I sat on the couch, and Case closed the distance after I patted the spot next to me. I kept my hands on my lap, but moved to catch his gaze. When he tried to look away, though, I grabbed his chin. "Hey, look at me, big guy." I waited until his eyes met mine. "It will be okay. I'll talk to Mrs. Johnson and see if we can't get this sorted out."

I pulled my hands away and reached for the remote, but Case stopped me. His hand grabbed my wrist, and he pulled me into a hug. I wrapped my arms around his waist as he nestled his face into my neck. "I want to tell you, and I promise I'll explain soon. I just—I need more time to figure some things out."

I smiled and moved my hands up and down his back. "I'll be here when you're ready, Case. I'm not going anywhere."

case

"Bus is here!" Townes shouted from the hallway.

I gathered the last few things I needed to put into my bag; athletic tape, snacks, and a change of clothes for after the game. "Be right there!"

We had been in Atlanta for almost a week and had spent our free time doing press and going over footage. The only time we could relax was during dinner, and when we were sleeping. I tossed the last thing I needed into my duffel when my phone lit up. I yanked it off the charger and opened the picture from Basil.

She and Hollis were sitting on Basil's couch. The coffee table she finally bought was littered with snacks and drinks as they both threw up peace signs at the camera. I read her text and grinned.

BASIL

Good luck tonight. Remember to stay outta that box ;)

I took a minute and looked at the picture. I was mesmerized by just how beautiful Basil was in it. My eyes traced over her dark braided hair, and how the ends landed past the number ten on the Jersey she was wearing. I smiled and coasted over her again.

I tried to talk to her about that night, the one I spent watching my team from the penalty box. Word had gotten out, and some guys on the other team were talking about Basil. I snapped. All of this was my fault. My plan, before I started throwing punches, was to take Basil out. I needed to clear the air between us and let her know how I felt. To let her know the reason I didn't kiss her at Riley's was because–I couldn't trust myself to hold back.

But also, I still hadn't told her about Aubrey. I couldn't keep expecting Basil to show up for me when I wasn't being honest with her. It hurt, at times when she seemed like she was retreating back into the shell she wore when we first met, and I hated it. We had two more days in Atlanta, but the second we landed, I planned on talking to her. I was going to be honest and hope she could forgive me.

It was what kept me from fucking her senseless at Riley's. I didn't want any secrets between us when I took her for the first time.

"Come on, Case!" Townes said from the hotel room door. I sent a quick heart reaction to the message before I tossed my phone into the bag.

"Coming!"

Two weeks ago, when Coach Warner told me I was being pulled from the assistant coach position due to the accusation against Basil, I was distraught. I didn't know how to process that all that shit with Aubrey had come back to bite me in the ass. Anytime I texted her and demanded she stop fueling these rumors, it was always the same response.

Date me again and it'll all work out.

Maybe you shouldn't have gone back on our agreement.

You might not have thought it was real, but I did.

I had to call Jasmine after that last one, to try to under-stand why whatever she was doing to help wasn't working. The articles were still being taken down when we caught them, but they were still coming. When Aubrey offered I pay her off to stop, I laughed and hung up the phone. Since then, she's stopped calling and texting. But guilt had pooled in my stomach.

Two more days, then I could talk to Basil.

The bus ride to the arena was quiet. Everyone was busy doing their pre-game rituals to get their minds in the right headspace. Something I didn't do the night after Warner talked to me, which put me in a bad mood before the game even started. Some of the guys liked to recite affirmations to themselves, others talked to their partners for pep talks. A few guys did weird things, like tying their shoes a certain way or only doing things in a certain number all week.

My routine was simple. I imagined skating out into the arena, and I was the only person the crowd was cheering for. In the past, I'd imagine people who meant the most to me cheering the most; Mom, Dad, but Basil had taken their spot these past few months. She stood just on the other side of the Plexiglas, cheering my name as I went through our warm ups. Then, she cheered louder when I made the winning score.

I continued that line of thinking as the bus got to the arena and we headed inside to get ready. As I passed Warner, he placed a hand on my shoulder. "Let's not be the first ones to throw punches tonight, okay?"

"You got it, coach."

We all headed to the locker room and got ready, and it was just as quiet in here as it was on the bus. If not more.

Townes grabbed his goalie mask and sat next to me on the bench. "We need to talk about some stuff after the game."

"Is everything okay?" I asked him while I kept my focus on tying my skates.

Townes shook his head and rubbed a tattooed hand over his beard. "Have you talked to Basil yet?"

I looked at him once my laces were done, and saw he was just as serious as I was. Townes was my best friend, and I knew he meant well, but he also had a tendency to get everyone else to do uncomfortable things when they weren't ready.

"I'm talking to her when we get back home."

"Why haven't you told her yet?"

"Why are you up my ass about this? We've had this conversation too many times for you to keep bringing it up," I barked at him, earning the attention of the team.

Townes stood and whirled around to point at me. "I'm bringing it up because it's already cost you the coaching thing. I don't want it to cost you her. So get your head out of your ass and talk to her like an adult Whitlock."

Townes walked past Warner and stood on the opposite end of the locker room, where some of the other guys stood. I ignored the curious stares as I found my place beside coach and then we headed for the rink. The sound of the cheering crowd grew louder and louder as we walked, and became deafening once we skated onto the rink. We paired off and started our warm-up routine on the ice, making sure we stayed on our side while the other team stayed on theirs.

We had a few minutes before the game started, so those of us who were done waited by the penalty box. Scottie and I were lost in casual conversation, going over the mistletoe Riley left in all his guest rooms, when someone skated over. It was hard to miss the smug look on Leo

Campbell's face when we saw him. He was one of the starting left-wingers for Atlanta's team, but how he still had a contract with them was beyond me. The guy had gotten into more fights than anyone I knew in the industry, and his missing teeth proved that. Scottie glared at Leo when he leaned against the sideboard.

"Sup Whitlock," he looked at Scottie, "Lancaster."

I could be professional, even though this guy got under my skin.

Leo's smirk grew more sinister when he looked at me. "Heard things aren't so good between you and Aubrey. Man, that's a shitty thing you did going and cheating on her."

Scottie shot me a concerned glance, and I didn't blame him. I was positive it looked like I was about to punch the guy. But I won't repeat what happened last game. I shrugged and held Leo's gaze. "So the papers say. You shouldn't believe everything you see, Campbell."

The whistle blew and everyone scattered, but not before Leo shot me an accusatory stare. I didn't know what his deal was, but I couldn't think about that right now. I took my place in the center and got ready for the puck to drop. It didn't take long to block everything out until all I saw was the puck, my team, and the other team's goal. The puck hit the ice, and I moved. At the last second, when my stick grazed the puck, I was blocked. The other team's center took possession and skated past me.

Atlanta had a strong defense, which made it hard for Scottie and Connor to steal the puck back, but we had something they didn't.

Townes—the best goalie in the league.

He managed to block every attempt they made at scoring, and it was obvious they were getting frustrated. One of the players skated toward Townes, but they left an opening.

Scottie came out of nowhere and took back the puck before he flew down the rink. He and I passed the puck to one another, making sure to stay out of Riley's way as he helped defend us from the opposing team. There was a small opening in their defense, and Scottie took the shot. The puck slid into their goal and the crowd cheered.

It was like that the entire game; us struggling to take the puck, while the other team struggled to defend their goal and get the puck into ours. By the last period, we were tied up, with them having more penalties. We needed at least one more opening and then we could fend them off until the final buzzer. I was trying to keep one of the other team's defenders away from Connor, who had a clear shot at their goal, when Campbell came up and slammed into him. There was a small scuffle on the sideboard, and I saw Campbell throw his head back, getting ready to connect it with Connors.

But Connor moved at the last second, and Campbell ended up smacking his head onto the Plexiglas. Connor managed to get away from him and skated fast so he could reach me to pass the puck. I took it and made my way down the ice. I noticed a small opening to the goalie's left, and I took the shot before I lost it. The puck hit the back net at the same time the final buzzer rang. As the crowd cheered, my teammates gathered around me. There was a lot of pushing and celebratory conversation, but my gaze stayed on Campbell.

That smug look he had earlier was back as he skated over, and he didn't stop when he started talking. "Let me know when you're done with that girl you've been seeing. Might take a trip up to Denver to see if she's worth hanging around."

Anger rushed through me as he continued past me, but I couldn't find it in me to go after him. I needed to talk to Jasmine, or coach, or *someone* who could fix this. We all went back to the locker rooms to change and get ready for a night out after our win.

Scottie came up beside me. "What did Campbell say?" he asked, crossing his arms.

I leaned my head back against the locker and stared at the ceiling. "Something about coming up to Denver when I'm 'done with that girl I've been seeing'."

His brows creased together. "Basil? Dude, how are you still having this problem?"

"I don't know," I said as frustration crawled up my chest and into my throat. He shook his head and walked away, knowing we weren't going to have a productive conversation with me like this. I appreciated that, unlike Townes, Scottie knew when to push a conversation. After everyone showered and changed, we drove back to the hotel. Townes and I made it to our room, but I was the only one who started to undress.

"You're not coming?" Townes asked as he met Scottie in the hallway.

I shook my head as I took off my socks. "Not in the mood. I'll see you guys when you get back."

Townes and Scottie shared a knowing look before Townes shut the door behind him. I ordered room service after I changed and grabbed my phone before sitting on the bed.

I smiled and started a Facetime call with Basil. She answered on the third ring with a smile. "Hey, big guy."

Those two words hit me in my chest, and my smile widened. The first time she called me that, I thought that I didn't like it. That, the uncomfortable feeling in my chest was discomfort, but it was different somehow. It took time before I realized I just wasn't used to being called something endearing by anyone who wasn't my mother.

"Hey sunshine," I said as I took a moment to admire her. She had changed out of the jersey and into those pajamas that drove me crazy. Her long, messy hair draped her shoulders, and her eyes lit up in a way that, even over the phone, drew my attention to them. She pulled the popcorn out of the microwave and poured it into a bowl while I watched her from wherever she propped her phone up.

"Which Harry Potter are you watching?"

"Da ird on," she said around a mouthful of popcorn. I chuckled and picked up the remote for the hotel television, hoping I could find the series on pay-per-view. I put it in the search bar, but nothing came up.

"Damn."

"What?" Basil asked as she settled on the couch.

"I wanted to watch it with you, but the hotel doesn't have it to buy."

There was a shuffling noise and when I looked at my phone, I saw Basil's television. The opening scene played for the third movie in the series.

"What's this?"

Basil peeked her head from above the screen. "Well, you wanted to watch it, so that's what we're doing."

She moved out of view then, and even though I couldn't see her, I knew her cheeks were turning pink. It made me smile. There was a knock at the door, and I grabbed food before settling back on the bed.

Basil and I watched that movie until I heard her soft snores on the other end of the phone, and I didn't bother hanging up. Even as my eyes felt heavy and I let sleep pull me under, too.

basil

I should have stayed home. When I walked through the door to Mom's earlier, I noticed the tension in the air. She wasn't happy, and I needed to appease her frustration somehow. But also, my car was on its last leg and I wasn't sure how the drive home would go.

It started when Case left for Atlanta and had been getting worse each day. I wouldn't have the money to fix it until next week, either. So all I could do was hope it would last until then. The current condition of my car served as a great distraction from Mom's bad mood.

When I tried to grab bowls and utensils to set the table, she kicked me out. So, I planted myself on the couch and kept Socks company as I thought of things that could be wrong with the old Honda. The lab sat on my feet, a demand for more scratches.

"I've covered every inch of your oversized stomach. Where am I missing?" I asked him, and he responded by shaking his head. "Ah, gotcha." I reached down and started scratching the backs of his ears. Socks let out a satisfied growl and leaned back into my touch.

"Come eat," Mom bit out as she set down the serving dish a little too hard. I nodded and let Socks outside before sitting down.

I watched as Mom served herself before taking a large sip of her wine. Now, mom didn't drink often, because when she did, she had a hard time pacing herself. I gave her a soft smile as I started loading the soup into my bowl.

"Is everything okay?" I asked.

Mom slammed down her spoon and leveled me with a harsh stare. Her features were perfect, not a wrinkle in sight as she looked at me. The only evidence of her anger came from her eyes. The piercing blues had darkened as she became overwhelmed with emotion. She smirked, but it was too tight, and I braced myself for what was about to come.

"How was your date?"

Is that what the attitude was about? I leaned back in my seat and set my spoon down as I looked at her. "Horrible."

Mom scoffed and took another sip of wine. "Tell me what happened. I'd *love* to hear your side of the story."

My mouth opened in disbelief, but Mom shrugged and kept her eyes on me as she waited. What did she hear? And who did she hear it from? More importantly, why was she choosing to believe someone else without hearing what happened from her daughter first?

"Okay." I sat up straighter and took a breath. "Well, aside from Beau's horrible, reckless driving, he was incredibly rude to the waitstaff. He talked down to me, insinuated I could have a better job solely based on my looks, and he ordered for me."

Mom blinked. "Basil, you're upset he ordered your food? You should be more appreciative of men being chivalrous."

Of all the things she decided to take away from what went wrong that night, that was it? I stared at her as I tried to find the words that would convey how frustrated I was—without causing more of a fight. Three deep breaths.

Three.

Two.

"It wasn't that he ordered my food for me, Mom. It's that he didn't care to ask about allergies or what I liked before he did it. He just assumed that because he was better than me, I would blindly go along with whatever he did. He ordered me scallops, Mom."

Until we realized how much easier my allergy was to manage than others, Mom was overly cautious with me around food growing up. So while I didn't expect her to be as upset as I was, I expected her to have some sympathy. One time, Uncle Vernon invited us to his place for a Fourth of July party and had a crab boil. That was the first time I ever saw Mom get mad at anyone she didn't work with.

She huffed in annoyance and I kept mine hidden. "You could have sent it back."

I couldn't believe this. "What did he tell you, Mom?" I asked.

I had to know. What did Beau or his dad tell my mom to make her think I was the reason the date didn't go well? Hell, why did it matter so much to her, anyway?

Mom stood and walked over to the entryway table. She rifled through her purse and came back with her phone. I watched as she tapped away on the screen, searching for something. "I thought–given what happened between your father and I–that I raised you right. That you knew how hurtful it is to betray someone you love. And yet you go and do this—" She turned her screen toward me and my eyes latched onto the headline.

MYSTERY WOMAN IDENTITY SOLVED!

Below the headline was a picture of Case and me walking out of the training facility. In a panic, I grabbed her phone to read more. My heart sank at the words "Mistress" and "Manipulated" that were being associated with me. What was going on? How long had it been going on?

Why was I finding this out from my mother?

When I didn't say anything right away, Mom scoffed and ran her fingers along the rim of her wineglass. "You became the very thing that tore your father's and I's marriage apart."

I looked at her and felt the only emotional tether I had to her snap. Our relationship had already been fragile, and I wasn't surprised it finally broke. But I was surprised this was the reason. That something I didn't know about or had no control over would lead to that kind of accusation.

I needed to leave.

Without so much as a glance at her, I stood from the chair and grabbed my coat from the hall closet. She didn't bother to get up and instead finished her wine.

The chilling wind bit my cheeks when I stepped outside, but I ignored it as I kicked through the snow to get to my car. Another reason I should have stayed home–the incoming snowstorm. I sent up a silent prayer that my car was going to work on the first try because I couldn't be stuck here tonight. When the car stuttered to life, relief fell over my body, and I tried to keep the tears at bay as I drove off. I had too many questions and no answers, and I didn't know what I wanted to do.

Case got in earlier today, but seeing him was the last thing on my mind. I needed to figure things out for myself before I talked to him, so I could ask him the right questions.

Why didn't he tell me?

Why did he let people talk about me like I was a horrible person?

How long had this been going on behind my back?

The questions spiraled through my mind as I finally took the off-ramp that led to my apartment. But one kept coming back; why was I letting myself get so worked up? I had never told Case about the resentment I held toward my mom, and how my view of love had shaped me. I wasn't sure if I was more hurt by him keeping me in the dark, or because of what my mom said.

I came up to the first stop sign, and when I pushed on the gas pedal—my car died. There was a moment of silence before I yelled and smacked the steering wheel. I was stuck less than five miles from my apartment, and it started snowing. Once I let my car know how I felt, I dug my phone from my pocket and ignored the way my hands were already getting cold. I tapped on the screen, and when it didn't turn on, I held the power button, only to be greeted with the no battery sign.

My head hit the headrest, and I started shaking from the mix of anxiety and adrenaline. It was a two-hour walk from home, and I wasn't dressed for the cold. Everything outside was covered in a thick blanket of snow and the wind was picking up speed. Usually, I kept blankets stashed in my trunk, but they were at home.

I had been too lazy to put them back after I washed them.

I sat there for a minute and contemplated my options, which were; to stay where I was, or try to hitchhike. Or I could walk home.

It took exactly five seconds for me to brace myself against the cold. I unfurled the collar of my sweater over my nose and hoped it would be enough to break the wind, so when it hit my face, it wasn't as bad. Once that was in place, I grabbed the hand warmers I kept in the center console and got out of the car. As I walked, I stayed under the street lamps, so if anyone lost control of their car, at least they'd be able to avoid me.

I made it twenty minutes before my hand warmers decided to stop working. Everything hurt and I couldn't feel my toes. I alternated between walking and jogging to stay warm when rubbing my hands together wasn't good enough. I lasted another mile before I could no longer feel my body and kicked a piece of ice in frustration when a car drove by. The car slowed, and the hairs on my neck stood up when it stopped a few feet ahead of me. My throat and chest started to hurt with how heavy I was breathing as I tried to keep my anxiety at bay.

I should have grabbed the pepper spray from the center console.

I turned around and continued walking. There was another street I could take. It was out of the way, but I wasn't walking past that car. This was stupid. I couldn't believe I decided to walk home while it was freezing outside. I took two steps before someone yelled at me.

"Basil!"

I stopped moving. The cold had clearly gotten to my brain if I had been hallucinating voices. That sounded a lot like Case.

"Goddamn it." I heard him mutter under his breath.

Yup, that was him.

My head whipped around to see him grabbing something from the back of his car before he jogged toward me.

"What the hell are you doing?" Anger laced his words as he threw a thick wool-lined jacket around me. "Put your arms in."

I looked at him, and anger surged from the coldest

parts of my body. Was it misplaced? I wasn't sure, but I couldn't help it. Case held my stare as he waited for me to listen and put my arms into the sleeves.

"Leave me alone," I said as I pushed past him. My apartment wasn't that much farther. I'd be fine.

"What? Basil put the fucking jacket on and get in the car," Case said as he caught up with me.

"No. Leave me alone."

Case stepped in front of me, and I stopped just short of running into him. When I glanced up and saw the worry in those green eyes, it just made me angrier. We stared at each other as I felt myself unravel. When he texted me when his plane landed, I was so excited to see him. Couldn't wait to be wrapped up in his warmth, but now, I didn't want anything to do with him. I needed space so I could figure out why he kept secrets that involved me.

When Case spoke again, his voice came out rough. "I'm only going to say this once. Either you get in the car, or I'm going to put you in there myself."

I straightened and tried to step around him. I wasn't getting in the car. "Leav—"

He picked me up before the word left my mouth. One arm wrapped around my legs and the other on my waist, then in one swift movement, Case lifted me over his shoulder like a sack of potatoes. I smacked his back with my numb hands. "Put me down!"

"No," he said, and his voice left no room for argument. That didn't stop me from trying to get out of his grip. I wiggled under him as he carried me to the car. He opened the door and placed me inside. I wasn't going to give him the satisfaction of seeing me relax into the heated seats, so I flipped him off instead. Case shook his head in annoyance before he shut the door and walked around to get in.

He tossed a blanket from the backseat over my lap before he drove off. "Stubborn girl."

Pressure welled behind my eyes. I wasn't going to cry, though, not here. I would wait until after he dropped me off, when I could do it in the privacy of my bedroom.

I felt stupid, and not because I was delusional for thinking I could walk home when the temperature was in the single digits. Stupid, because I let my emotions get the better of me. I was hurt and confused because *why* didn't he talk to me? Why was I so upset about him hurting feelings I didn't tell him I had? A normal friend would be a little irritated, sure.

Hey, I wish you would have told me about this. Please don't let it happen again.

Why couldn't I feel like that?

The smallest tear fell. I wiped it away quickly and hoped Case didn't notice.

It wasn't long before Case pulled into my apartment's parking lot. He got out and walked around to open my door. "Put the coat on."

I stood and shoved the coat into his chest. "You can leave. I'm not going to freeze to death inside my apartment."

Case followed me as I made my way to the door. "Great. That means I can spend less time worrying about your health and more time figuring out what's going on with you."

I whirled around once the door was unlocked. "I don't want to talk to you, Case."

"Then let me talk." His voice came out as a plea as his eyes darted between mine. The anger was still there, but so was something else, and I didn't recognize it. "You're upset and I don't know why. Tell me so I can try to fix it. Please, Basil."

With a huff, I stomped into the apartment. Case followed and watched as I turned on him with my arms crossed. Of all the questions I asked myself and the answers he needed to give me—I didn't know what I wanted first. But if he wanted to talk, then he could talk about the blonde he was dating before we met, and what I had to do with their break-up.

I leaned against the couch and shrugged.

"Who is Aubrey?"

case

All the anger and concern drained from my body.

Basil rubbed her hands against her arms before a shiver took over her body. I wanted to bundle her up, lay her on the couch, and demand she rested up before we talked. She wasn't going to allow that, though. I didn't think I could get close enough without her pushing me away. I had to explain myself and ask for forgiveness. I would beg if that was what it took—she was too important for me to lose.

She never took her eyes off mine. "Who is Aubrey, Case?" She asked through a shiver.

I couldn't talk to her like this when she was freezing and her lips were turning blue. I needed to fix a lot of things, but her well-being was going to come first. It always would.

I started toward the kitchen and as I passed her said, "Sit."

Basil grabbed the throw blanket and wrapped it around her before she sat down. She kept her focus on the TV while I made my way into the kitchen. I filled her kettle, and as I waited for the water to boil, a thousand questions filtered through my mind.

How did Basil find out?

Why was she outside walking in single-digit temperatures? And why didn't she call me?

I didn't know the answers to those questions yet, but I would in time. All I had to do was answer Basil's questions first and hope she didn't hate me when I answered them. I grabbed a tea bag from the pantry and looked at Basil as I set it in a mug. She still faced the television, but I could see how she worked the blanket nervously between her hands.

I couldn't look away from her as I started talking. "Aubrey and I were in the same friend group in college. We weren't exactly friends, but we got along." Basil shifted on the couch and I saw how she tilted her head back toward me. I kept my focus on the water as I waited for it to boil. "We had a few classes together and hung out sometimes, but we never dated. We lost contact after I graduated."

I took the kettle and filled the mug. After I added honey and lemon, I took it to Basil and made sure she grabbed it from my hands. I needed to watch her drink it, so I knew she was helping herself warm up. I sat on the opposite end of the couch and looked at her.

"I had just been named captain for the Peaks, and she hit me up. Aubrey had moved out here for modeling, and after a few weeks of hanging out, asked me to be her fake boyfriend. She had already been here for six months and was struggling. She didn't want to move back home, and I wanted to help her out. Everyone deserves a chance, right?"

Basil kept her focus on the tea, but I knew she was listening.

"We agreed to a year. And by the end of it, she wanted more. So, I called it off. Basil, the thing between me and Aubrey wasn't real. I—" My brows pulled in as my eyes roamed over her face, searching for a sign she understood. "I fucked up," I said, resigned, as I looked at the floor.

It was quiet for a moment as I waited for Basil to say something.

She took a deep breath. "When?"

She didn't give me the chance to speak before she continued.

"When did you call it off, Case? Can you tell me why my name is being smeared in fucking sports magazines?" Basil asked as her grip around the mug tightened. When I looked at her, what I *saw*—it felt like someone had taken my already beat-up heart and crushed it to dust.

Basil was crying.

I kept my distance, even though every fiber of my being begged to close it. To pull her into my arms and promise everything would work out. I knew she would be upset. But seeing how much it affected her, and how it made me feel—was unexpected.

I cleared my throat. "I called it off at the first party we went to, the one when we got food with Townes. She showed up because I hadn't planned any dates or outings, and I was tired of it. She was asking for more of my time than what we agreed, and I just couldn't do it anymore." I shifted closer to her and waited for her to pull away again. When she didn't, I continued. "Aubrey spread a rumor, saying I cheated on her. Because in some fucked up way she thought her career was still tied to mine. I swear Basil, the articles were taken down the second they—"

"There were *more*?" she asked as she set the mug on the ground and stood from the couch. The blanket fell to the floor, and she shivered again. "When were you going to tell me, Case? Why didn't you tell me this was happening? I heard your coach mention something about your image and the teams. Mr. Clein blames me for you leaving. He thinks it's my fault."

With each word she threw at me, I grabbed them and tucked it into my body. The reasons started to add up and realization hit me. I could lose her because of this, because I wasn't honest like I said I'd be.

Basil's voice was soft, and she held onto her arms as she stared at me. "My mother said I wasn't any better than the woman who tore apart her marriage." Her tears came in full force now as she tried to keep herself together.

I withheld the truth because I was so sure I could handle everything. But, I couldn't handle this.

Basil let out a shaky breath as she tried to collect herself, and I never looked away. Another round of tears streamed down her red cheeks, and it physically hurt that I couldn't do anything. If I so much as breathe in her direction—I was afraid that would be it. That she'd tell me to leave, and all of this would be over.

It would hurt, but it was okay. Because if she told me to leave—I could walk away grateful. Grateful I got to love her silently. When she fell asleep watching movies. When she curled up to experience new worlds between white pages.

And when she smiled—god, that smile. If she told me to leave, I would be broken. Because I would rather stay and love her silently forever than lose her.

"I feel stupid, Case," Basil said as she hunched over to place her hands on her legs, and tears fell from her eyes. She kept her head down and talked into her knees. "I hate this. I hate what my mother said and I hate that I found out from her. I waited. I knew something was bothering you. And I knew you would tell me. I just—" Her voice broke again, and I had enough.

I stood from my seat and walked over to her. I prepared for her to step out of my reach when I held out my arms, but when she didn't move, I wrapped them around her. Basil dropped like she could finally let the weight of her worries take over because she had the support. I kept us steady as we kneeled to the floor. I rested against the couch and Basil settled against my chest.

I didn't know how long we sat there, but I combed my fingers through Basil's hair as her tears became less frequent. When she was done, I expected her to pull away again—demand I leave and never see her again. I prepared myself for it, but when she looked at me, I didn't see the anger that fueled her. This was softer, sadder–it was hurt.

I hated myself for being the one responsible for it.

Basil pushed off me to retrieve the blanket and her tea before she sat on the couch. I leaned my head back and waited, but she never said anything.

So, I filled the silence. "Why were you out walking in the snow, Basil?" If I didn't know better, I would have mistaken her strangled chuckle for a cough.

"My car broke down and my phone died. I didn't see another option." She looked over the armrest of the couch and raised a brow. "How did you find me?"

"I was on my way to your house when I saw you."

"How'd you know it was me?"

"Because everyone else I know is smart enough to wear a thick enough jacket when it's freezing outside." My voice lacked its intended teasing tone, and we fell back into silence. The only sound that filled the apartment was the wind blowing against the windows. I thought Basil had fallen asleep after a while and sat up to find her staring into the mug.

"I'm still mad, Case, and really hurt."

"I know," I said as I sat next to her. "I was planning on telling you tonight if that makes you feel any better?"

"You should have told me when it first started, Case," she said as she pinned me with a stare.

I reached out and grabbed the mug from her, setting it

on the table before I reached for her hands. "You're right. There's no excusing what I did, and there's nothing I can do that will make it right. I can ask your forgiveness and pretend everything is going to go back to the way it was. But that's not how trust works. I broke yours, and I'll spend however long it takes to build that back up again. But Basil, can you promise me one thing?" I rubbed my thumb over her wrist and noticed how her pulse raced under my touch.

"You're not in any position to ask for promises."

The words didn't hold any malice, but they hurt anyway.

I focused on her pulse point as I stared at her. "Promise me you won't ever do something so reckless again. If you're having car trouble, people trouble, any kind of trouble—call someone. Call me, please. I'll always answer your calls."

Basil looked at me with hooded eyes, and I was suddenly taken back to another night not too long ago. When she looked at me like that, and I wanted to kiss her. When I wanted to do so much more.

I wanted to kiss away her tears and show her love in all the ways I couldn't convey with three little words.

We sat there in the quietness of her apartment, and I knew it wasn't intentional, but Basil fell asleep. When I stood to leave, to give her the space she needed, her arms tightened around my torso.

"Stay," she commanded in her sleep-filled voice.

I stayed.

I wiggled out of her grasp to turn off the lights before sitting back where I was before. I fixed the blanket, so it covered us both, and soon enough, Basil's soft sounds lulled me to sleep.

———

Townes's car was in my driveway when I pulled up, and I braced myself for the lecture he was going to give.

When I opened the door, I was greeted with the smell of chocolate and found Scottie over the stove when I rounded the corner into the kitchen. He wore a Kiss the Chef apron that I knew did not belong to me, and I didn't know if he even cooked enough for it to be his. I glanced at Townes, who sat at the island with Hayley. She saw me first.

"Uncle Casey!" she yelled as she hopped down from the barstool. Her dark curls bounced as I swept her up in my arms and hugged her. She'd been calling me Casey since she started living with Townes, and our attempts at correcting her hadn't worked.

"Hi Haybug. What are you guys doing?" I asked as I walked over to her Townes.

Hayley lifted a small finger and pointed at my chest. "You're in trouble."

I looked between the guys. "What did you tell her?"

"They didn't say nuthin Uncle Casey. But Uncle T's forehead has been stuck like that all morning." She pointed to Townes, and he leveled me with an unhappy stare. I set Hayley down and looked at Scottie.

He shrugged over the stove. "Don't look at me. I'm just here to feed you guys."

"You're here to listen to us bicker," Townes countered, never tearing his gaze away.

Scottie whirled around and placed a hand on his chest at the same time his mouth flew open. "How dare you accuse me of such a thing!" He turned and flipped the pancake onto a stack he had at his side. Then he looked at Hayley. "Come on Haybug, these meanies don't get any pancakes."

"Yes!" She ran to his side. "Can we watch Moana too?"

Townes and I watched as they disappeared into the living room, and then he turned to face me. "What happened?" he asked, that scowl deepening. I called him this morning when I left Basil's because I knew she'd want to be alone when she woke up. While I didn't go into detail, he knew it was about her and promptly came over.

I crossed my arms and leaned against the island. "Basil found out." I waited for some sort of outburst, an 'I told you so', but nothing came. Townes stayed silent as he looked at me. He leaned back in the barstool and crossed his arms. His scowl loosened a fraction.

"Elaborate."

My mind went back to last night, and just the memory of Basil—and how broken she was—made my chest ache. So, I told him everything. Where I found her and how she refused to get in the car, that I wasn't anything but a publicity stunt to Aubrey. I kept the things Basil said to myself. We all knew I hurt her. I didn't need to expose her like that.

Townes leaned forward and rested his arms on the countertop. He stayed like that for a while before he shook his head. "Isn't the wedding this weekend?"

"Yeah," I said. I had already prepared myself for when Basil told me she was going by herself.

Townes looked at the granite before he stood and put his hand on my back as he walked past me. "Better practice your 'forgive me for being an ass' speech, then." He kept walking until he rounded the corner that led to the living room. "Scottie, exactly how many chocolate chips did you put in those pancakes?"

basil

Case and I hadn't talked all week, and the only time he reached out was to tell me he sent my car to a mechanic.

Which—was nice of him—but I was still too pissed to be happy about it.

The morning after Case left, I went down an internet rabbit hole. There were so many online forums about Case and Aubrey and their breakup, but I couldn't find any articles. So, I guess Case was honest about that.

The forums surprised me. They weren't at all what I was expecting. While my mom had accused me of being the reason Case and Aubrey's 'relationship' was torn apart, that wasn't what everyone else was saying. My chest felt like it was being torn in two as I read things like, "Looks happier than ever" and "He deserves his privacy, let him be."

But the kind words from strangers didn't make up for the fact that Case withheld information from me. If I hadn't been the topic of conversation, I wouldn't have cared.

I groaned as I absentmindedly skated around the rink, not paying attention to the kids as they did their drills.

Until Michael skated in front of me, and I almost knocked him over.

"Are you okay?" I asked as I tried to reel in my thoughts.

Michael nodded, but his face was overshadowed with concern when he looked at me. "Yeah, but Coach, are you okay?"

Aiden skated over then, and scoffed. "Of course she's not. Coach Whitlock's gone, and she misses him."

I cleared my throat and placed my hands on my hips. "Why aren't you guys doing your drills?" Aiden skated off and took his previous position in front of the goal. Michael, however, wrapped his arms around my waist before he looked up.

"I miss him too, Coach," he said with a smile before skating off to join the other kids.

I did my best to keep my mind from wandering for the remainder of practice and kept my distance from the parents when it was over. While Mr. Clein was the only one who had expressed his grievances about Case being gone —I could see the other parents thought the same thing. They whispered, and their smiles lacked their usual kindness. So, I kept to myself and took my time collecting the cones from the rink after saying goodbye to the kids. I also waited a few extra minutes before leaving the rink, because being ambushed by a parent was not something I could handle today.

Once everything was put away and my skates were in my locker, I grabbed my phone from my purse and opened the text notification.

HOLLIS

Here!

Be out in a sec

I waved goodbye to Daniel and found Hollis's car parked right by the door. Which I appreciated, because the parking lot was covered in patches of ice from last night's storm. She had the same reaction Case did when I told her about my stroll through the snow and made me buy two jackets to keep in my car. Along with another pack of hand warmers and a portable charger.

"Hi," I said as I got in the car.

"How was practice?" she asked as she started pulling out of the parking lot.

I laid my head back on the headrest and turned to look at her. "Fine, the kids asked about Case again." I expected another round of insults from Hollis about Case, but they never came. Instead, she hummed under her breath and tapped her fingers on the wheel. Hollis was hiding something.

I turned in my seat to face her fully and pulled my brows in question. "What?"

"What?"

"Don't 'what' my 'what,' Hollis Shay. What's going on? You're being weird." I poked her side.

Hollis bit her lip and glanced in the rearview mirror. "I don't know what you're talking about."

I huffed and decided silence was going to be my best option for the rest of the short drive. We reached the apartment in a few minutes, and as I got out, I turned to Hollis. "Want to come inside?" I asked. She hadn't been over much since she moved, and I missed her.

She shook her head and gave me a soft look. "Not today, but we'll get together soon."

I nodded and got out of the car. Hollis waited until I got to my door before she drove off—which was strange. Normally, she waited until I was inside before she left. I shook off the weird feeling that crawled up my back and opened the door.

Only to stop when I found Case baking in my kitchen.

"Hi Basil," he said as he tilted his head toward me, and I could see the hint of a smile on his face.

I missed that smile—even if I was mad at him.

"What are you doing here?" I asked as I made my way to him. When he turned to face me, I was taken aback by what I saw. He might be smiling, but everything else was wrong. His hair was a mess, he had bags under his eyes, and his usual air of confidence was gone. A small part of me was glad to see it because, in a way, it validated my feelings. That he cared about hurting me. The bigger part of me, though, hurt to see him like this, and I wanted to fix it. Make everything better, but that wasn't my job—it was his.

I was still trying to figure out how to tell him about my feelings and why I was so hurt.

Case looked back down at the bowl and added a couple of eggs before he reached for the sugar. "Baking." He started opening drawers. "Where are your measuring cups?"

I pointed to the drawer closest to the sink before crossing my arms. "I can see that, but how did you get inside?"

"Hollis let me in and—yes, Basil. She sat me down and lectured me for four hours when I visited with Scottie a couple of days ago," he said when my jaw dropped. It was hard to believe that Hollis, the woman who had been cursing his name all week, let him into my apartment. Maybe she and I needed to reevaluate each other's key privileges.

"Flour?" Case asked as he looked around the pantry. With a resigned sigh, I walked over to the fridge and reached up to grab the canister from the top of it. But when I reached for it, I accidentally moved it backward.

Case chuckled from behind me, "I got it, you go sit down."

I moved to the side before he got close enough for my body to react to his proximity. Not that it worked very well. As he stepped in front of me, I caught a whiff of that clean, masculine scent and a tingle traveled down my back. I leaned against the counter. "No, you can either tell me why you're here or leave."

He turned toward me and *winked.* "If I leave, then you won't get brownies."

"I'll finish making them myself."

"No, you won't, because I'll take everything with me. And I promise, you're going to want these, ones," he said as he started chopping up a chocolate bar, and my stomach chose that moment to let Case know how hungry I was. When he faced me this time, the smile on his face wasn't as bright, and it made my heart ache. "Grab a banana and go sit down, sunshine. We'll talk when I put these in the oven."

Reluctantly, I grabbed a couple of bananas from the fruit bowl before I went and sat on the couch. While I found a movie to watch, Case finished up in the kitchen. He put the brownies into the oven and then washed the dishes. He hesitated for a moment before finally walking over and sat at the other end of the couch. We watched the movie, but neither of us paid any attention.

Case cleared his throat, and his voice wobbled when he spoke. "Basil," he took a steadying breath before he continued, "I know sorry can't magically fix what I did."

I turned the volume down and turned to face him, pulling one leg up as I leaned into the couch. Case held my gaze and continued. "I thought that, by not telling you what was happening, that I was protecting you. Because you don't deserve any misplaced negativity. Aubrey's out here trying to tarnish your name, and I thought I was doing everything I could to prevent that, but it didn't stop.

I swear to you, I was going to tell you when I got back into town, but it was too late."

As I sat and listened as Case struggled to get the words out, he looked at me with a seriousness I wasn't used to and I watched as fear and determination danced in his eyes when he spoke again. "If you don't want to see me again, I understand. When I didn't tell you about those articles, I took away your ability to decide for yourself. You should have been the one telling me how you wanted the situation handled."

Case and I stared at each other until the timer went off. He walked into the kitchen and took the brownies out of the oven, only to put them right back in. When he sat down, I noticed how his hands shook before he locked his fingers together.

I chuckled, not because anything was funny, but because I needed to stop the building pressure in my throat. Even though I was hurt and angry—despite those emotions softening—I couldn't help but forgive him. I always knew I would.

I had given Case so many pieces of me, and he made them fit perfectly in with his own. We were an imperfect puzzle with jagged edges and pieces we were still searching for. All we had done was add another piece. The puzzle wasn't finished, and it might never be, but I wanted to keep working on it—until those jagged pieces made the perfect picture of us.

I leaned toward Case until I was close enough to place my hand on his leg. There was a shift in his gaze. The fear was gone and in its place was something that—I think shared a name with what I felt in my chest whenever I was with him.

"Case, let me make this clear." I watched the way his chest heaved in silent, heavy breaths before I continued. "I'm not forgiving you because you said sorry, I'm forgiving you because I—" I let the word fall silently in the space between us, and my brows tensed together. "Because I don't want to waste anymore time being mad at you."

Case stared at me, and something shifted between us. It was warm and familiar. I recognized it from the night he picked me up from my date with Beau, and from Riley's party right before he told me goodnight. The air grew thicker the longer we sat in silence. I watched the movement in Case's neck when he swallowed and my cheeks warmed.

I wasn't going to give in, though, not yet.

The second timer went off, and Case walked off into the kitchen. He took the brownies out of the oven and they smelled familiar. I came up behind him and watched as he turned off the oven and set the brownies to the side to cool.

"What recipe is that?" I asked him as I inched closer to get a better look. There was something different about these, but I couldn't place it.

Case smirked from my side and put my oven mitts back on their little hook on the fridge. "Rhonda's."

I almost tore a muscle in my neck with how fast I turned to face him. "Rhonda's? How the fuck did you get the recipe?"

He walked away then and took his seat on the couch. I silently followed, but kept my focus on the brownies and wondered how long they had to cool down before I could eat one. Case threw an arm along the back of the couch and rolled his head, his eyes on me as I sat down. "I convinced her you were too good for me, and I needed to apologize to you." He moved the blanket over us once I was in a comfortable position.

"I'm not too good for you, Case," I said as I switched movies to something we'd actually watch. If anything, he was too good for me. He came and apologized even when he hadn't forgiven himself because he put my feelings above his own. I was scared, and I didn't deserve that, but wanted it anyway.

Case leaned his head on mine and sighed. "Well, believe it or not, it's true." A beat of silence followed before Case asked. "Do you still want me to be your date to your dad's wedding?"

I glanced at the clock and realized we had less than twelve hours before we were supposed to make the drive to Breckenridge for the weekend. So, with a smile he couldn't see, I answered.

"Yes."

"Can I still act like your boyfriend? You know, to save you from any uncomfortable questions from nosey family members?"

I rested my head back against him and kept my gaze forward as I thought about it. Case acting like my boyfriend would mean putting on a show, and I didn't know if I was strong enough to handle that. I closed my eyes and answered without confidence. "Yes."

case

I left Basil sleeping on the couch when I ran home to grab my suit, and when I came back—more than half of the brownies were gone.

If it wasn't glaringly obvious from the half-empty pan, the crumbs that littered the floor toward her bedroom were a dead giveaway. I chuckled and swept up the mess while Basil got ready to leave, then wrapped the pan in foil before setting it in the fridge. She came out of her room shortly after with a suitcase behind her and a backpack slung over her shoulder. She smiled when she looked at me, and that was a look I would never take for granted again.

"Ready to go, big guy?" she asked as she tried to get the bags down the narrow hallway.

I chuckled and grabbed the suitcase. "We're only going to be gone for the weekend. How much stuff do you have in here?"

Basil shut and locked the door behind us and walked ahead of me to the car. "Have you ever been to Breckenridge in February? You can never be too prepared."

I put her suitcase into the trunk before going around

and getting in. Basil was all ready to go; coffee in hand, slippers on, and hair thrown haphazardly on her head.

She was stunning, and I was incredibly lucky she decided to forgive me. Because when I walked into that apartment—I wasn't expecting her to. She could have said that she didn't want to be *whatever we were* anymore, and I would have come to terms with that. But she forgave me, and we spent the night watching Harry Potter and eating a reasonable amount of brownies. Well, mine was reasonable —Basil's first slice was the size of her plate, so I cut her off.

Because they were a lot of work and I wanted more for later. She obviously had other plans. Basil yawned and sipped her coffee while she tried to find something to listen to.

"What's your dad like?" I asked her to fill the silence.

Basil didn't look at me when she shrugged and clicked on a song. "Don't know, I haven't talked to him since high school."

I raised a brow and reached for my coffee. "And he invited you to his wedding?"

"Yeah," she said before the car dove into silence again. I could tell she didn't want me to press, so I stayed silent. At some point, Basil fell asleep. Her head rested on the window and her soft snores filled the car.

We got into town just before seven, and the morning sunrise spilled oranges and pinks across the sky. Basil woke up once we pulled into the hotel parking lot. Apparently, her dad had paid for all the accommodations and picked one of the nicer hotels in the small mountain town. Once we were out of the car, we took our time stretching—both sore from the car ride—and I made the mistake of glancing at Basil. As she raised her arms over her head, the hemline of her shirt rode up.

I had seen that sliver of skin before, but this time was different. I wanted to touch her—to see if her skin was as soft as I thought it was. I wondered what noises she would make if I peppered kisses down that inch of skin until I landed at her hip and—

"Case!" Basil said as she snapped her fingers.

I cleared my throat and picked up my bag. "Sorry."

"You okay? Need a nap?" she asked with a smirk as she weaved her arm through mine. When I looked down at her, she scoffed and tugged where our arms were linked. "You wanted to act like my boyfriend, remember? This is boyfriend-y stuff."

I wasn't going to argue with her. We walked through the doors of the hotel and checked in at the desk, where Basil thought it was a great place to run her hand up and down my back while I signed our parking valet. The woman at the desk handed us our room keys, and we headed upstairs. Basil enthusiastically took a key from me and opened the door, only to stop in her tracks when she made it three feet inside.

Well, shit.

"At least there's a couch," I said as I set our bags down at the end of the king-size bed.

The only bed.

I noticed the fireplace as I crossed the room, and hummed when I looked out the window. "Mountain view. Nice." When I turned around, Basil was still standing there, glancing between; me, the bed, and the couch. In an attempt to lighten the mood, I smiled and winked. "You don't think this is couple-y stuff?"

Basil's mouth dropped, and I laughed. "Kidding sunshine. Do you want me to go back downstairs and get a separate room?"

Her face flushed the lightest shade of pink, but she shook her head. "No, it's fine. One of us can sleep on the couch." I nodded and moved my bags over, only for Basil to shake her head. "Case, no offense, but you're huge. I'll sleep on the couch."

"Don't be ridiculous, I'll be fine," I said, feeling my muscles ache as I looked at the small piece of furniture. I could fit if I slept in the fetal position. Or what if I put one leg on the back of the couch, and one stretched out on the ground?

I would make it work.

Basil shook her head a second before her phone rang in her pocket. She pulled it out and tossed me an apologetic smile before walking out the door. As she talked in the hallway, I started to unpack my bag. As I put my clothes into the small dresser drawers and my toiletries in the bathroom, Basil came back inside and grabbed her jacket.

"That was my dad. He wants me to meet him downstairs for a little bit. I'm going to get some food when I'm done. Want me to text you? You can come with me?" She said it like a question, and as nice as it sounded, I was too tired to do anything but sleep. I had gotten up a couple hours before she did and the coffee on the drive didn't help.

I pointed to the couch. "I'm going to take a nap, but if you could bring me back something, that would be nice. I'm not picky."

She nodded and turned to walk out the door again, but not before glancing back with that dazzling smile. "I'll be back soon."

———

Soon was measured in a long nap, a trip to the hotel lobby for a snack, and a shower.

When the clock ticked past five, I figured I had enough time to wash away the day so I could relax for the rest of the night. I wasn't sure what was taking Basil so long, so I would find a place that offered delivery when I was done. That was the plan–until I stepped under the hot water and my mind started to drift.

I was no longer plagued by an old memory, one where Basil and I were on my couch with inches between us. No, this wasn't a memory. It could have been though, if I had given in to the urge to kiss Basil with the mistletoe between us. I had wanted to pull her into my lap, to kiss her hard enough that she couldn't doubt my intentions. I would have drawn sounds from her lips before I slipped my hand over her mouth to keep her quiet and whispered pretty words in her ear.

With a groan, I wrapped my hand around my cock and gave it a long, slow tug. I rest my head against the tile as I fucked my hand, imagining—wishing—it was something softer. Maybe I wouldn't have fucked Basil that night. I could just have easily laid down, hauled her over me, and watched her pretty face as she fucked mine. A shudder ran through me as I continued stroking, and my breathing became heavy as I lost myself in the illusion. One I had crafted more often than I could count.

"Basil—" I groaned as heat pooled in my stomach. The head of my cock became increasingly sensitive the more I stroked it.

I was so close—just another few—

"Case? Are you okay?"

Fuck.

My body instantly ran cold. I cleared my throat and tried to rein in whatever control I had left. "Yeah, be out in a second." I finished up and turned off the water. I dried and threw on the clothes I brought in the bathroom with me. Then, I checked myself in the mirror to make sure I looked, well, like I wasn't just thinking of Basil.

When I came out of the bathroom, though, my control snapped. Basil was lying on the bed, wearing the jersey she never gave back. It rested against her mid-thigh—giving me the perfect view of her ass. She looked back at me and smiled before she pointed to the unopened takeout box next to her.

"Hope you're still hungry. Sorry, it took so long."

I was hungry, but not for whatever she brought back. I sat on the bed and pulled the food into my lap with a strangled smile. "Thanks."

Basil looked at me with creased brows. She sat up and turned to face me with her legs crossed.

"Hey, are you okay?" she asked, tapping my knee. I met her gaze, an excuse ready on my tongue, but stopped short. Even in the darkness of the room—with the fireplace and movie lighting up the small space—I could see it. The deep red that crept up from her neck to her cheeks.

I tilted my head and opened my mouth, trying not to smirk. "How long have you been back?"

"Huh? Not long. I got back and knocked on the door. That's it."

I looked at her and the way she fisted the shirt in the space between her legs. Her hair cascaded over her shoulders in messy waves. There was no denying the heated look in those eyes when she finally looked at me again. I wouldn't leave her wanting *anything* tonight.

I narrowed my eyes and moved my food to the side. "Why did you ask if I was okay?"

Basil sucked in a breath. "I heard my name and–uh–I don't know. I thought you might have been–hurt?"

She was rambling as she continued working the jersey between her hands. My eyes flicked to her at the same time my head tilted. My voice came out rough when I spoke. "I was, in a way. But tell me sunshine, what other reason could have caused me to *possibly* say your name?"

To her credit, she didn't shy away as I moved closer. My knee brushed hers and as she sat there, I took the chance to watch her take in deep, heated breaths. I watched as her breasts moved up and down under my shirt before my gaze dipped to the spot between her legs. And when she tried to squirm away, I wondered—how wet was she?

"Come here," I commanded as I grabbed her wrist. Basil stared at me for a moment, and I could see her thinking of her options. Of course, if Basil said no, then that would be it. She'd sleep on the bed, and I'd sleep on the couch. We'd wake up tomorrow and would go to this wedding pretending like nothing happened. Like nothing had ever happened.

But I was tired of pretending, and I hoped I wasn't too late.

She surprised me. Basil straddled my hips and with a thick voice, she asked, "Why did you say my name, Case?"

I licked my bottom lip and pleaded, "Can I kiss you? Please? Then I'll show you."

Basil didn't finish her first nod before I closed the distance. I moved my hands to grip Basil's hips and moaned into her mouth when she moved against me. I realized then that she wasn't wearing anything under the jersey.

I was still so fucking turned on, and the release that was stolen from me only made me want her more. But tonight wasn't about me. She wanted to know why I said her name? I'd show her. We were a clash of heat and tongues as I worked my way into her mouth. I slid a hand up to the back of her head as I deepened the kiss.

Basil grabbed the bottom of her shirt and started to pull it up. I gripped her hands and bit the skin at her collarbone, stopping her. "Not tonight, pretty girl." I trailed kisses back up her neck until I reached the soft skin under her ear. "You want to know what I was imagining while I was fucking my hand?" I watched as her skin prickled under my breath and laced my fingers through her hair. "Sit on my fucking face."

I set Basil aside so I could slide up the bed, closer to the headboard. Then I hauled her over me. As I looked up, I could see the hesitation on her face. Her cheeks were flushed and her lips were swollen. She looked divine, and I bet she tasted it, too.

"Case, are you sure? I–I don't want to–"

"I'll be fine," I said as I placed light kisses on her inner thigh. "Let me worship this pretty pussy, baby." Another kiss. "You deserve it, sunshine. Please?"

She nodded and lowered herself down, but it wasn't right. I wrapped my arms around her thighs and tugged. Basil moaned and threw her head back when my tongue glided over her clit. "I. Said. Sit."

Basil moaned again and rested her head on the headboard. Her fingers clawed at my scalp while I worked her with my tongue. This was perfect—more than perfect. I held Basil down as she squirmed over me and I took my time. I licked and sucked, but it wasn't enough. She tasted better than I had imagined and I wanted more. My grip tightened as I continued to devour her. Basil was a writhing mess above me as she grinded against my face.

"Fuck, Case I–I'm–."

She moved faster. I held on tighter and helped her catch her release. Soon it would be my cock making her say my name—screaming it until her voice became hoarse and all she could manage were breathy moans. Basil's fingers tightened in my hair as she shuddered over me, and I moaned into her as she came on my tongue. Eventually, her hips slowed, and she slumped over. I placed a gentle kiss on her thigh before I helped her off and pulled her down to rest next to me.

Her breathing was heavy, and I placed a kiss on her forehead. She glanced up and her eyes were full of bliss and sleep. "What about you?" she asked as her hand traced down to my hard cock. But this was never about me. I stopped her and laced our fingers together before pulling our hands to my chest.

"I'll be fine, Basil. Now, go to sleep."

When her eyes closed, I reached for the remote and turned off the movie. Then I adjusted the blanket over us both. Basil reached for me when my head hit the pillow, and I couldn't help but give her a few lazy, sleep-filled kisses.

"Hey, Case?" she hummed as she settled her head back onto my chest.

I smiled. "Yes, sunshine?"

"You can sleep in the bed tonight. It's okay."

basil

Not sure if it was the exquisite hotel bed or the post-orgasm bliss—but I slept great.

Then I woke up and was overwhelmed with anxiety. About last night, when Case touched me—said things. So there I laid—with Case to my back, his arm curled around my stomach, and his leg between mine. His soft breaths tickled my neck while my thoughts spiraled.

When my dad asked to talk to me yesterday, I was expecting a short 'thanks for coming, see you later.' Not 'Get to know your estranged family before the wedding.' That was what kept me for so long, and I still had to grab dinner. I knew Case would be hungry, so I ran to the closest restaurant to grab food before I headed back to the hotel.

Everything seemed fine when I got back to the room.

I heard the shower running and headed straight to the king-sized bed. I set the food down, and mid-bite, I heard something. It was the softest sound, but I didn't know if it was one of pain or something else. So, I stood in front of the bathroom door, and that was when I heard it again.

Now, I didn't make it a habit to eavesdrop on people

who were in the shower. I didn't know if I was hearing things, or if Case slipped and fell and was waking up from being unconscious. I wouldn't barge into the bathroom unless I knew he needed help. It was quiet for a moment, and as I turned to walk back to the bed, I heard my name. And the way it carried through the door made me freeze.

I didn't know what caused him to say my name the way he did, but I liked it. And I wanted to hear it again.

I panicked, but only a little. I couldn't stand there and listen, but I also couldn't just go about my business like Case wasn't doing whatever it was he was doing. The ragged way he answered lit something in me. With a surge of confidence, I rummaged through my bag. I put on the jersey I hadn't given back yet and stripped my underwear. Not something I'd usually do, but again—confidence. I sat on the bed and opened my food just as the bathroom door clicked shut, and when I looked at Case—I knew.

I knew I wasn't hearing or imagining things.

He wanted me like I wanted him. I just wasn't sure how much of myself I was brave enough to hand over.

Case's arm tightened around me before he pulled me closer to his front. He placed a gentle kiss behind my ear and sighed. "Morning, beautiful."

I loved his morning voice. It sounded soft and vulnerable, and I needed to hear it again. I turned in his arms until I was face-to-face with the space between his neck and chest. With a soft touch, I traced his collarbone, memorizing his skin against mine before I moved down to memorize the other parts of him. The light dusting of hair tickled my fingers as I trailed over his chest, then I trailed my way up to his jawline. Case peered down at me, and I was expecting a smile. Not the creased brows that chased away the tiredness from his green eyes.

My eyes traveled between his as I tried to think of where we went from here. I was scared to go forward, but we couldn't go back. Not when we had come so far. I settled my gaze on his chest and snuggled closer. "What are we, Case?"

He dragged his fingers under my shirt and over my skin. They traced light circles that made me melt into him even more. When he spoke, his voice was lower, like he was as nervous as I was. "We can be whatever you want, sunshine. If you want last night to be a one-time thing, that's fine. But listen Basil–" I looked up at him and was caught up in the way he looked at me. His eyes spoke in ways he'd never been able to out loud. He moved a hand to cup my jaw and held me there. "I don't care what you want us to be. So long as I'm with you, I'm happy. And I hope you're happy, too."

I stared at him as his words sank in, but the way his voice tightened caught my attention. I didn't want him to think I was anything *but* happy. Was I terrified? Sure. But not for reasons he might think.

I was terrified because all these feelings I had for him were ones I'd been taught to run from. Terrified because I had never felt such comfort with anyone else, and terrified because that same feeling was the only thing keeping me from him.

With a soft smile, I held his gaze, and I hoped he heard the honesty in my words. "There's a lot I don't know, Case. But, being right here–with you? It feels right. I haven't been this happy in a long time."

The relief that overcame Case was palpable as he let out a heavy breath and grinned, promising a dimple that never followed through. "Me too."

Without dropping my smile, I untangled myself from Case and sat on the edge of the bed. I stretched my arms over my head, and the action pulled the shirt up and I was suddenly aware of just how exposed I was. The hairs on my neck stood up as I felt Case's heated stare. I cleared my throat and dropped my hands as I glanced at the clock. I stood to face him, and couldn't look away.

He looked so comfortable laying there, with the comforter bundled around his waist and his hair a mess. My body warmed under his lazy gaze. "I'm going to grab some coffee. Do you want to come?"

"Sure." He lifted the blanket, and my mind turned to mush as my eyes dragged over him. Case stopped moving and when I looked at him, I blushed for a different reason. The way his eyes held mine at me had heat pooling in my stomach, and I was torn between getting coffee and jumping back into bed.

"Careful, sunshine. I can't have you testing me this early in the morning."

I quickly grabbed my bag, headed to the bathroom, and tried to control my breathing.

As I got ready, I made sure to put on enough layers. Then Case checked me when I met him downstairs in the lobby. He tugged on the collar of my jacket and pulled me closer so he could run his hands over my arms. Once he was sure I wouldn't freeze on him again, he gestured toward the door and we left.

After a short drive to the main street, we parked and walked to the first coffee shop we saw. We walked through the café door and I noticed two things; the first was all the antique decor that lined the walls. The second was how busy it was. Almost everyone inside was dressed in snow pants and goggles. As if they were here to grab something quick before they headed up to the ski resort.

"I'm going to the bathroom, be right back." Case waited until I nodded before he pushed his way through the crowd.

As I waited for him to come back, I recognized my family members who filed into the café. Distant cousins, aunts, and uncles. People I never had the chance to have a relationship with. I met most of them yesterday, and they all gave polite nods when we made eye contact before going about their business. A man walked up to me then. He wore a knit beanie and a thick wool sweater, and the way the corners of his eyes creased when he smiled told me he was older.

He cleared his throat. "Can I buy you a coffee?"

"Uh—"

"Sorry. I hope it's not too forward. I saw you in line and just—I had to ask you."

I glanced behind him just as Case came into view, and I gave him a polite smile. "I'm flattered, but no thank you," I said. The man nodded with a small smile and walked to the back of the line. Case watched the man as he came to stand next to me. Then he placed a hand on my waist and pulled me to his side.

I hid my smirk until we got to the counter and ordered. Case led me to the end of the counter with his hand on my back and kept it there while we waited. I traced the floral design that was engraved on the side of the counter, and when I looked up, I caught him staring at the man from earlier. I tapped his chest to earn his attention.

"You're not jealous, are you?" I asked as I tried to hide the smile that tugged on my lips.

Case rolled his eyes, and with a smirk, pulled me closer to him. "Not jealous, just—I don't want to share."

I smiled into his chest, and a moment later our names were called. We grabbed the cups and started heading to the door. It opened as I reached for the handle, and I almost collided with a stunning woman. She looked to be around my mom's age, but this woman looked softer.

Her tight brown curls framed her face, and the green jacket she wore made her stunning blue eyes pop. We stared at each other, and when I realized people were staring at us—I knew.

This was the woman my dad was marrying.

I felt like air had been stolen from my lungs as we stared at one another, Case leaned in and concern laced his voice. "Basil?"

"Excuse me," I said to the woman before I grabbed Case's hand and led him out of the café. My mind spiraled as we walked to the car. My mother described the woman who ruined her marriage as a horrible person. Someone whose only goal in life was to ruin others, no matter the cost. But that wasn't who I ran into.

It didn't take much to recognize how kind she was, and it ruined another construct Mom built for me. How many more would come crumbling down?

Case kept a gentle hand on my leg as we drove back to the hotel, and neither of us spoke as my mind tried to work itself out. After we parked and walked inside, he turned on the fireplace and joined me on the bed. I sipped my coffee and closed my eyes.

"Do you want to talk about it?" he asked.

I rested my head on his shoulder. "Not right now. Want to watch a movie instead?"

"Sure, we've got some time. Which one?" he asked as he reached for the remote.

I sipped my drink again before answering. "Doesn't matter, just something to pass the time."

Case clicked through the channels until he found an old Western movie. We settled back onto the bed, and he pulled me onto his chest. As I laid there with Case, I realized something. Somewhere between the soft touches, the gentle words, and the acts of kindness during anger, something happened.

The lies my mother led me to believe had started to crumble. And the one I believed the longest—about love leading to heartache–had crumbled a long time ago.

basil

The first time I saw Case in a suit, he was doing an interview. I was at home, ready to change the channel, when he, Townes, Scottie, and the rest of the team walked up on stage and sat at a long table. Townes still looked intimidating despite his tattoos being covered, Scottie looked confident, and Case—Case looked like he was the universe's favorite.

My ovaries still hadn't recovered from that one instance, and now they were about to explode again from seeing it in person.

When I walked out of the bathroom, I stopped. Case stood in front of the mirror and was adjusting his tie. I couldn't bring myself to blink, move closer, or even breathe correctly until he turned his head. He moved from the mirror and started closing the distance between us. His eyes dragged up my body with every step until he was in front of me, and then his eyes were on mine.

My hair fell in loose curls over the dress I found on clearance. The dark blue satin fabric clung to my body. The neckline dipped to the space between my breasts, and

I had never felt more self-conscious about their smaller size until now.

Case's voice was rough when he finally spoke. "Wow. Basil, you're," his eyes dragged over me once again and he let out a shuttered breath, "exquisite."

I blushed under his stare, but smiled and smoothed the fabric down my sides. "Come on, we don't want to be late."

"*You* don't want to be late," Case teased as he winked and grabbed my jacket before he helped me put it on. Once we were both ready, we walked to the car and admired how nice everyone looked as we all left the hotel. The ride to the venue was twenty-minutes, and I spent the entire time being eaten up by nerves. Aside from yesterday, my dad and I hadn't spoken. I didn't know what to expect from him tonight. Was he going to ignore me like he had done the past ten years? Was I here so he could make a statement?

The questions continued even as we pulled into the church parking lot. Case opened my door and held my hand as I steadied a heel on the gravel. Then he laced our fingers together before we walked inside. The white vaulted ceilings made the space feel even more massive. Light pink roses lined the aisle that led up to an arch on the stage. The nerves finally made their way into my throat, and I tore my hand from Case's. His face was soft as he looked at me.

He took a step closer and leaned in. "We can still leave if you want, sunshine. Just say the word."

"No, it's okay," I said as I looked around the room again. Everyone was taking their seats as we walked around to find ours.

My Uncle Ronald stopped us with a smile. "Your seats are in the front row."

Case and I thanked him before we exchanged confused looks. We found two small nameplates on the dark wood seats, one for each of us. I did my best to keep my face neutral as I sat down, but Case had to place a hand on my leg to keep it from moving. I didn't know why my dad wanted us sitting in the front, but that was another thing I could ask him later.

The ceremony started soon after we sat down. Music filled the room and everyone stood. Case held my hand as we watched all the people walk down the aisle.

My father.

The bridal party.

The ring bearer and the flower girl.

Then finally, the woman my dad was marrying. She looked more beautiful than she did this morning, in her ballroom-style wedding gown. I tracked every movement as she walked up to my father and watched as she smiled. It was the kind that was unbashful and overwhelmed with happiness. I couldn't help but smile along with her, but it wasn't a reaction to her happiness. It was realizing that, *that* was how I looked when I was with Case.

He must have noticed it, too. Because his hands tightened around my leg, and he held on throughout the entire ceremony. A constant, gentle reminder that he was there if I needed him.

———

The dance floor was filled with people, all of whom had a drink in hand.

My father and his new wife were sitting at their table, talking with everyone who came up and gave their congratulations. Meanwhile, I had been waiting for an opening to say goodnight and leave with Case. He had excused himself a few minutes ago to get us some drinks, and I didn't notice my father walk up until he spoke.

"Hi," he said before he gestured to the empty seat next to me. "May I?"

I nodded and watched him sit and lean back in the chair. He tapped the table, and I recognized the look on his face—he was deep in thought. I only recognized it because it was the same face I made. "Are you having fun?" he asked, and again, I nodded because I didn't know what to say to him.

A wedding reception wasn't the ideal place to have a heart-to-heart with your estranged father. Or so I thought. He leveled me with a stare, and I peered into eyes much like my own when he said. "I know this isn't the best time, but I need to know what your mother told you after I left."

"Not wasting any time, huh?" I asked, trying to lighten my mood.

My father chuckled and shook his head. "I've wasted enough of it, Basil, and I'm done."

I nodded, surprised by his admission, and chewed on my bottom lip. "She told me you cheated, and that was really it," I said. There were plenty of times growing up when I would beg for more information, but she never said anything.

The music grew louder, and my father leaned over the table. "Let's talk somewhere else."

Without waiting for an answer, he stood and started walking toward the patio. I grabbed my jacket and followed him. Once we were outside, he leaned against the railing and looked out at the view. Lights from the town at the bottom of the mountain danced in the dark, and I watched my breath fog when I sighed. It felt nice out here.

My father's face was tense when he spoke again. "Basil, you should know your mother and I—we had already filed for divorce before I left."

"What?" I asked as I felt the blood drain from my body. That wasn't what she told me, not even close. I didn't even know divorce was part of the equation. Sure, there were days they weren't happy. But I didn't think it was that bad. He nodded, but kept his focus on the town.

"Your mother had a lot of dreams, Basil, and she accomplished a lot of them. But starting a family as young as we did was not one of them. Things were fine for a few years, but then something happened. I don't know who changed first. All I know is I was waking up and looking at a woman I didn't know anymore." He looked at me then, and his voice became solemn when he continued. "I've missed you so much, Basil, and I need you to know I never stopped trying to be in your life."

An involuntary scoff came out of me, and my jaw dropped. "I think you and I remember things very differently. You stopped calling when I got to middle school."

He rubbed his hands over his face, and the look he gave me was that of complete defeat. "When your mother and I split, we didn't have any sort of court agreement. Which I was fine with. We both wanted what was best for you. But then one day your mother demanded I start paying child support." I didn't like the dark turn his voice took, but I waited anyway. "Basil. Your mother went behind my back and took me to court for custody. She claimed that I never paid child support and wasn't in your life. The judge granted her full custody. That's why I lost contact with you."

I knew my mom could be a lot to handle at times, and made some questionable decisions. But I never imagined she could do something so cruel. I shook my head, and a sob escaped. He reached for my hand, and I didn't pull away when he touched me. "You deserve to know the truth, Basil, and I want you to know that I love you. That didn't change when your mom cut me off."

All I could do was nod when he squeezed my hand in

assurance. Someone came up behind us and my father turned to face them.

"Ah, you must be Case," he held out a hand, "Otto."

I kept my gaze forward even as my father turned back to me. He held out a hand and dropped it a moment later. "Thank you for coming, Basil. I—I'll talk to you later. If you'd like," he said.

Then my dad looked between us before he walked back inside. I wasn't alone for even a second before Case wrapped his arms around my shoulders and pulled me into a hug.

He held me as I fell apart. I didn't understand how my own mother could lie to me my entire childhood. She took away my ability to believe in things that made life wonderful. But if there was anything I knew for certain, it was that she would never get the chance to do it again. Case rested his head on mine and asked, "What do you wanna do?"

I didn't say the first thing that came to mind, so I went with the second thing.

"Can we leave? Maybe get some ice cream?"

Case nodded before placing a gentle yet hesitant kiss on the top of my head. "Of course."

So, with only a glance at my father, we walked to the car and headed back to town. Case stopped at the first store he found, and we walked inside. The people that were out gave us curious glances, whether because of our attire or because an NHL hockey captain was walking around their local grocery store, I wasn't sure. We walked down the freezer aisle and each picked our flavors; mint chocolate chip for me, and rocky road for Case.

After we paid, we got back in the car and drove the short distance back to the hotel. I couldn't help but think things over during the drive, mostly about how I didn't realize just how much my mom molded me to be like her. Not in every way, but in the ways that mattered—at least to me. I never questioned her when she swore off men and suggested I do the same. Never batted an eye when she poked me with her sharp words and never told her to stop.

The one thing that kept tugging in my mind, though—was how I was constantly asking Case to be honest with me—when I couldn't even be honest with myself. It wasn't fair for me to ask him for more than what I was willing to give, and it stopped now.

I needed to be honest with him.

Case parked in the empty parking lot and opened my door. But this time, I didn't take his hand when he offered it. Instead—with determination fueling my body—I walked past him and to the doors. He followed me and waited as I tried to open the door with shaky hands. Once the door beeped, I marched inside. Case turned on the fireplace at the same time I whirled around and opened my mouth to speak. The three words flew out before I could stop them.

"I love you."

case

I love you.

I blinked and wondered if my previous head injuries had finally caught up to me. But no, Basil stood there and looked just as surprised as I was by her words. Her eyes were glassy, and her bottom lip trembled as she tried to hold herself together. I closed the distance between us and dragged her to the bed. I grabbed our ice cream from the bag and opened hers before I handed it to her. The way her breaths came in fast, unsteady bursts caused me to place a hand on her thigh.

When she controlled her breathing, she started taking small bites.

The crackling of the fireplace filled the silence while we ate. Basil was halfway done with her ice cream before she took a deep breath. "When I was younger, I remember seeing how my parents looked at each other. Like they hung the moon and the stars the other one looked at. So, when my dad left, and I saw my mom fall apart—I thought it was safer to swear it off." Basil stabbed her spoon into the container and took a bite big enough to give her a brain freeze. Which—it did. I rubbed my hand over her leg as her nose scrunched and she shook her head.

"It's cold."

"It's ice cream."

Basil hummed and took another bite, but this time, she kept her eyes on the fireplace. She shook her head. "It was stupid of me to think like that—that just because she's cynical about love that I had to be too. She made me think love was fragile, and when it broke, it ripped you apart in the process. I used to think, 'How could anyone want to open themselves up to that kind of pain?' It didn't make sense for a long time." She set the ice cream on the ground and shifted until she was facing me. "But then you came along."

I raised a brow and smirked. "Me?"

"Yeah, you. I was perfectly happy with where I was in life, but you managed to make it better. And—I realized I wasn't being fair to you, Case."

"What do you mean?" I asked.

Basil lowered her head and stared into her lap as she continued. "I feel like I was asking a lot of you. Asking you to tell me when things were bothering you, but I wasn't ready to do the same. And I don't want to be the one to ask more than what I'm willing to give." When she raised her head, I saw a stray tear trail down her flushed cheeks. Shit, I hated seeing her cry. "And I—I'm really sorry, Case."

I grabbed her cheeks and placed a kiss on her forehead before peering into her eyes again. "You have nothing to be sorry for, Basil?"

"Yes, I do. I'm sorry I wasn't honest with you sooner about how I feel. And for blowing up about the whole Aubrey thing. I think it was more of a reaction to my mom comparing me to a person I thought was horrible. I shouldn't have done that."

My thumb caught another tear and wiped it away. "Those are some pretty big feelings, Basil. But do you want to know something?"

"What?"

I leaned in and pressed my forehead to hers. "I would give you anything you asked. Even if you never told me any of this, I would still do it. I wasn't going anywhere."

"You weren't?" she asked in a quiet voice.

"Basil, I was ready to live my entire life being nothing more than your friend. I wasn't going to love you any less if you didn't feel the same way. You're too important to me," I said, and I watched as her eyes widened.

When she spoke, it came out as a whisper, like she was repeating a secret. "You love me?"

I wiped away another tear. "Basil, I fell for you that day you came into my life, and haven't bothered to stop."

She sniffled and let out a strangled cough. "Fuck, I didn't want to cry." Basil moved to wipe her cheeks, but I caught her hands and pinned them to her side. Then, with feather-light pressure, I leaned in and kissed them away. Basil softened under me and arched her chest up into me. I groaned and kissed down until I hovered an inch above her lips.

"You've had a long night Basil," I said, as I tried to hold myself back.

She let out a shaky breath. "Do you not want to?" Her voice was smaller than before, and I moved one of her hands to place it on my cock. She sucked in a breath and I started kissing her neck.

"Listen to me," I said as soon as I reached her ear. "Fucking you is *all* I want to do. But I'm trying my damnedest to be a gentleman right now. We can go to bed, and you can sleep on it, sunshine. We don't have to do anything you don't want to."

I pulled away to find her chest was as red as her cheeks. Her breathing came in heavy pants as her gaze held mine, and we stared at each other for a moment before she stood. She took a few steps toward the mirror. "You're right, we should go to bed."

My pants tightened even more as I watched Basil collect her hair over a shoulder. Her bare skin tempted me, even in the fire-lit room. She looked at me through the reflection and raised a brow.

"Can you help me unzip?"

I stood and walked over to her, and with each step, I committed her to memory. But while she was beautiful in that dress, it didn't compare to how breathtaking she was all the time. I came up behind her and took in every inch of precious skin that was exposed as I unzipped the dress. Basil watched me in the mirror, her eyes full of heat as I worked the zipper down to her lower back. She shuddered when I caressed the skin there before I moved my hands to the straps of her dress. I ran my finger under the thin fabric and lowered my head to place a kiss on her shoulder.

"This dress," I said as I dropped the flimsy fabric to rest over her shoulder. I moved my hands to her waist. "Is going to haunt my dreams. I wanted to rip it off you when you came out of that bathroom."

She arched against me as I moved my hand to her stomach. "You can rip it off now."

"Oh, I'm not going to do that, pretty girl. It's too nice for that," I said as I moved my hand up to cup her breast. Basil let out a soft moan and sunk back into me. *Perfect*, she was so fucking perfect. "Take it off," I told her before I removed my hands. She wasted no time stripping the dress, leaving her only in a lacy bra and a thong to match. My hands clenched and unclenched with indecision. Where to touch her, where to kiss her—fuck—where to start?

Before I could decide, Basil turned around and held my gaze as she tilted her chin.

"Case," she said.

The word left her lips on a plea, but I needed to hear the words.

"I need you to kiss me."

I gripped the back of her head and pulled her into me. I moaned into her before I nipped her bottom lip with my teeth. Basil opened her mouth, and I took my time licking every inch I could reach. She stumbled backward, so I bent down, hooked my hands under her ass, and lifted her. She wrapped her arms around my neck as I walked us back to the bed. I laid Basil down, and she hissed when I ran my hand over her bra.

"Case—" she breathed out. I angled my knee between her legs before I started kissing my way down her neck. I took my time licking and sucking on her sensitive skin. Basil bucked her hips against me when I nipped at her collarbone, and I chuckled.

"Do you know how many times I've thought of this?" I asked as I placed a kiss just above the fabric of her bra. "You writhing under me? While I take my time worshiping every inch of you." I hooked a finger over the material and pulled it down, exposing her to me. "Fuck. You're perfect Basil," I said before I flicked my tongue against her nipple, and I reveled in the way Basil writhed under me when I took her in my mouth.

I took my time here too, licking and sucking as I fixated on Basil's sounds. When I was done, I moved to the other one, and Basil ran her hands through my hair. I groaned when she gripped and her nails scratched against my scalp. I released her nipple and kissed her again. Basil moved a hand and attempted to shove it between us.

I grasped her wrist and placed it above her head. "You need to use your words, sunshine. Tell me what you need."

She moaned again when I kissed my way down between her breasts and over her stomach.

"I need you to stop teasing me, Case," she said as I kissed the space between her belly button and the hemline of her underwear.

"I don't know what you're talking about," I said with a grin before I pulled down her underwear to place a kiss on her hipbone. Basil groaned and bucked her hips. I looked up and found her staring down at me with soft, pleading eyes.

Her breaths came faster now. "I need you to fuck me, Case."

Her underwear was off in one fell swoop before my name even left her mouth. I moved up to kiss her, and we were a clash of teeth, tongue, and hands as she worked the buttons of my shirt. Once that was off, I stood and took the rest of my suit off. Basil's eyes grew more heated when I stood before her and stroked myself. She bit her lip, and a second later I was on the bed again. I gripped her bare waist and pulled her toward me.

I aligned myself at her entrance and paused. "Shit, condom." I pulled back to reach for my pants on the floor, but Basil stopped me.

Her cheeks were red as she looked at me. "I—I'm on the pill. And I haven't been with anyone in a long time." Her voice came out soft, and I leaned down to kiss her again.

"It's been a while for me too, and I've been tested. Are you sure?"

She looked at me through her lashes and nodded.

I positioned myself again and held her gaze as I sank into her. My entire body tightened as pleasure ripped through me. She felt so *fucking* good. Basil moaned and raked her nails over my skin, my back, and my arms, as she tried to find a place to hold on to. I set my forehead on hers and asked, "Are you okay?"

"Yes, just—give me a second."

I did as she said and placed soft kisses over her face. When she nodded, I sank the rest of the way in, and when I bottomed out—Basil let out the most delicious moan that threatened to snap the only shred of control I had.

"Careful sunshine, make that sound again and I don't think I'll be able to hold back."

"I don't want you to hold back," she said as I eased myself back. My breath was shaky, and Basil spoke again as she held my gaze. "I want you to give me everything, Case."

A groan escaped me a second before I slammed back into her, and the sound she made went straight to my cock. I fucked her like she asked, harder and harder, until we were both seeing stars. "You sound so pretty, baby." Basil opened her eyes, and her mouth hung open as I leaned in. We both gasped at the new angle. "You're doing such a good job letting me fuck this little pussy."

"Case," Basil breathed, and I knew what she was going to say—because I was already close too.

"Use your words, baby girl," I said as I struggled to hold on. She deserved to finish first.

She deserved everything.

Basil tightened around me and grabbed the back of my neck before she pulled me closer and against my lips with a groan she said, "I'm coming." She shattered around me, and I followed soon after. We breathed heavily against each other as I slumped to her side and pulled her into me.

Basil turned in my arms and with a tired voice said, "I have to pee."

I kissed her forehead. "I'll be here."

I watched as she untangled herself from my arms and disappeared into the bathroom. I took the time to adjust the comforter and pillows, so that way when she came back, all I had to do was wrap my arms around her waist again. When she came back, she adjusted the blanket before she rested her head on the pillow.

"Hey, Basil?" I asked as I fought the sleep that threatened to take over. She hummed and tilted her head back slightly. I leaned in and kissed her temple. And in the softest words I could manage, told her. "I love you, too."

CHAPTER 35

basil

I woke up alone and found a note and some coffee sitting on the nightstand.

My body was blissfully sore as I rolled over and hugged the pillow closer to my body. My skin tingled as I remembered all the spots Case loved, and my heart wasn't in any better condition—Case loved me back. He whispered it before my eyes shut and I let sleep take me, but it was all I dreamed about.

I read the note again—he had to take a phone call with Jasmine because something important came up that couldn't wait until we got back to town. I didn't know how long he had been gone, or when he would be back. So, I sat up, stretched, and went to find some clothes. By the time I was dressed and had my teeth brushed, my phone rang. I picked up the video call and set my phone on the counter, where Hollis got the perfect view of the fancy bathroom.

"Okay, please tell me that's one of those hotels that give you robes. How soft are they?" she asked as she glanced around the room.

I chuckled and started braiding my hair. "Oddly enough, no robes. But there is a fireplace."

I wasn't sure what she saw on my face, but she placed her red pen on the table and raised a brow. "Well, that sounds romantic."

I blushed. "It is."

Hollis slammed her hands on the table and grinned. "I fucking knew it! Tell me everything, and I mean everything, B," she said. I finished tying off my hair and took the phone back to the bed.

"I'll tell you everything when I get home."

She snickered. "Too busy getting busy, huh? It's fine, I understand."

I rolled my eyes and pulled the blankets over me before I grabbed the coffee. It was the same thing I ordered yesterday—I didn't realize Case noticed. That realization made me smile as I stared down at the small heart that was drawn on the lid. When I glanced back at my phone, I noticed Hollis grinning bigger than before.

"What?"

"I'm happy for you. I don't know what you two talked about, but I'm glad you did. You deserve him, B."

I was glad too. I had never been that honest with anyone before, and it left my chest feeling lighter. While I didn't tell Hollis the conversation between Case and me—because I wanted that to stay ours—I did tell her about the conversation I had with my father. How my mom kept us apart and lied to us both. She and I would talk when I knew I wouldn't blow up on her.

By the time I finished telling Hollis, a shadow had dimmed her bright face. Her blonde brows were furrowed and her mouth sat in a tight line. She was pissed. "What's your mom's address again?"

"No, you're not stuffing her gutters with eggs again."

"I'm not going to do *that*. Besides, it didn't work well

the last time, anyway," she said with a shrug. I opened my mouth to say something, but the lock on the door beeped. I quickly said goodbye to Hollis and was on my feet before Case opened the door completely. When our eyes met, my heart stopped. How was it I found a man who loved me before I knew I felt the same way?

I smiled. "Hi."

Case grinned and my eyes darted to that dimple. It was the only thing I searched for to know if his smile was true. Case always gave me those dimpled grins.

"Hey," Case said before he took three steps and hauled me into him. His lips met mine, and I melted into his chest.

It was over quickly, and I whined when we broke apart. "I wasn't done," I pouted.

He placed a kiss on my forehead and said, "We can finish later. Because right now, we've got to go."

"Where are we going?" I asked as he pushed past me to grab my purse from the couch.

"Into town," he said as he slung my purse over his shoulder and grabbed my coat from the closet. Once I was bundled, he grabbed my hand and interlaced our fingers. Case led me out of the room and to the car. I laughed once we pulled out of the parking lot, and he tilted his head. That smile was still there.

"What?" he asked before he grabbed my hand again.

I shook my head. "You're just so excited. Mind telling me where we're going?"

"I'd rather it be a surprise."

My brows creased as he kissed the back of my hand. "I don't like surprises."

Case turned on the main road that led into town and looked at me again. "You'll like this one."

I sighed and attempted to bring my hand back so I could cross my arms, but Case held on and gave me an exaggerated look of shock. "Are you going to pout?" he asked. I tried my best not to smile as the sight of the town came into view.

"No," I told him.

"You'll like it, I promise. Now, let me hold your hand." He looked at me with soft eyes. "Please?"

I let my eyes roam over him before I placed my hand in his. "Fine."

Case grinned and turned his attention back to the road. A few minutes later, we parked in and started walking to the far side of town. The crowd grew until it was crowded enough that Case made me walk in front of him. He placed his hands on my waist and guided me through the bodies until we came across a clearing.

No—it wasn't a clearing. It was half of the main street that had been blocked off. Shops were closed, and the streets were full of giant cubes of ice. Well, some of them were cubes, others were being carved out by people on ladders. I tilted my head back to look at Case. "What is this?"

"An ice sculpting festival."

I stared forward and glanced up and down the street at the beautiful artwork that was being created. Some of the sculptures were finished, but they were too far away. I grabbed Case's hand and tried to pull him in the direction I wanted to go. But he didn't move, and when I turned to face him, I noticed his cheeks were flushed. And I didn't think it was from the cold weather. "Everything okay?"

"Yeah, I just—I want to make sure this is a proper date. Want to grab some food?"

If my heart could swell so much it would burst out of my chest—it would have happened by now. Honestly, it would have happened the night he gave me those jolly ranchers. I let Case take me to a nearby restaurant, where he had made reservations weeks before we were coming here. We enjoyed each other's company over giant bowls of soup. Once we were done, Case dragged me to a local bookstore, and I spent a half hour browsing the weathered shelves and piling books into Case's waiting hands.

By the time we left the bookstore, the weather had grown colder, and more people were walking up and down the sidewalk. All admiring the ice that was starting to take shape. We started on the farthest end of the street and worked our way up to where it was the busiest. We walked by cherubs, Vikings, flowers, and intricate architecture. I watched as the artist meticulously carved into the ice and wondered how someone could have that kind of vision.

To take a giant cube, see something beautiful, and make it come to life was amazing.

The only reason we left was because I started to shiver. Case gave me a few packets of hand warmers and led me to the car. Once his door was shut and we headed back to the hotel, he asked. "Did you have fun? Was it okay?"

I grinned so big my cheeks hurt. "Case, it was amazing. Seriously, we need to come back next year and do it again."

"I'll reserve our room for this time next year then," he said with a smile.

There was something about those words—next year. Anxiety dug its way through all the happiness I'd been feeling all day and planted itself in my chest. Would we really make it that far? Were we going to make it farther?

Or was our time fleeting?

I wasn't scared to love him anymore, but I was terrified of what came next. All the what ifs. Because if anything happened and I lost him—it would be for good. Case must have realized my mind was spiraling because he rested a hand on my leg and furrowed his brows.

"Talk to me."

I took a deep breath before I told him. "It scares me— just—a lot can happen in a year. I've never had a timeline longer than a month because back then—I knew things wouldn't work out." I waited anxiously as Case thought something over. It wasn't until we parked that he turned in his seat and grabbed my face in his hands. He leaned over and kissed me. I didn't think I'd ever get used to it. The way I felt with his lips on mine was—magical. Case smiled when we broke apart, and his gaze trailed over my face before landing on my own.

"We can come back next month. Next week? We'll start small, if that's what you're comfortable with."

I leaned in and gave him a quick kiss before I smiled. "Have I told you today that I love you?"

Case grinned and shut off the car, "Only in every smile I see when you look at me, sunshine. Come on, it's cold," he said before getting out of the car. I joined him and we walked in together. Once we were back in the room, his phone rang. He let out a groan and ran a hand over his face before looking at me. I don't know who was calling, but I knew Case didn't want to deal with it.

"I've got to take this. It shouldn't take very long. Be right back," he said before he walked out into the hallway. When the door clicked shut, I set my coat on the bed and turned on the fireplace.

After the room warmed up to a suitable temperature, I took off the other layers of clothes I was wearing and grabbed my toiletry bag. Might as well shower while I waited for Case to finish up his phone call.

basil

Case was lying on the bed when I came out of the bathroom, and the sight was nearly my undoing.

He wore a pair of black briefs and nothing else. The light from the fireplace cast shadows over him, but the light dipped and curved over every muscle it touched. Heat pooled in my stomach as my eyes traced over him. How could anyone be so beautiful? I took a step forward, and Case turned to face me. When he went to stand, I put my hand out, and it shook as I said, "No—jus—just lay back down. Please."

Without hesitation, Case rested back against the head-board and watched as I walked closer to him. His eyes heated with every step until the only thing I could see when I stood in front of him was how much he wanted me.

I swallowed back my nerves and kept my breath steady when I spoke. "Close your eyes," I said.

Case hesitated for a moment, taking his time to look over me once more before finally closing them. I lifted my hand and gently placed it on his face. I traced over the masculine angles, starting at the straight bridge of his nose, before I moved down to his jaw. My fingers backtracked to his thick brows; I took my time to memorize everything I could. Case shuddered when I ran my fingers through his hair, and he smiled as he leaned into my touch.

"What are you doing, sunshine?"

I had to think about it for a few minutes. His eyes were still closed when I started massaging his scalp. "You're always the first one to reach out for me. I want to make up for that."

"You don't need to do that, Basil," he said as he turned his head to place a kiss on the inside of my wrist.

I continued moving my fingers, scratching his scalp. "Shh, be quiet."

We sat there for another few minutes; me taking in all the small things about Case I hadn't noticed before. Like how light freckles scattered the tops of his cheekbones, and the small scar he had at the top of his forehead. I filed the information away and wondered how often Case had done this. What small, insignificant things had he taken and cherished in his mind?

Case's eyes opened as soon as my hands fell to his shoulders, and he gripped my thighs and tugged me closer.

"Tell me something," I said as I stared down at him. He tilted his head up and waited for me to keep going. "Is this how you thought we'd end up together?" I asked, my voice coming out as a whisper.

Case's grip tightened slightly as he smiled. "Not at all."

I crossed my arms behind his head and shrugged. "Enlighten me then. How'd you picture it?"

Something shifted in Case's eyes as he peered into mine, and I couldn't look away. He hummed, and I twirled a strand of his hair around my finger. I couldn't tell if he needed a haircut or not—I kind of liked the shaggy look he had going on. Case drummed his fingers along my inner thigh before he finally spoke.

"It was going to be after the wedding. I was going to invite you over, make you some brownies, and then I was going to list all the ways I started falling for you. How it started when we first met, and how I knew from that moment you were all I wanted. There were so many times I saw you reading, or coaching the kids, and all I wanted to do was put my arms around you. I would have told you—that—the fact you're so undeniably *you* is what drew me in. You don't shy away from your feelings, Basil, and I think that's beautiful. Then," his gaze dipped to my mouth, "I would have asked to kiss you."

My heart felt like it was being compressed in my chest from the love it was trying to contain. I licked my bottom lip as my breathing grew heavy. "And if I had said yes?"

Heat pooled in my stomach and traveled to the space between my legs. That sensation grew with every stroke of his fingers against my legs, and I wished I hadn't put on pants. I needed to feel him against my skin.

Case smirked, but it was dark and teasing as he stood. My chest was against his abdomen, and I tilted my head to hold his gaze. He cupped my cheek and leaned down to kiss me, but it was softer than all the others. Like he was showing me how our first kiss should have been if things had been different. I wrapped my hands around his wrists, a silent plea for more, but the kiss never changed. Case broke away, and his hooded eyes peered into mine.

"Then what?" I asked as I leaned closer.

Case trailed a hand until it rested at the nape of my neck. His voice came out rough when he spoke again. "Then I would have taken you on every surface in my house until you couldn't walk and still begged for more."

He kissed me then, and just like the times before, I sunk into his grasp. Letting him hold me as I got lost in the way his mouth moved with mine. It was dominating, desperate, and only intensified when he dragged his tongue on my bottom lip, asking for entrance I was never going to deny. Case's other hand fisted the bottom of my shirt while the other pulled my head back. He moved down to my neck and only pulled away to remove my shirt. "Go lay down," he commanded.

I sat on the bed and only leaned back when he crawled over me. He quickly removed his shirt before placing himself over my chest. I took shallow breaths as his own moved over my skin.

"Beautiful." A kiss on my collarbone.

"Magnificent." A kiss on my breast.

"You consume me, Basil." A kiss just below my belly button.

His hands rested on either side of me as he lazily traced his lips over my exposed skin, pausing every so often to kiss and gently suck. I didn't last long before I was squirming under him, needing him to touch me.

"Case, touch me." I arched my back under him and let out a whine when he pulled back an inch. "Please."

Slowly, he moved closer. Teasing the waistband of my pants with a promise. He whispered, "You're so pretty when you beg."

In one swift movement, my bra was being unclasped, and Case was on me. I gasped when his mouth enveloped my nipple. My skin prickled, and I moaned into the dark space above me. He released me, but only to switch to my other breast as his hand worked the fabric over my hips. Something came over me when he started trailing kisses down my body, his path clear. I sat up and got to my knees. Case raised a brow, but before he could ask any questions, I pulled at his pants and unbuckled the belt with steady fingers.

He stood and removed his pants before taking his place again in front of me. I held his gaze as I reached out and stroked his cock and reveled in the way his eyes rolled back. The sight of him writhing under my touch only emboldened me more, and I pushed on his chest until his head hit the pillow. This time, I took my time kissing down his body, over the light dusting of hair on his chest, to the muscles that lined his abdomen. When I looked up at him through my lashes, he was breathing heavily as he grasped the sheets with both hands.

I teased the head of his cock with a slow lick. "Fuck," he groaned, trying his best to not buck his hips. I licked him from base to tip before I finally wrapped my lips around his cock and took him as far as I could down my throat. Case's hand was in my hair then, grabbing and using it to guide me in the way he liked.

"You're doing so good, baby—fuck." He said as I sucked on my way back up. I flicked my tongue over the tip, and Case lost it. He pulled me up and flipped me over onto my stomach. Case took his time kissing his way up my spine. My skin prickled after every kiss, and I let my head fall into the comforter. Case's breath tickled the shell of my ear when he reached it. "Let me know if it's too much."

I nodded and felt him shift behind me. A second later, Case was pushing inside me and I moaned into the bed. Case laced his fingers through my hair and pulled my head up. "Let me hear those pretty noises," he said with a thrust. It didn't take long for him to find his rhythm, and I became a moaning mess under him.

"Fuck, baby. Do you know what you do to me?"

Pound.

"Know how many times I've fucked my hand? Wishing I was inside you?"

Pound.

"You take me so fucking good."

Pound.

I arched under him, angling him deeper. I tilted my head to the side so I could find his heated gaze. "You act like you're the only one who did that."

Case pulled out, but I didn't have time to miss the sensation. Because he was flipping me over and hauling my leg over his shoulder before he sheathed himself again. I kept my eyes on him as I continued in between moans. "I thought of you so much, Case. Fucked my fingers, wishing I had your cock inside me instead."

"Jesus," Case said under his breath a second before he picked up speed. His hands roamed my body, tracing my stomach, and pinching my nipples before he dropped one to rub my clit. Case swallowed my moan with a kiss as he continued to thrust in and out of me. I was burning. Overwhelmed by all the wonderful sensations. I'd had sex before, but it was nothing like this. With every thrust, kiss, touch—Case was engraving himself into my soul.

Every touch was filled with nothing but love, longing, and every other emotion I couldn't name at the moment.

Case rubbed my clit faster, and I gasped under him. "Case if you keep doing that I—"

"I know. You're going to come," he said as he kissed me. "I'm close too, pretty girl."

Case didn't relent in his touch or the way he fucked me. I clawed at his back as that heat grew and felt myself shatter when he nipped at my neck. Case followed soon after, muffling his moans with another soul-crushing kiss.

We laid there, exhausted and sweaty. Case rolled to the side and pulled me to his front. I couldn't help but smile into the pillow. He was so warm and comfortable. My eyes grew heavy, and I was a second away from letting sleep pull me under when Case moved. I looked at him with creased brows, but he chuckled and grabbed my hands.

"What are you doing?"

"I need to shower, and you're going to keep my company," he said before he dragged me into the bathroom. When he turned the water on and turned to face me, I crossed my arms and raised a brow. All he did was pull me in by the waist and wink. "I'm also not done with you yet."

case

"She wants to what?" Townes asked as he slammed a hand on the countertop.

Hayley looked at him with a raised brow and answered with so much sass I didn't understand how it fit inside her body. "Uncle T, remember what you told me when I get big feelings? Deep breaths," she said as she exaggerated deep breaths through her nose, and out her mouth. Townes pinched the bridge of his nose and did as she suggested.

"Does he always listen to you?" Basil asked Hayley— who sat in her lap while she colored in the new coloring book Scottie bought for her.

Hayley shrugged. "Nana said I'm wrapped around his finger."

Basil grinned and smoothed away a wild curl from Hayley's face. "It's the other way around girlie-pop."

I glanced around the room at everyone and sighed. We had a serious problem that needed to be dealt with, and we were already getting off track. When Basil and I got back from the wedding, Warner asked me to meet him as soon as I could. So, I spent a couple extra hours with Basil before I headed to the training center. The news he told me made my stomach churn, and I needed help from everyone to figure out what to do.

"Question," Basil said, raising her hand. We all looked at her. "Why haven't you sent a cease-and-desist letter? Shouldn't that have worked? I don't understand why Aubrey has this much power."

Townes leaned back and crossed his arms. "He has, but she's either ignored it or she never got it."

As aggravating as it was—he was right. I had Jasmine send many letters telling Aubrey to stop, not for my sake but for Basil's. When she told me, though, about the comments she read on public forums, it eased the guilt. I was willing to let it go, let the situation run its course until everyone forgot about it. But Aubrey had other ideas—sue me. According to her, because of the breakup—that she made public—she had been painted in a bad light by the public and had lost quite a few work opportunities.

I sighed and leaned my head against the fridge. "I don't either."

I had been going back and forth since I got the news about what to do. Sure, I could pay her the money and be rid of this whole thing, but I couldn't. That wasn't how I was raised, and I didn't want to use money to get rid of a problem like this—I was too honest for that.

"Something's not right about all of this," Townes said.

I nodded in agreement. "Yeah, I think so too. I'll get with Jasmine or something and see what she can find."

Townes and Hayley nodded, but when I glanced at Basil, she was chewing on the inside of her lip. I wanted to ask her what was on her mind, but her phone rang. She glanced at the caller ID and shot me a look I'd been waiting for since the wedding.

It was her mom.

Basil put on a fake smile and set Hayley to the side before stepping out to answer the call. Once she turned the corner, and Townes was sure she wouldn't hear, he spoke up. "Don't fuck that up, Case," he said as he pointed to where Basil disappeared.

I tilted my head toward him and smiled. "I already did, and she's still here."

Townes's mouth lifted a fraction of a centimeter, and I knew that was the most I'd get from him. He was happy for me, and I was grateful for it. Especially since I intended to hold on to Basil forever, she was mine, and I was going to spend every second I could cherishing her.

"She's super pretty. I like her," Hayley proclaimed from her coloring book.

I rustled her hair, and she tried to swat my hand away with a giggle. "Thanks, Haybug, I was waiting for your approval."

Basil walked around the corner, and the look on her face said everything. She hid her nerves behind a yawn. "Okay, well, I think it's time I head home for the night."

"Let me walk you out," I told her as I pushed off the counter. Basil said goodnight to Townes and Hayley, and I walked with her outside. She shivered against the wind, and I ran back inside to grab the hoodie I left on my chair.

"Thanks," she said as I helped lower it over her head.

I couldn't stop looking at her. Basil was beautiful—she always was—but seeing her wear my clothes just did something to me. I leaned in and gave her a quick kiss. She sighed against me but pushed me away before it could turn into more.

"What did your mom want?"

She rolled her eyes and fidgeted with the keys. "To know if I was done being dramatic and when I was coming over for dinner again."

"I don't like your mom," I said as I clenched my jaw.

Basil scoffed and glanced down. She kicked a stray rock that was on the driveway. "Yeah, I don't like her either sometimes." Her voice was thick, and she tried to hide it behind a weak chuckle. I put my finger under her chin and tilted her head until we were looking at each other.

"Do you want me to come with you?"

Panic settled into her features, and she fumbled with her words. "N—no, that's okay."

I smirked and leaned down. "Give me a date and I'll pick you up at six." I kissed her quickly before I stepped back. I still couldn't get enough of her. Basil stood there in a daze, but she didn't argue. Instead, she smiled before she turned around and walked toward her car. It wasn't until she was pulling out of the driveway that I went back inside, where Hayley was waiting for me.

She gave me a knowing smile before she skipped off while singing, "Casey and Basil sitting in a tree—" Her voice disappeared when she rounded the corner. And I couldn't help but laugh as I followed her.

———

Basil's leg was shaking the entire car.

I picked her up at six like I told her I would, and she spent the entire ride to her mom's being eaten by her nerves. We pulled into the driveway, and I set my hand down on her leg. She sent me an apologetic smile. "Sorry."

"Hey. There's nothing to apologize for." I cupped her cheek and ran my thumb across her smooth skin. "I'm here for you."

She closed her eyes as she nestled into my hand. Then she took a few steadying breaths before she nodded. I placed a chaste kiss on her cheek before I opened my door. Basil walked around and met me at the stairs that led to the door. She straightened and knocked three times before taking a small step back.

There was a steady thumping coming from inside, and I didn't realize it came from the dog until he ran out the door when it opened. The fat, black lab ran into Basil's legs and almost knocked her over. But she didn't mind. Instead, she giggled and bent down to pet the dog's stomach. When she was done, it walked over to me—giving me bruises on my legs from its tail as I scratched behind its ears.

"Oh, I am so sorry about him! Socks get inside." A cold voice called from the doorway.

I peered up and was surprised at what I saw. This woman wasn't anything like Basil, and as hard as I tried to find any similarities—I couldn't. She gave me a calculated smile and held out her hand. When I didn't take it, her smile turned cold.

"Jean," she said before turning around and waving a hand. "Come on in, you two!"

Basil spared me a glance before she walked ahead of me. After everything she had told me about her mom, I didn't feel like being very nice. The only reason I was here was to support Basil. Because her happiness and well-being were all I cared about. The lab, Socks, followed us into the dining room where the table was already set.

Jean looked at Basil with a tense smile as she sat down. "I wasn't expecting your boyfriend to join us, honey."

I placed my hand on Basil's leg under the table to reassure her. I wasn't going to let her mom hurt her again. Basil straightened in her seat and exhaled, then her attention shifted to her mom. When she spoke, her voice was steady. "Mom, I'm not here to make small talk."

"Oh? Are you here to apologize for running out after our last conversation? Because Basil, sweetie, that was incredibly rude, and I raised you better than that."

Basil's body stiffened under me, and I started rubbing small circles with my fingers. "If anyone was being rude, it was *you*."

Jean's demeanor finally shifted as shock crossed her face. "Excuse me?"

"I'm sick and tired of how you talk to me."

"Honey, I only say things that——"

Basil's face tightened, and she scoffed. "That what? Make you feel better about yourself?"

Jean reached across the table for Basil, her eyes darting between us. But Basil pulled her hand away and gripped mine under the table. Jean's brows creased as she tried to smile, but it was all wrong. Her control had slipped, and she knew it. She shot me a panicked look and cleared her throat before leaning back against her seat. "I don't think this is an appropriate conversation to have in front of company."

"Well, you were comfortable making assumptions about both of us last time I was here, so I don't see the problem, Mom." There was a heavy weight of silence that fell between the two women, but I made sure to continue those small circles. Jean opened her mouth to speak, but Basil spoke first. "Dad told me what you did."

The horror that crossed Jean's face was comical and Basil leaned forward, her voice shaky when she continued. "And I've been wracking my brain all weekend, trying to come up with an excuse for *you*. Because even though I never understood why you used your words to hurt me—I thought for the longest time it was you doing what was best for me. As your daughter. But I talked to Dad before we left and realized you did it to him, too. The one person you claimed to love wholly and without conditions—you pushed him away."

"Basil, I——"

"No. I'm talking," Basil said, the words snapping out of her. "I'm only here to tell you that you were wrong." She gripped my hand tighter. "You've always told me love would lead to heartache. But you didn't realize that whatever you felt when Dad left wasn't that—it was the loss of control. And you're about to experience it again."

Basil didn't wait for her mom to respond. Instead, she stood from the chair and hauled me toward the door. She gave Socks a scratch behind his ear and said a teary goodbye before walking through the threshold. I gripped her hand tighter before she got into the car, and grabbed it again when I was inside.

We pulled out of the driveway and Basil took in deep, steady breaths, trying to calm herself as the streetlights strobed across her face. When I pulled up to her apartment and shut the car off, I turned to face her. I wasn't going to ask if she was okay. Because I knew how hard it was for her to cut off ties with her mom—even though it was justified. So, I didn't say anything and instead, I got out so I could open her door. Then we walked inside and she sat on the couch while I made her tea.

"What do you want to do?" I asked her as I placed her mug on the coffee table. Basil shrugged and threw a thick blanket over my legs. I wrapped my arm around her waist and pulled her close.

She traced a finger over my chest and sighed. "Other than consider therapy? No clue."

"How about we watch a movie, relax, and start again tomorrow?"

Basil looked up at me, and I brushed away a strand of hair. "What about you, Case? With Aubrey, what's going to happen?"

"I have no idea. I'm still waiting for Jasmine to get back to me."

Basil let out a snort before she stilled. She stayed silent

long enough I began to worry. But before I could ask her what was going on, she was reaching for her phone. "What are you doing?"

She held the phone up to her ear and gave me a worried grin. "Hoping my relationship with my father isn't so bad that he's not willing to help me."

basil

I couldn't wait for the kids' game to be over, and not because it meant I got to hang out with Case before his game tonight. But because I could finally talk to him about what my dad said.

He invited me over for lunch earlier this week after our phone call two weeks ago, and I left with great news. I knew growing up that he worked a lot. He was often hired as a private investigator and had wicked computer skills that I guess were still put to use. So when I asked him if he could look into the whole Aubrey situation, he was more than happy to help.

He told me everything over soup and sandwiches at the spot we frequented when I was younger. I was happy to see it hadn't been shut down like my mom led me to believe.

The final buzzer rang, and the kids cheered on the ice before lining up to shake hands with the other team. It was bittersweet that the season was ending, and we only had a few more weeks together. Some had already signed up for next season, and some signed up to try another sport. I smiled as they made their way to the bench and sat to guzzle water.

"Amazing job today, guys!" I said as I placed my clipboard under my arm. The kids smiled as they nodded their heads. As they finished up and gathered their gear, I stood at the side to talk with some parents whose kids hadn't yet decided what they wanted to do. According to their kids, they were hesitant because they were aging out of my group. I wouldn't be their coach next season and it was discouraging. While I more than appreciated they were comfortable with me, I encouraged the parents that the other coaches were just as—if not more—qualified than I was.

Once our conversation ended, I turned around and stopped when I saw Mr. Clein sauntering over. The last time we talked was when he accused me of being the reason Case was removed from the team. Which, as I found out, was the decision of Coach Warner. He was concerned about the publicity Case was getting and didn't want that attention directed at me or the training center.

I hauled my bag over my shoulder and met the man with a leveled stare. "Was there something you needed, Mr. Clein?"

"Yes," he said, crossing his arms. "I've been trying to understand why Mr. Whitlock was removed from the team. His coach and the program director haven't said anything, and if you value your job, then you'll tell me."

I stared at him in shock. When did I start letting people talk to me like this? Sure, Mr. Clein had always had his… edges. But who did he think he was bossing me around like I worked for him? The season was almost over—I didn't care about hurting feelings anymore.

"That sounds like a threat," I told him, tightening my grip on the strap of my bag. He adjusted his stupid cuff links before he put his hands in his pocket.

"Because it is. I find you incompetent and you blew your only shot at the help you so desperately need. So, I insist you start talking so Mr. Whitlock, or anyone else for that matter, can help you."

I felt like a fish with how many times my mouth opened and closed as I searched for a response. Mr. Clein chuckled and turned around. But at the last second, I ran to his front. Blocking him from leaving. He peered down at me and all I saw was red.

"How fucking dare you," I stated. My hand had started to hurt because of how tight my grip was. Mr. Clein blinked and opened his mouth to say something, but I wouldn't let him. "Since the day we met, you've given me shit for no reason. You've always complained about what you think I'm doing wrong, and looking down your nose at me because you don't think I'm good enough."

"Ms. Andrews—" Mr. Clein started.

"Coach. I am Coach Andrews to you." I took in a deep breath to calm myself. "This team is successful because I do a damn good job coaching these kids. They're successful because they work as a team and help each other every time they're on the ice. And having Case on this team did nothing but give them more confidence, which hasn't been lacking since he left."

I dropped my bag and slung it over my opposite shoulder as I turned to leave. I called behind me as I walked away. "Talk to whoever will make you feel better. Have a good weekend."

Thankfully, most of the kids and their parents had already left, so I could stomp out to my car without garnering any looks. I threw my bag into the passenger seat and smacked my steering wheel. My phone rang as I turned on the car, and I had to take a few more calming breaths before answering.

"Hi, Dad."

"Hey, how are you?" he asked. I leaned my head back and sighed. "That bad, huh? You guys lose?"

I shook my head and rubbed my hands over my eyes. "No, we won. Just dealing with parents can be really aggravating sometimes. But that's a conversation for a different day. What's up?" I asked as I pulled out of the parking lot and headed home.

"Right," he said before clearing his throat. "I was calling about the tickets."

"Oh, are you and Erin not able to make it?" I asked. It was hard to hide my disappointment. I was looking forward to seeing them at the game tonight.

"That's not it. I was just wondering if you wanted us to pay you back for them. I know they can get quite expensive."

I sighed and smiled to myself. "No, it's fine. Case has it taken care of."

A beat of silence passed between us, and the question that's been itching my brain since the wedding came out. "Um, Dad?"

"Yes?" He sounded so sincere, and memories from when I was younger came to mind. When he and I would make breakfast on Sunday mornings, when he helped me learn to sew—and I kept pricking my finger. My eyes watered as I remembered everything and then grew jealous of the time we lost because of the one person who was supposed to love us both unconditionally.

"I was curious—about Erin. When did you two meet?"

The sound of Dad's chuckle was accompanied by rustling like he was sitting down. "If you're wondering if she was the one I left your mother for, then the answer is no."

I don't know why I was relieved by that, but I was.

"It took me a long time to find her, actually. I kept looking for what I had with your mother and when I found it—well—those relationships never lasted." His voice turned solemn when he spoke, and I kept quiet as I nodded along. It made sense—when you live with that kind of toxicity for so long, it's all you know. I was glad he managed to get out of that cycle.

"Then I found Erin, and it took some getting used to Basil. I won't lie. I wasn't used to feeling safe with someone. But she showed me the kind of love I deserved every day for the past four years." His next sentence came out softer. "She looked at me the same way I see Case look at you, Basil. I hope you know how lucky you are, hon."

Shit—I was crying. I wiped away a tear as I pulled into my parking spot and tried to keep my voice from breaking when I spoke. "Yeah, I know Dad."

"Okay, well," He cleared his own throat and I swore I heard a sniffle—good to know where I got my sensitive side from. "I'll see you tonight."

"Yeah, see you tonight," I said before hanging up, only to stay in my car a few minutes longer. Tonight was going to be—a lot—and I needed to mentally prepare myself for it. I got out of my car knowing one thing and one thing only—if I was brave enough to jab a hockey captain in the chest, then I was brave enough to face a fake ex-girlfriend.

A few hours later, Hollis and I walked into the arena, and we immediately found my dad and Erin. They wore matching jerseys and Erin waved at us—aggressively. I laughed and looped my free arm through Hollis's.

"Are they even hockey fans?" Hollis asked as we walked closer.

I simply shrugged and kept my attention on the stairs. "No clue, but who's going to turn down free hockey tickets?"

Hollis raised a brow. "You did. Well, you tried the first time Case got tickets."

I rolled my eyes playfully and walked down the last two steps before we reached our seats. Erin took the popcorn from my hands and gave them to my dad before she wrapped me in a tight hug. I tensed under her, but I didn't think she noticed. Because her smile was just as bright when she pulled away as it was when she went in for the hug.

"Basil, these seats are *amazing*! Thank you so much for inviting us," she said as she let me go.

I smiled and sat in my seat. "Of course, though—are you a hockey fan?" I asked as I reached into the popcorn container. Hollis had already set her feet on the sideboard and was watching the guys do their pre-game stretches.

Erin nodded. "Used to watch it with my parents growing up. I've been trying to get your dad interested, but he's more of a football guy," she said with a teasing frown.

Dad threw his hands up in surrender, and Erin placed a kiss on his cheek. I was so caught up in watching them that I didn't notice the tapping on the glass. Case was on the other side and beamed when I finally looked at him. He didn't stay long. Scottie yelled something at him from where he was on the ice. So Case placed a gloved hand over his heart two times before he skated away. Two times for the two-syllable word he loved to call me.

Sunshine. The gesture warmed my heart, and I felt my cheeks heat.

Once he reached Scottie, I let my eyes wander around the arena. They stopped when they found Aubrey. She sat front and center and was chatting with a player from the other team.

My heart started beating faster, and my hands were sweating. I elbowed Hollis in her side and she tore her gaze away from whoever she was looking at on the ice and whirled her head around. "What is it with you jabbing me tonight?"

"Look," I said, pointing at where Aubrey sat. "Found her. Should we wait until she goes to the bathroom and follow her or something?"

Hollis raised a brow. "You said you had a plan."

I waved a hand. "Eh, I had half a plan," I said as I tried to figure out how this was going to work. Hollis and I needed to get her somewhere where there weren't many people. Somewhere she wouldn't feel pressured to lie to any listening ears. I chewed on my inner cheek in between sips of beer.

It would have to be after halftime when everyone was here to catch the last half of the game. That's when I'd get her. So, I sat back in my seat and divided my attention between her and the ice. This game was brutal, just like it was the last time the Peaks played Atlanta. When Hollis and I watched that game in my living room, I kept wincing anytime Scottie or Case were smashed into the sideboards. I knew they had pads and stuff on, but still—it only protected them so much.

Seeing it in person wasn't any better. I cringed every time someone was hit, then yelled extra loud when they had to sit in the penalty box. The second half wasn't any better, and I was so caught up in the action that I almost missed Aubrey walking through the crowd of people—heading to the doors. I turned on Hollis and tugged on her arm.

"What?" she asked, her eyes wide with excitement.

"Aubrey. Let's go," I said before I turned to my dad and Erin to excuse ourselves. Then, we made our way past the bodies of people to catch up with her. This thing she was going to end.

Now.

basil

Hollis and I caught Aubrey at the concession stand. She had just grabbed her food and was walking back when she spotted us. Her eyes narrowed a split second before she slipped on a mask of annoyance. There weren't many people out here, but she spoke like someone was watching.

"Haven't you caused enough trouble?" she asked as she shifted her weight to one side, popping a hip. My eyes scanned over her and I took in how *polished* she seemed. Her hair was slicked back into a perfect ponytail, and it looked exceptionally healthy for how blonde it was. Her skin was free from any imperfections, and her figure—well —she was a sports model for a reason.

I could see why she and Case were labeled a power couple. Because they complimented each other well. But she never wanted anything more than the opportunities he gave her. I watched Hollis pull her phone from her pocket, and I stood straighter as I stared at Aubrey.

I could do this.

"I think you're the one who's caused problems, not me."

The laugh she let out echoed around us. "Me? I'm not the one who destroyed a happy relationship, babe."

My skin crawled, but I kept my face neutral as I tilted my head and creased my brows. "A relationship that wasn't even real?" I asked, and she stood to her full height and peered down at me with her mouth in a tight line. A few people walked past us, but they didn't look.

Her next words came out sharp. "I don't know what you've been told, but that relationship was the realest thing I'd ever experienced. And you ruined it."

"Okay look—I get it. You're upset, but Case and I weren't together while you guys were doing your thing. We just worked together, that's literally it," I said, holding up my hands. More people trickled out of the arena doors, and I knew my time was fleeting. "But all the shit you pulled? Those articles? The money? It's too much."

Aubrey's brows pulled tight, and her shoulders fell. "What do you mean '*those*' articles?"

"The ones you kept encouraging? Interviews about your failed relationship and how it was my fault?"

I watched as Aubrey took a step back. She shook her head as her eyes darted across the floor.

"And there's the fact you're trying to sue him—like he's the reason your career has gone down the drain," I said.

Aubrey held up a manicured finger and looked at me with a level of confusion I was hoping to see. "Hold on, I'm still trying to wrap my head around the fact that there's more than one article. I only brought it up one time."

"But you kept telling Case—"

"Yeah, I was desperate and begging, but that was it."

A small crowd had formed now, but I had to keep going. While I didn't like Aubrey, it wasn't fair to keep her in the dark when she was involved in this whole thing. I tilted my head and put my hands in my pocket, my fingers rubbing on the edges of the folded paper that was in my pocket. "You know Jasmine? The team's PR manager?"

She looked more confused now. "Yeah? What does she have to do with anything?"

"A lot actually," I said before I took out the paper and handed it to her. Her skepticism was overwhelming, but she grabbed the paper, anyway. She opened it and began reading.

"What is this?" she asked as she held out the paper.

I raised a brow and smirked. "How about we talk about this with everyone? The game's about over. Follow me."

I turned around and looped my arm with Hollis's as we walked toward the team's locker room. Aubrey took a minute before she followed us, and she kept her distance. We made it past security and waited outside the locker room doors. The game had just finished by the time we got there—so it was only a matter of time before we'd see the team. What I wasn't expecting, though, was to see Jasmine. She walked toward the locker rooms with her head down at her phone.

"Jazz?" Aubrey asked as Jasmine bulldozed past her.

She stopped her in tracks and turned on her heels with a nervous smile. "Aubs? What are you doing back here?"

Aubrey stepped away when Jasmine moved in for a hug. "I could ask you the same thing. Aren't you supposed to be at some dinner thing? That's what you said when I invited you." While Aubrey kept her voice level, I could hear her anger steadily rising.

Jasmine stepped back and shook her head. "It ended early, so I figured I'd stop by and see how the game went."

Hollis leaned in and whispered, "I'll be out front, and I'll text you the file just in case you need it."

I nodded, and no one paid attention to her as she walked off.

"Hm," Aubrey said as she bit the inside of her cheek. Jasmine nodded and turned back around, unsure of what else to say. But when she saw me, she stopped.

"Hi, I don't think we've officially met. I'm Basil," I said with a smile as I held out my hand.

Jasmine crossed her arms. "I know. You're the reason I've been so busy these past couple of months. I guess I should thank you for the job security."

"Oh, no need for thanks," I said, crossing my arms and mirroring her stance. "Considering you're the reason for your workload."

Jasmine narrowed her eyes, but as she opened her mouth to speak, she was interrupted.

"Ah! You're all here." A booming voice called from behind. We all looked at the end of the hallway to see Warner smiling and waving us over. The team came up behind him, but no one stopped as they headed our way. We walked against the athletes, and I was almost to their coach when I felt a gentle grip on my wrist. I looked up and found Case, sweaty and breathing hard. He glanced over to where Jasmine and Aubrey stood before meeting my eyes again.

"I'll be there in a few minutes."

I nodded and placed a chaste kiss on his cheek before I continued walking to Warner's side. He crossed his arms and looked at the three of us. "Well, this is going to be an interesting conversation. Come on."

He turned and led us down the hallway toward an empty office. I glanced at Jasmine, who was anxiously scratching the side of her thumb. She tossed a mocking smile when she noticed my stare, and I did nothing but face forward. Once we were all crammed into the office, Warner shut the door behind him and took a spot on the corner of the desk. His brown eyes dragged over all of us before landing on me.

"Basil, I understand you've got something important you wanted to discuss with all of us?"

All eyes were on me as I nodded. "I'd like to discuss with all of you the cheating allegations that have been running around the past few months."

Jasmine groaned, "Why? Are you here to apologize for all the stress you've caused?"

Aubrey shot her a look, and there was nothing but anger in her voice as she spoke. "How about you listen to what she has to say?"

"Why are you on her side? She's the reason you and Case aren't together anymore," Jasmine quipped back.

Warner stood and pointed to either side of the room. "We're here to listen, now separate."

I snickered as Jasmine's eyes widened, and her mouth opened. "I'm not a child, Donovan. You can't talk to me like that."

"Then stop acting like it," he said as he sat back down. "Continue, Basil."

I nodded and took a deep breath. "I did some digging and found that Aubrey hasn't been causing as many issues as you thought," I said as I kept my eyes locked on Warner's. "She only mentioned her and Case's breakup once, and that article was removed. But as you both know, there were more." My eyes glanced at Jasmine, and her face was starting to turn red. "It was weird, right? That Aubrey was holding this over Case's head and kept talking about it? Then she wanted to sue him?"

"Right?" Warner said, his attention shifted to Jasmine as she tried to keep her cool. She was scratching the side of her finger again.

I smiled. "Well, I know a guy. And when I brought up everything that happened, he agreed it was weird. So, he was able to do some work and track down the guys who published the articles. Then, he was able to get the emails from where the information was sent. But the weird thing was—it came from Jasmine's computer."

"This is crazy," Jasmine said. She took a step toward Warner and held out her hands. "She doesn't know what she's talking about."

"I think she does, actually," Aubrey said, holding out the paper from earlier. She placed it in Warner's waiting hand just as Case walked into the office. He wrapped an arm around my waist and pulled me into his side as Warner scanned the information he was given.

Over lunch with my dad, he had written down everything I needed. Emails, phone numbers, and the IP address of Jasmine's computer. She sent false information to reporters who kept running stories about me and Case. But she kept Aubrey—her cousin—in the dark about it. So, while Aubrey was still begging for Case to get back with her, she never made it a public spectacle. And when Case mentioned what Aubrey said about paying her off— Jasmine ran with it.

"Why did you do this?" Aubrey asked with shaking hands. Her eyes were glassy from the tears that threatened to spill over.

Jasmine let out an irritated sigh. "Do you know how it would look if you had to go back home, Aubs? After everything I've done to keep you here?"

"What are you talking about?"

"God, how clueless can you be? Did you really think you got the best manager by chance? No, Jameson owed me a favor. Your dad wanted me to look out for you after you moved here because you're the favorite of the family. I wasn't about to subject myself to their ridicule if you went back home."

Aubrey looked at Jasmine as emotions played out on her face, but she never said anything.

After a tense few minutes of silence, Warner looked up.

"Jasmine, I'll need to speak with you for a few moments. Everyone else, you're free to go."

We exited the office, and I sent Warner the file Hollis had sent. It was a recording of the conversation Aubrey and I had when I approached her. While I didn't particularly care about her career, it was wrong for any blame to fall on her. After all, it wasn't her feeding information to those who ran the stories.

Aubrey didn't stay to hang out and chat when we reached the front of the building. She had given us a solid nod before she walked outside. Case and I watched her, his hands drawing small shapes on my lower back. We heard footsteps and turned around to see Scottie, Townes, and Hollis walking up. The guys were freshly showered and had their duffels slung over their backs. Hollis wrapped her arms around me.

"Everything went well?"

"Yeah, everything's fine."

"Good," she said with a smile.

Scottie threw an arm over her shoulder and tilted his head. "We have a lot to celebrate then. Come on."

I watched as Townes's attention snagged at where Scottie and Hollis's bodies were connected. But he deepened his scowl and walked off before I could try to decipher what I just saw. We followed Townes, but after everyone had walked through the door, Case stopped me. He gently grasped my head between his calloused hands and smiled down.

"I love you, Basil," he said before he kissed me. So many emotions flowed into me, but I couldn't concentrate on what they were. Because they flowed freely, no longer blocked by those heavy feelings of anxiety and fear. He pulled away and rested his forehead on mine as he laced our fingers together.

"I love you, too, Case."

He smiled. "Good, because you're mine forever."

epilogue

Case

10 months later…

"Are you ready?" Basil asked from the bottom of the steps. Her footsteps echoed behind her words. I shoved the small black box into my pocket before I slung my bag over my shoulder. She appeared in the doorway and my breath stopped. I swore, she got more and more beautiful every day. After the whole thing with Jasmine—Basil cut her hair. It was grown out now from the jaw-length bob she initially got, now it was long enough to dust the tops of her collarbones.

The kids that moved up to the next level love her new look, though some of them didn't recognize her. Basil was stressed most of the summer when she was coaching the girl's soccer team—worried Mr. Clein had gone through with his threat. But to both of our surprise, he gave her a very heartfelt apology for his behavior, and she hadn't seen him since.

She also moved in six months ago, and I hope I never get tired of waking up next to her. I walked past her and placed a kiss on her forehead before smiling down at her.

"I was waiting on you," I teased as I smacked her butt when I passed her.

She stared after me with an open mouth as she fought a smile. "Case Whitlock, you know damn well I'm always the first one ready."

The first day she moved in—she asked when we were going back to Breckenridge. She loved the ice sculpting festival and hadn't stopped talking about going back. I think she's secretly hoped to move there one day, probably after I retire.

The drive this time was different. Basil had the windows rolled down and the music blasting. I couldn't help but join in. She wanted to book the same hotel we stayed in last year, but I wanted something a bit more lavish. Did I lie and say the hotel was booked out for the month? Yes—but for good reason.

We pulled into the driveway of the Airbnb and Basil couldn't help but look at it. It was built on a slope, and the porch in the back overlooked the beautiful town. Gigantic windows were stacked on one side and were framed by dark metal—which complimented the stonework on the lower half of the home.

"Case, this is beautiful," she said as she got out of the car.

My hands started to sweat as I kept my distance behind Basil as she walked up to the front door. "It's open," I said, relieved I managed to get the words out without them sounding shaky.

It all happened in slow motion. Basil opened the door, and I watched as her head swiveled over the roses and candles our friends helped set out. Townes, Scottie, Hollis, and Hayley stood back in the kitchen. I followed Basil inside, and when she turned around, her eyes were full of unfallen tears.

"Case?"

I wiped my hands on my pants before reaching into my pocket.

"I uh—" I had to clear my throat to keep tears from spilling over. I got down on one knee, never looking away from Basil. "I was prepared to love you from a distance, Basil. And for the longest time, I thought that was my only option. But the longer I watched you, the harder it was to convince myself of that. You, Basil, never do anything without giving it your all. Coaching, your friendships, *us*. And I hope you'll allow me the chance to continue doing that with you. I've loved you since you poked me in the chest a year ago, and I hope you'll let me love you until we're old and have gray hair." I opened the box. "Will you marry me?"

Basil wasted no time. She threw herself into my arms and managed a "yes" between happy sobs. I pulled her back far enough to slip the ring on her finger and kissed her like our forever hadn't started yet.

about the author

Ashlynne has loved writing from an early age but stopped when motherhood became her priority. In January 2021 she re-kindled her love of reading and in April 2023 decided it was time to start writing again.

She writes sweet stories filled with tension that will have you reading until the early morning.